CW01645551

Pagan Death

Sam Taw

This is a work of fiction. Names, characters, organisations, places, events, and incidents are either products of the author's imagination or are used fictitiously.

Copyright © 2019 Sam Nash writing as Sam Taw. All rights reserved.

No part of this book, or any portion thereof, may be reproduced, stored in a retrieval system or transmitted in any form or by any means, electronic, mechanical, photocopying, recording, or otherwise, without the express written permission of the publisher or author.

Cover art supplied by Carantoc Publishing Ltd
First edition, 2019
ISBN 978-1-9160051-8-1
Carantoc Publishing Ltd.
www.carantocpublishing.com

Author Note:

Evidence supporting life in the Late Bronze Age emerges almost on a daily basis, thus is the changing nature of archaeological theories. While much of the story is grounded in fact, some aspects are products of the author's imagination, for example, previous historical theory suggested that trading could have taken place between Phoenicians and Cornish settlers in this era. This has now been refuted as unlikely, and yet it makes a compelling storyline. While I have tried to find conclusive proof to support the story, there may be some inaccuracies as new digs unearth the truth.

Please note that this product was created by a British author. Except for Cornish words, slang and dialogue, spelling and grammar is corrected to **British English**. There are also scenes which may offend more sensitive readers. It is not deemed suitable for children.

To Old Pop, for his love of long forgotten things.

CHAPTER ONE

Curse this rain. My old bones ache. Why Eseld can't perform this ritual closer to home is a mystery. Not that the Goddess of Lakes and Seas will listen to her. It's been nigh on ten springs, and it continues to pour. I should have worn my winter furs. At least it'll get warmer later around the fire pits at the feast. Get a drop of warm ale in my gut. That'll do me nicely. Shame about that servant girl. I rather liked her. It seems such a waste to just slit her throat and let her blood course into the current. The least they can do is to keep her skinny little body covered until her time comes. Poor mite is shaking more than I. No wonder, I suppose. Who would want to go in such a way? Five and twenty heads of families all looking on while she shivers in the rain, her arse sticking out for all to see. No, that is no way to go. I suppose that's what you get when you're caught in between your Chieftain's furs; his spiteful second wife chooses you for sacrifice. Give Eseld credit where it's due though, she can certainly put on a good show.

The Sun broke through the low mists and glinted from the ripples on the River Exe. Its swollen waters lapped at the jetty planks on which Eseld stood. For once, we had caught a break in the storms. Pulling back the hood of her cloak, she raised her arms in the air. "Oh, good and gentle goddess, have mercy on us. We cannot survive another failed harvest. Our meagre grain stores rot before we can make bread, our animals grow sick and die, our hunting grounds shrink in the floods." This she said with such conviction, that she gripped the blade in her fist too tight. Blood trickled down her wrists. "Spare us your wrath, and we will honour you for all eternity."

The tribal Metern, Chieftain Aebba, stamped his foot against the planking. "Get on with it, woman." He lifted his heavy woollen tunic and pulled out his pintel and then proceeded to piss from the end of the pontoon. Eseld gasped, her look of horror transforming into a seething stare. Aebba's first wife, Cryda covered her mouth with the back of her hand and chuckled. She stood between the Ordoviches Tribe visitors, come to trade for our tin. They are shorter than our kinsfolk, but their calf muscles bulge when they walk. Must be all the mountains they climb.

Eseld stood and waited for Aebba to complete the evacuation of his bladder, and then turned her back to him. "Forgive him, great lady, for our Metern's water is no disrespect, but a form of blessing."

At this Aebba laughed so heartily, I thought he might lose his footing and slip into the river himself.

Eseld would not be dissuaded from her performance. With the entire royal court lined up along the bank in awe, she urged the continuance of the ceremony. "We give unto thee our riches. Paega, you first my darling boy." Eseld beckoned to her eldest child. He looked up at her and shrugged. "Your sword, son." She urged.

"No, you can't be serious? I've only had it for two moons, it's the keenest edge in the land."

"All the more reason to give it unto our lady." Eseld beckoned him onto the jetty. Paega growled under his breath, unhooking the belt securing the weapon to his hip. He stomped down the walkway, the planks bowing under his gait.

Dangling the bronze sword and scabbard over the surging river, his pained expression converted into a scowl. The prime metalwork sunk beneath the muddy surface and vanished. He turned on his mother. "Happy now?" He spat, before clumping back to shore.

His little sister removed a copper bangle from her arm, scurried onto the platform and threw it down near her feet. "For our lady," she muttered.

Aebba patted her head. "Good girl. Run along now."

"And what will the Ruvane sacrifice?" Eseld sneered.

Aebba's first wife and tribal Ruvane, Cryda, glided forwards, crossing paths with the youngster. She touched her shoulder and descended the embankment to the platform. Not to be outdone by such pageantry, Cryda stretched out her arms and pulled back the hood of her cloak. Her golden hair twisted and braided, and secured by a finely carved horn comb. This she removed and held in her outstretched palm.

"This was a gift from my royal father, the Metern of the Cantii. I offer it to our lady with love." Tipping her hand, the comb fell into the silted mud banks. Slaves rushed forwards, clamouring to retrieve the article first, wading waist deep in the filth. A bony slave of no more than fifteen springs swooped down, cleaning it on his rough tunic before handing it back to Cryda.

She rewarded the creature with a smile before launching the comb high into the air. Everyone watched it land in the fast-flowing channel, to be carried down to the sea. Cryda looked to the visitors, who in turn fidgeted under her gaze.

One of them ventured, "A fine offering, Ruvane Cryda." While the second felt obliged to remove his own pin badge and toss it into the Exe.

When all the material goods were delivered unto the goddess, Eseld grabbed the slave girl by the arm and shoved her to the end of the dock. Tears streamed down her ruddy cheeks as she hugged herself and shivered. Her pale naked body faced the opposite bank.

Eseld cupped a beaker of woad, daubing the girl's back with symbols she had learnt from a childhood with the Priest Sect. Spirals and interlocking runes appeared in blue, while Eseld chanted her incantations and rolled her eyes to the back of her head as though she was possessed by some lordly spirit. Chilled, I edged closer to the warmth of my pony, skirting behind Cryda and her Ordo Tribe visitors.

Eseld looked around at her audience. The Chieftain was losing interest. He fiddled with his beard and then sought out Cryda's glance, winking and sticking out his tongue in playful banter. She giggled and effused in return, toying with her collar in a coy, yet seductive manner. Aebba licked his lips. "Quicken your pace, wife. This damp air will rot my toes before you are done." He jogged Eseld's elbow with such force, she jabbed the blade into the slave girl's arm, who squealed and darted away. Eseld caught hold of her hair before she could make her escape.

With a stream of priestly words, Eseld raised the knife to the shrieking girl's throat and sliced it across her windpipe. Crimson spurts showered Eseld, making Aebba pace backwards from the splatter to preserve his finery. With eyes wild and mouth foaming blood red, Eseld held her juddering body over a basin on the jetty, catching a measure of the girl's steaming blood. When the writhing ceased, Eseld pushed her into the river, and stood basking in the spectacle. Slave blood dripped from her chin and hands.

Eseld stepped up to the Metern, and painted a spot of blood on his forehead between his brows. He braced himself as it trickled down his nose.

"Are you finished, woman? Can we get back to feasting and celebrating our visitors now?" Aebba brushed Eseld backwards and returned to his horse, leaving the slaves to clear up the mess. I stooped to gather a bunch of fresh watercress and clambered up onto my pony. His body heat and musky smell was a welcome relief after the fetid stench of slave innards.

Eseld is playing a risky game. If her sacrifice fails to stop the rains, Aebba will have another reason to cast her aside. Their union did little to unite the clans as Aebba had hoped. Eseld's father, leader of the Priest Sect, had forged an uneasy alliance with the Durotridge Tribe, east of Exeter. Their constant forays onto our lands stretched the limits of our warriors. Aebba sent riders to patrol the borders, leaving Exeter and the mines on the west coast unguarded. Before the priests could mount an attack, Aebba invited Eseld and her father to the Chieftain encampment, with the intention of bartering for their union. Aebba made token promises to her father about adopting their faith and rituals, and consulting them before major decisions, knowing full well that their nomadic existence would test communications.

The coup was averted, but the threat remained. He had no love for Eseld. That he reserves for Cryda, she of Cantii Chieftain blood. It is his third wife I pity the most, a young maiden of the Ordoviches Tribe. Their marriage opened the way for copper trading with the wealthiest tribe in all of Kembra. It was not such a good deal f the young Brea, forced to adopt a Dumnoni name at time of their binding ceremony. This little maiden endured six springs of Aebba's advances and still she remains without child. I saw she had a fresh crop of bruises yesterday. I must mix her a tincture to ease her suffering. She is the only woman in the camp I can stomach.

Our journey back along the riverbank to Exeter was delayed when Cryda's royal waggon got bogged. Aebba would not wait until the oxen could be hitched from a nearby homestead, galloping off to his throne room and a quart of warm ale. I left the safety of the procession and ambled back through the shacks and huts with one warrior to protect me and a couple of slaves eager to be rid of the mud. The closer we got to camp, the more insistent the beggars and waifs became. Their shredded rags did nothing to hide their protruding bones. Some were covered in sores and cankers. I hope to the goddess that these rains stop and we can plant new crops. I handed out what metal nuggets I had with me, and heeled the pony's flanks to hurry him into the Metern's encampment. Slipping down onto the mounting block, I trudged along the boardwalks and into the long house. Aebba had already stripped off his wet shoes and leggings and was drying himself against the fire.

"Nephew!" I yelled from the door flap. "I need more supplies and I am out of tin ingots."

He lifted his tunic and turned to heat his bum cheeks. "Speak to Paega. He'll set you up."

"You really should do something about the growing numbers of starving and homeless at your gates."

"We do. They get the left over scraps my dogs don't want." He chortled. I could see he had already been at the ale.

"I mean it, Aebba. These are desperate times, and if you don't trade with the Frynks for some grain, you could have an uprising on your hands." I let the door flap fall and paced closer. It was hard not to strike a belligerent stance.

"Is this how you speak to your Chief, Aunt?"

"No one is around to hear us. Besides, I pulled you from your poor mother's loins. Great lump you were too. If I cannot give you my advice, there is no hope left for the Dumnonii."

He glared at me; his chin dipped to his chest. After a few moments of uncomfortable silence regarding each other, he relented. "Fine. I'll look into it. Now give me peace, old woman, or I'll have you whipped." The grin plastered across his face countered his angry brow. He was teasing his old aunt. I shuffled away content that he had heard me.

By noon, our whole party had returned and Eseld was in high spirits, directing the slaves and arranging the roasting spits and sweet offerings. I slipped away. With a plentiful supply of tin in my pouch, I hurried back to my hut and secreted all but a couple of ingots in my hidden trove. Not even my slaves know of its whereabouts.

Despite the creeping chill, I braved the new rains to check on my herb plot. All too often the young boys allow our herd to trample the hurdle fencing and let them graze on the young shoots before I can make them into tinctures and ointments. As it happens, all was well, but some of the seedlings had perished in the boggy conditions. With my pony kitted out with haulage bags, I sharpened my blade on the grinding stone and headed into the woods. It was a bit early, and altogether too cold for mushrooms, but I reckoned on a fair bit of willow bark and milk thistle. I had just cut a few withies for scraping my teeth and was stripping them of leaves, when I heard talking close to the riverbank. A deep lyrical tone of a man and another whose voice I know well. Leaving my labours, I picked my way between the undergrowth to catch their words.

Cryda fawned over the Ordo visitor, twirling her hair around a finger and leaning on his shoulder. They mumbled so that I could not make out their speech, but from their choice of secluded meeting place, they were not discussing the weather. As she whispered something into his ear, the Ordo's brows rose in surprise. What had she suggested? There were more low conspiratorial utterances and then she moved away. She then slipped off a thick, tin bracelet from her wrist and gave it to him. His eyes nearly bulged from their sockets. That was greater wealth than he would see in his whole lifetime. He turned the bangle around in his hands, examining the fine scratch marks and decorations on its surface. Beaming with delight, he nodded to Cryda.

My foot slipped from the tree root on which I balanced. I landed with a thud and a groan. Spooked, Cryda gathered up her linens and ran from the forest. I picked myself up and rubbed my ankle. By the time I got to my feet, they had both gone. It's a good job I harvested the willow bark first. Chewing on the bitter fibres, I let the juices numb the pain and my pony take my weight back to my hut. The slaves stowed the plants and roots in my growing collection of jars and beakers, and warmed some water over the fire to bathe and bind my grazes.

What a fine sight I shall make at the feast this evening. Wearing my best tunic and with beads woven into my white hair, I hobbled across the boardwalks to the Long Hut at sundown. It was my intention to secure a spot as close to the fires as possible. I know from my many weary years; how tedious these events can be. At least I would be warm and well fed. With one of Aebba's furs over my shoulders and my feet toasting nicely, I settled down for the evening's entertainment.

The Metern and Ruvane Cryda made their spectacular entrance, late as is their custom, and glowing from the afternoon antics. I rather suspect Cryda had ignited his lust through guilt, for she had a furtive look about her which darted between everyone present, carefully avoiding the Ordo visitor.

Aebba hoisted himself onto his favourite bench at the head of the hut, his hefty rump cushioned with layers of skins and furs, stuffed with the fleece from our sheep.

His bronze cup filled with warmed ale, he sat content to survey his lot. Cryda sat to his left, her own chaise similarly decked out, for the lengthy feast ahead. Aebba's lesser wives, Eseld and the mousy Brea, sat beneath him, their chaise low to the ground and draughty. Eseld scowled from her lowly position, no doubt brewing up ways to best Cryda and gain Aebba's favour. The family elders sat closer to the door. Their conversations were awkward and stilted.

Each head of the family, rose from their bench and presented Cryda with lavish gifts, from carved bead necklaces to wolf fur hats. Eseld seethed. Every now and then, she would turn in her seat to smile at Paega, sitting in his lofty position to the right of Aebba. He was her one and only lauded achievement. The eldest child and heir to all of Dumnonium, that's if Cryda's twin boys do not decide to challenge him.

In due course, the beer flowed, mellowing tempers and relaxing tongues. A solitary piper blew sweet tunes into our ears as we filled our bellies with roasted boar and roots. The wind howled through the door flap, accompanied by a torrential downpour. One of the slaves lifted a wooden panel over the gap, shutting out the worst of the wild weather.

"Looks like your sacrifice this morning was a waste of time, Eseld." Cryda taunted, grinning at the Ordo man sitting alongside her.

Eseld stood up and turned to the Chief's plate, snatching the leftover bones from a bird he had eaten. She scraped off the remaining meat and sinews and rattled them inside her cupped hands, chanting garbled words and imbuing them with a curse or spirit blown from her own mouth.

"Oh, great lady, show me the future of this tribe. What will be the fate of Aebba and his kin?" She threw the bones down on the table before the Metern and plucked a copper comb from her hair. With careful prodding of the hairpin and a gasp of horror, she said, "You have mocked the Lady of the Lakes, you shall know her wrath."

Aebba picked up a bird wing and threw it at Eseld's head. "Enough with the omens and signs, woman. It rains just as the wind blows, the seas swell, the night comes. It rains because it can. Night kills day, rain kills sun. The rain is victorious until the sun gains strength."

"My Chief, it is more than ten cycles since this wet scourge has come to punish us, to spoil our crops and flood our homes. This is come about because you scoff at our lady. Ruin will be our fate." She replied, returning the pin to her hair.

"I am Metern of the Dumnonii and she will do my bidding. Enough rituals, enough sacrifices. Know your place, woman, and be silent!" Aebba belched and thumped his chest with a clenched fist. Muttering beneath his breath, he said "This is what comes of marrying the daughter of priests."

"My Chief?" Eseld enquired, although she surely heard him as well as I had done.

"Nothing. Bring my daughter over here. Where is my Derwa?"

"Why, Aebba?"

"I want to look upon her beauty."

Frowning, Eseld walked to her daughter sitting next to me near the fire. She took her by the hand and led her to her father's table. The young maiden kept her head bowed. I could see her little hands shaking behind her back.

"Hmm." He contemplated, leaning forwards to take Derwa by the chin and lift her face up to his. "You are sent by the gods, in spite of your mother." At this, the child smiled. "Hmm," the Chief murmured again. "I think you could be right, Cryda. She is ready to make a fine tribal Ruvane."

Eseld and the girl almost swooned in shock.

The Chieftain continued, still holding his daughter's chin. "How would you like to live in the mountains and give birth to the future Metern of the Ordoviches?"

CHAPTER TWO

Eseld held her breath, but I could see her temper boiling to the surface. Her pinched face slackened as she thought of a ready retort. “Aebba, our daughter is too young to wed. She is still a child. Can’t we find a better match for our Ordo visitors?”

“Nonsense. Derwa is more than ready, aren’t you girl?” Aebba stared at his daughter with an intensity that would freeze the hearts of the hardiest foe. My niece trembled in his clutches, too afraid to gain say her lord and father. A slow nod, assisted by Aebba’s hand came from the child.

Eseld looked deeply distressed, she flounced closer to the Chief, bending low to his ear. “Husband, I would speak with you in private about this. Can we not leave the matter for another day?”

“No.” He bleated, his anger growing once more. He let go his daughter with a slight shove, which propelled her back towards her seat. “There is nothing to discuss. Are our visitors happy with this arrangement?” Aebba waited for the taller of the Ordos to nod his agreement, before gesturing for Eseld to leave his presence. “The matter is settled.” He drained his cup dry and held it aloft for a refill. Eseld gave her daughter a reassuring smile and both returned to their seats.

Cryda's face broke into a self-satisfied grin. She placed her jewelled hand on Aebba's arm, who in turn patted her with affection. It did not take long for the Metern's humour to ease, particularly as Cryda's hand slipped from his arm to beneath the table, and from Aebba's expression, to his nether regions.

The sweet offerings and meats were varied and plentiful. I cast a thought to those starving wretches at our gates. It curbed my hunger for indulgence. Most of the guests on my table were reduced to picking at morsels left on their plates, content to avail themselves of more alcohol at the expense of food. A ham hock, roasted with a thick honey glaze, sat almost untouched less than a foot from my seat. I called a serving slave over to my table. He bent low to hear me.

"Is the rain heavy right now?"

"No, Fur Benyn, it is much lighter than before. Thank the goddess."

"Hmm." I wish they would not call me that. I may be a benyn, but I am far from wise. Could be worse, I suppose. At least he didn't call me a wise *old* woman. The piper began playing his jolly little tunes, in an attempt to enliven the crowds. I took advantage of the increased banter and noise to hoist myself from my seat. I instructed the slave to carry the platter with the ham hock, and follow me out of the Long Hut.

Aebba caught sight of me fumbling with the door panel. "Making a run for it, Aunt? Taking off with my food and my slaves?" His booming laughter seemed to fill the hall. It was shortly followed by raucous merriment from his guests, keen to prolong his genial mood. I ignored him. He may be swift to laughter, but his changes in temperament are like quicksilver, especially when inebriated. I kicked the foot of a warrior near to the door, who hopped up and helped me move the wooden panel. The slave and I headed out into the damp night, picking our way along the criss-cross of board walks through the muddy compound to the gates.

The guard tower was manned by a young lad whose injuries I had stitched less than a week before. I yelled up to him, imploring him to open the gates. He called down to me, asking for my name and nature of business. The moment he recognised me, he scurried down the ladder to greet me.

"Fur Benyn, it is not safe for you out there after dark, not even with a guard."

"I want to get this cooked boar out to those in need. It is not right that gluttony exists alongside such starvation." I pointed towards the gates and out into the settlement.

"You are kindness itself, Fur Benyn, but I cannot let you pass. I would be strung up by the Chief if I was the cause of your death. Let the slave go alone, or let me take it into the shacks."

I swear I could see him dribbling at the thought of getting his mucky hands on the ham. One word from me and it would be gobbled up by the night watch in no time. As much as the slave deserve better quality rations for a change, the same result would occur if I left it in his capable hands. I peered down at the knife tucked into his belt. "Give me your blade. I will cut the meat into sections and see you take it to each hut." He looked at me without comprehension. His mouth twisted into the dimples in his cheeks. "You heard me, and be quick about it. I have need for sleep at my age and it's late."

I stood in the opened gateway, watching the guard and slave, deliver each chunk of meat according to my instruction. Under torchlight, I could see the harried mothers appear at the entrance to each shack. With tears in their eyes, each would rip apart the ham and divide it among their children. Not one of them took a bite for themselves, yet their hollow faces betrayed their hunger. These were the families whose menfolk had perished, by fair means or foul. The struggle to fill the bellies of their young kept them lean and desperate. Daily foraging in the forest, yielded fewer squirrels each moon. The rains were sent to test us all.

With my conscience a little lighter, I turned to amble back into the Long Hut. That was when the sound of thunderous hooves caught my attention. The guard heard it too. He pushed the slave and I back into the compound, and hurried to close the gates behind us. Climbing the ladder, he reached the lookout as the rider approached.

I could hear the snorting and puffing from the horse. A loud voice called out, "Open the gates, I come with news from the borders."

"Speak your news here and I will tell the Metern." The guard bellowed back.

"Let me through, or my cousin Eseld will choose you for her next sacrifice." That seemed to spur the guard into action. He spilled through the opening before the gates were fully opened, his horse foamed with salty sweat. I prodded the slave to run and fetch the Lady Eseld, and stood watching the commotion, keen to hear the tidings. The man and I regarded each other, me with curiosity, and him with disdain. He did not dismount, but instead fingered the handle of a large axe secured to the horse with leather strapping. His face bore the marks of ritual cutting and tattoos to garner the support of the gods. It set him apart from our men, identifying him as a warrior priest. His regard of me was cursory. I was of no interest or threat to his welfare, but he remained vigilant as the crowd of guards left their stations to watch him.

Eseld scrambled from the Long Hut and along the board walks to greet him. His demeanour altered to concern. He slid from his horse and laid a hand upon her shoulder, touching his forehead to hers. "Cousin." He murmured.

Eseld reached up and mirrored his greeting. As they parted, the warrior grimaced, straightening his leg. "You are hurt, cousin?" Eseld enquired.

"A scratch some days ago, that does not want to heal." He rested his arm over Eseld's shoulder, an intimacy that would have drawn Aebba's scorn if he had seen. She did not register the infringement of his touch as overstepping his position. She was the second wife to the Metern of the Dumnonii, none other than selected servants may impose themselves upon her. I observed their familiarity, the instant ease with which they conversed together, the closeness of their bodies as she aided him along the planking. This was more than kinship.

"You must have the wound dressed properly." Eseld finally noticed me lurking in the shadows, and called to me. "Meliora, will you tend to my injured cousin?"

I so seldom hear my name called, that it took a moment to register. She must have thought I had lost my wits. "Bring him to my hut." I said, and then to the slave, I called out; "Fetch me hot water, and lots of torches. I need to see what I am doing." As the boy ran, I called after him. "Bring me comfrey leaves too." At this the boy stopped, his shoulders slumped as if he were about to receive a beating. I squinted into the darkness at his pathetic form. "What is it now?"

"Fur Benyn, I do not know comfrey from watercress."

I grumbled, but I understood his distress. "Then get the water and light. And hurry, boy." Eseld seemed reluctant to let go of her cousin as he spilled onto the edge of my bed and unwrapped his bloodied leg. The guard from the lookout post carried a torch, its spitting flames guttering in the squall above me as I went out to my herbs and gathered all that I needed. On my return, I found Eseld and the warrior in an embrace, confirming my suspicions of their closeness.

Eseld deflected. "I see that you have grains laid out on rushes by the door, Meliora. Is this one of your magical tests?"

"It is." I said, guarding my reply. I knew what was filtering through her devious mind. I had used the same test on her before she fell heavy with young Derwa. She was listing all the potential maids in the camp who could be with child. I was ready for her next question.

"And who would this test be for?"

"Never you mind. Help me get his leggings unbound. You seem to know your way around this man well enough." I could see her pout from my doorway. She let the matter drop. My threat was clear enough; push me and I will tell my nephew about your lover.

The warrior's leg stank like maggoty meat. A thin crust of a scab stuck to his clothing. He flinched when I yanked it free and putrid puss oozed freely. Eseld covered her nose and moved away. "This will smart a bit." I said in warning, as I poured hot water across his thigh and scraped the gunge from the raw flesh. I had seen injuries like this one before. A glancing blow from a sword, blunted on enemies' skulls, but still sharp enough to tear at thigh and breast. This warrior was lucky not to have lost his leg. The gash was longer than my hand.

Cleaned of festering flesh, I roughened the surface of one comfrey leaf, until the sap leaked out and smeared it with a thick layer of honey. He braced again as I pressed it into the wound. A few more leaves over the top and I secured them in place with cord spun from fleece. The colour drained from his face. He thanked me with a surprising level of humility.

He glanced up to Eseld. I guessed that they both craved privacy, but I would not budge. I wanted to hear the news as much as she.

"Did my father send you? How is my mother? What news have you, cousin?" Her impatience was almost as acute as my own.

"We were attacked. Our warriors had a large herd of ponies rounded up from the moors. We had them fenced in an enclosure at Uffculme, ready to break them. It was only a short layover on our way to the Chard Barrows. You know how busy it is at this time of the year, Eseld." He held out his hand to hers for comfort. It was instinct that made her grab hold and squeeze. His eyes cast down to the rushes on my floor. "They came at night. A great hoard from the Durotriges Tribe. They made off with all the new horses, but not before they had burned and slashed our shelters and killed a terrible number of our clan." His hand tightened on hers. "My mother and sister now sit with the gods."

"What of my kin?" Every muscle in her body tensed for his announcement. She held her breath.

The warrior looked up, the glaze of waters filling his eyes. He swallowed. "Your father lives, but was badly wounded."

"And my mother?"

The warrior shook his head. Eseld crumpled into his arms and sobbed. I have to admit, I felt uncomfortable in their presence, and braved the rains while he comforted her. I heard him making shushing sounds, her cries muffled by his neck. Her grief started subtly, waves of disbelief and begging for the news to be false. It progressed into anger, her little fists pounding against his hollow sounding chest. Her hysteria built into a wailing cry that could pierce the stoniest of hearts. Finally, acceptance, the pitiful sobs muted once more. Beyond the entrance, I could still make out their words.

"If Aebba cannot protect his clans, he has no right to be Metern. Your father has sent me to warn the Chief that should further attacks occur, he will have no other choice but to forge an alliance with the Durotriges Tribe, if only to secure the lives of our people and livestock. You know what happened last time…"

Eseld's voice was faint but clear. "My father was set to become Metern himself."

"And you know what would follow that?" His voice was warm but stern. I detected the note of anxiety in his tone.

"The Alchemists at the west mines would either blockade the tin supply or take over leadership themselves."

"Right. And they have all the wealth in the world backing them. Who do we have, but a few old warriors and spindly priests? It's likely to end in a massacre. Where are Ruvane Cryda's sons?"

"Blydh is beyond the moors with our horsemen. Aebba received reports of raiding along the northern coastline. They are supposed to protect the borders right up to the Durotriges boundary." Eseld sniffed.

"And what of the other one?"

"There is no way of knowing where Tallack could be. Aebba gives him free rein to do just as he pleases. He has at least four boats now, three of them able to cross the sea to Iwerdon. He has even made raids in Frynk. He returns every now and then, buttering up Aebba and Cryda with plunder and slaves taken from the southern Kembra tribes. He won't be a problem." There was a spell of silence, broken only by the rustle and creaking of leather leggings and my bunk straining under their weight. My fear that their intimacies might get out of control was interrupted by Eseld's loud whispering. "I have an idea which may solve all our problems in one go. I will tell Aebba the news in the morning, nothing can be achieved by telling him now. He would only make light of my mother's death in front of the visiting Ordoviches leader, and I cannot bear that."

I flounced in, expecting to find them unclothed and poised for carnal relations. Instead, I found Eseld on her feet, dry eyed and plotting. She made for the entrance, pushing past me as though I were a mere inconvenience. Before leaving, she turned back to face her cousin. "I will find you a warm bunk for the night and some food. Stay and rest while your leg heals. Leave Aebba to me." It sounded more of a threat than a promise. Eseld left me with the warrior as he rebound his leggings and thanked me again for my healing services. He did at least have the grace to appear sheepish at his actions with the Lady Eseld, but my look of disapproval did little to sway his decision to stay in the encampment.

I watched him hobble towards the Long Hut, in Eseld's footsteps, but halt at the entrance. He obviously trusted his cousin more than I. What treacherous plan was she cooking up in her twisted mind?

CHAPTER THREE

The morning brought a cold wind and an early patient. Ruvane Cryda shook me awake in my bunk. I had my furs wrapped around me so tightly, I did not want to budge, not even for her.

"Do I still need to piss on the grains at your door." She said, peeling my coverings from me and prodding with a knuckle.

"Take a look for yourself." I grumbled, turning over and shutting my eyes to the intrusion. "If it has sprouted, you are. If it has spoiled, you are not."

"And what if it has done neither?" She asked, peering down at the patch of rushes, neatly laid with wheat and barley.

"Then squat, squeeze out another and come back tomorrow, but at a reasonable time." I heard her soft footfalls on the rushes and the stream of water spattering down between her legs.

"Are you sure this works?"

"You could always just wait and see. It has worked many times before." It was clear at this point that she was not going to let me sleep. Throwing off the furs, I edged to the side of my bunk. I glanced over at her as she dropped her dress down to her ankles and stepped off the grain patch. Her features were strained. "What is worrying you, Cryda? You have had children and lost others, may Cernonnus protect them, wherever they may be." I touched the carved amulet at my neck, bearing the god's likeness. "Why are you troubled this time?"

"I am not a young woman, Meliora. Would you not be concerned in my situation?" She came and sat by my side. I looked at her radiant skin, her wide eyes and good teeth. Compared to me, she was still in the first flushes of youth. There was little to endanger her life by another pregnancy; no more than the usual risks. I wondered whether the secrecy and worry could not have another foundation.

"Young enough, Cryda. There shouldn't be a problem." I said, keeping a watchful eye on her response. "Unless you know something that I don't?"

Her brow cinched together. "No, everything is fine. I shall return in the morning." She rose quickly, peeking from the doorway before hurrying out into the rain. I was left with the feeling that nothing was, in fact, fine. Should she prove to be with child, I got the sneaking suspicion that she was preparing me for my assistance in relieving her of the obligation of carrying it to birth. Now, why would she want to be rid of another potential heir to the great Chieftain Aebba? That is, if she is carrying his child.

With a new fire laid in my hut, I was loathed to go out into the frigid morning, but I was called to re-dress the wound of Eseld's cousin. A slave led me to a round house next to the Long Hut. This was a secluded shack, built especially for Eseld's children. She had insisted upon it before her binding ceremony. These days, only young Derwa slept there, but often it was given to clan leaders or other important visitors. Eseld must have moved her daughter from her bunk late into the night to accommodate her relative. I could guess as to why. It was just a stone's throw from Eseld's hut. It seems that she cared little for her reputation.

By noon, I got word that a woman close to the river needed my help. I grabbed my travel bag, a few tinctures, my best knives, and a length of cat gut, and mounted my pony. They are better used to the swelling waters down by the river. Most of their huts balanced on stilts. A few could actually hang a fishing line right from their home. Despite their best efforts though, they cannot stop their children falling for the dropsy. I crossed their sturdy bridges and followed their eldest boy into the family hut. The river seeped up the walls, blackened with mould.

Such a happy little soul, even between the coughing fits. He beamed up at me with a toothless smile, and I back at him. I squashed the flesh around his ankles. My fingers left deep impressions in the soft tissues. His drowsy eyes were surrounded by pockets of bad humours, probably a build-up of phlegm. There was nothing I could do to relieve his suffering. His poor mother would have to cradle him until his time came. I gave them a tonic of steeped willow bark, but I knew that he would not last out this moon.

The father tried to give me a fine boning blade in payment. It was his only metal, and one that assured food for his family. How could I deprive them of that? My short ride out to their encampment was not a waste of my time, I found a clump of fresh sprouting samphire on my way home. It's one of my favourite foods; lightly boiled, with a little butter and salt. It would have been even better if I had saved some of the roasted boar from last night. The night was drawing in when I passed through the forest to the Metern's encampment. I quickened my pace as the mist swirled around my pony's legs.

There are few noises in the night-time that frighten an old woman such as myself. I know the calls of the owls, the screech of the fox and the howl of the wolf. I know that animal attack is rare, and I can ward them off with fire or blade. I also know that there is little out there as dangerous as starving people, and they are growing in number daily. Jabbing my heels into my pony's flanks, I kicked him into a canter along the track closer to home.

As we neared the final bend, I heard branches snapping and the rustle of fabric. Someone was in a hurry. I drew my largest knife from its sheath, and held it across my lap ready to swipe, should the need arise. I certainly did not look like a woman of wealth. My muddy robes, and torn cuffs marked me out as a forager, but the horse alone was worth more than my life to some. The pony snorted, and bucked his head high. I held onto his mane, and steadied him with a pat and a few kind murmured words.

At the end of the thicket, a figure in a dark hood pushed through the undergrowth and joined the path. From the dainty hands, I could see it was a woman. That calmed my nerves a little.

"Ho there. Where are you headed?" I called out, but the woman ignored me, hurrying along the track. "Hail. I could walk with you. Hold fast." I kicked my pony to speed him to the lady's side. Since there was nowhere for her to hide, she lifted her hood away from her head. Eseld stared back at me, clearly framing the excuses for her behaviour.

"Meliora. I did not hear you. We can walk back to camp together." She shifted uneasily, moving the arm furthest from me to behind her back.

"What are you doing out here, it's almost dark?" I leaned back to see what she was hiding.

"Um…Derwa had a bad night. All that talk of binding her to the Ordo Tribe. I went in search of hedge nettle."

"On your own? You could have sent a slave for that, or ask me for that matter. Even dried nettle will sooth frayed nerves." She did not answer me. Her mouth opened and I watched the slow inhalation, but Eseld was never a quick thinker. "Where is it?" I pressed.

"Oh, um. I couldn't find any in the end." Her arm swung into view. A small pouch hung from her hand, crafted from the same fabric as her skirt. It had a wet stain of squashed berry seeping through the fibres. The kind of deep purple you get from blackberries, but they are only ripe in Autumn. She tucked it behind her once again, her alarm evident in her expression.

"Really? I saw masses of nettle just two nights past. What have you there?" I was so focused on the pouch, I hadn't realised that we were at the gates of the camp. The warrior in the lookout saw us and shouted down for the gates to be opened. Eseld used the distraction to her advantage and slipped away from me without reply.

I rode straight around to visit her cousin, half expecting to see her arrived there before me. He was alone. I dressed his wound with crushed plantain, and then returned to my own hut to clean my samphire for the pot. Whatever was Eseld doing in the woods? Solitary forays in the undergrowth are most unlike her; she rarely does anything without an audience.

By nightfall, I could hear the raucous laughter and music coming from the Long Hut, as Aebba continued to host the Ordos from Kembra. Tired from my labours, I ate my meagre food, made offerings to the gods, and then climbed under my furs for the night.

Rising with the sun, I checked the grains near my door before Cryda awoke. They had sprouted. How would she react to the news? I stoked the fire back into life and checked my stores. I had plenty of ingredients to mix a concoction to hasten the bleed, but would she ask me for the means to end the Chieftain's sixth child? Was she, perhaps carrying another's offspring?

I cracked my last duck egg into a beaker and nestled it in the embers. The yolk was tainted with blood. This is a very bad omen indeed. Whatever the gods have planned for our tribe, it will be blighted with sorrow. I dare not tell my nephew, Aebba, of my suspicions. He is likely to banish me from his good graces for such a warning, particularly after his show of contempt at the river sacrifice. Loathed as I was to eat such an article, my hunger and the memory of those starving mothers near to the gates reminded me of the sin of waste. It is my hope that I will not be cursed by this action.

With anxiety growing in the pit of my gut, I busied myself with the grinding of chalk lumps until Cryda's arrival. The goddess had finally blessed us with a morning without rain, allowing me to hear the hollow footsteps of her approach on the board walks. She came into my hut and crouched down near the rushes to examine the wheat. I watched her face as she processed the information before her. It was not the look of joy painting her expressions, but a numbed panic. We exchanged knowing glances for a long moment. I waited for her instruction but was surprised when she gathered herself up and rushed from my home instead. Not a word, not a sound was uttered. Was this the result of a secret tryst with a lover, right beneath Aebba's nose, or a genuine fear for her physical health? I could not tell.

The sun was high in the sky before I could decide what to do, such was my fear. In the end, I reasoned that this was Cryda's concern. Should she require my help, she need only ask. My silence, however, is my problem alone. I should have stayed in my hut for a second night, but I wanted to see if Cryda had chosen to tell Aebba.

For once, the weak sunshine dried off the livestock, making the evening chores more bearable and my attire warm and dry. I suppose I ought to let the slaves take care of them, but they are too careless with the fencing. I do not want my best milkers to escape.

When I got to the Long Hut, Eseld was taking the credit for the break in the rains. According to her, she has the ear of the goddess herself. Cryda flounced in wearing a new tunic and more metal than I have ever seen in one place before, but even she could not take the attention away from the second wife of Aebba.

Each family head paid tribute, stepping up to Eseld's table, bowing and offering her tokens of jewels or furs. I kept my beady eye on the Chieftain. He seemed to be allowing Eseld a moment to shine, content to chug back many cups of ale while bellowing orders to little Brea to bring him more food. His manner was pleasant, almost tame. It was obvious to me that Cryda had not told him about the child growing within her. From the smug glances Eseld threw at Cryda, I wondered if she hadn't guessed about her condition. Perhaps she had seen Cryda peeing on the seeds in my hut. Another heir would put Cryda's sons in a stronger position to become Chieftain, should Aebba fall.

I shuffled around the fire pit, towards my usual bench, but found it otherwise occupied. One of Derwa's little friends sat in my stead. She jumped up, in deference to me.

"Fur Benyn, forgive me. We did not think that you would join us this eve, or I would not have sat in your place."

Tapping her shoulder on my way past, I said, "Do not trouble yourself, child. I can find another warm bunk for my weary bones." And then to Derwa, I enquired, "Are you more settled, or shall you still be in need of some hedge nettle?"

"Hedge nettle, Aunt… why would I need that?" Her brow furrowed; her mouth contorted in puzzlement.

"Are you not anxious, worried, struggling to sleep? Does it not bother you that you will be sent to marry the Ordo Chief's eldest son?"

She giggled, turning to her friend. "Oh no, Aunt. My mother told me that would never happen."

Clearly, Eseld was confident that she could talk old Aebba out of selling his youngest to the Ordoviches, but it also confirmed my suspicions about the purpose for her trip to the woods.

I left the girls to their silliness and clambered up to the high benches next to Ruvane Cryda. "Make room for a little one?" I muttered, plonking myself down next to the Ordo guests, and wrapping myself in Aebba's furs.

Cryda did not looked pleased with my intrusion. Her eyes narrowed to slits. "Your place is down there with Eseld's mewling brood. This bench is for the Metern and his guests."

I sighed, a loud frustrated exhalation, taking my time to raise from my comfortable seat.

Aebba blustered in, catching the tail end of Cryda's rebuke. "Does my favourite aunt's presence offend you, wife?" He glared at Cryda for a protracted moment, and then burst into raucous laughter. "Let her stay, woman. She can regale our visitors with tales of my conquests." He launched himself onto the couch in the centre of the row.

Cryda's mouth pursed into that of a fish. "The Ordos must be tired of your tales by now, my love."

"And yet they never seem to tire of your company, wife." There was menace in his retort; a hint of annoyance. She pretended not to notice, clapping her hands together and ordering the slaves to bring forth the cooked birds. I beckoned a young lad over to fill my cup with ale. As he tipped the liquid from the pitcher, he misjudged the shift in weight. The edge of the pot clanged against my cup, knocking it to the ground. I did not want him to be punished for such a simple mistake, for Aebba can be a harsh master. Shooing him away, I bent low to retrieve the beaker and caught a shocking sight. The taller of the Ordo visitors, was touching Cryda beneath the table. It could not be mistaken for anything but a prior familiarity. I bit my lip and righted myself, trying not to betray my feelings. When Aebba turned his attention to back his guests, the Ordo's hands returned above the table. Cryda did not move a muscle, nor did her face give away their betrayal.

Aebba may have several slave girls in a night, or the option of taking many more wives, but he is our Metern. That is his right. The Ruvane does not enjoy such favour. She must stay clean and loyal to Aebba alone. I inwardly cursed the woman for placing me in such an awkward position. Aebba is my blood. I have a duty to tell him of her infidelities, and yet, I know what would be her fate if I do. No woman deserves such a humiliating and painful death, for laying with another man. May the goddess forgive me, I chose to stay quiet, at least for now.

By the time the servants brought out the platters of roasted deer, Aebba had taken much ale and seemed in good cheer. I watched closely as Cryda leaned across to the Metern, and whispered something in his ear. At first, he snapped his head around, and muttered something low under his breath. Whatever he said, Cryda's response was to nod with a wide grin plastered across her features. The Metern kissed her roughly, and then again softly, with more affection. He stood from his bench and lifted his cup.

"My friends and family, raise a cup to our fortunes. The gods have blessed us with another child. Ruvane Cryda carries my next son." Everyone stood and roared, raising their cups and beating their fists against the tables to congratulate the happy couple. "Bring the wines we traded with the Frynks. Let us all drink to Cryda's health. Maybe she will give me another set of twins." Another chorus of shouting and cheering followed, enough to deafen us all. With the Metern in such high spirits, almost all of his guests relaxed and enjoyed the brew made from rotting grapes. Now I understood why the taller Ordo struggled to give his host good wishes on his fortunes. If it was his child, as I suspected it most surely was, no one except the Ruvane and I would ever know. Eseld too, looked boiled from within to hear of the news. Whether she suspected foul play or not, no one would believe her assertions without proof. Cryda had stolen Eseld's glory once again.

I left the hut to make water sometime later, grabbing a torch from the boardwalk near the entrance to light my way. As I returned, I saw Eseld hurrying towards the round house where I knew her cousin to be. With all that I had witnessed this day, my senses were on high alert. Digging the torch into the mud, I left it behind, and tip toed after her, stopping at the doorway to listen to her words. I thought that she may be seeking comfort in his arms, but I was wrong. Eseld was helping the man to his feet and urging him to gather up his belongings ready to flee. Their conversation was hushed, but Eseld's clear tone was easy to make out.

"You have to return to the Priest Sect right now. Tell my father to make his move by the next full moon. I will ease the way."

CHAPTER FOUR

I got word from a slave girl that the crabs were biting well down in the estuary. Crab is a favourite of mine. The trouble is, that as soon as word spreads, everyone gets to the easy pickings before I have even mounted my pony. I'm too old to go hopping round the rock pools, not that there are any around here. Mud and silt are about all you'll get by this river. You have to go further east for the rocks. I'll leave that to the young ones. With the scraps from the last feast tucked into my bags, I wrapped up a bit of salted boar and led my sweet natured steed through the compound, and out of the gates.

No one pays me any mind. It's fairly regular for folks to fetch me, or send word to my hut when they need patching up, or herbs for a belly ache. I come and go as I please. This day, was better than most, for the rains held off for most of the night, and the muds were starting to dry off underfoot. It's a fair way down to the best crabbing spots. I stayed on the west bank, avoiding the worst of the marshland, taking a wide route through the meadows till I came to the red clays. I was tempted to fill a beaker with some, with a view to drying it in my hut, but I figured that my old pony had enough to carry, what with me and the crabs I intended to catch. Maybe I'll send a trusted slave to collect some, another day.

By the time I got to the crossing, where the waters begun to taste of salt, and the rivers snake and wind, parting and joining up between the sand banks, I was uncommonly hungry. The pony was glad of the rest. He stood and ate his fill of lush grasses, while I munched down on the hunk of meat from my saddle pack. While I nibbled, I unwound the catgut from my kit, and twisted it to a fine thread, tying on a bronze hook I brought back from the mines last summer.

There's a nice gradual slope to the spot I chose. I pulled off my leather turn shoes, and dangled my feet into the slow flowing current. I could see the fishermen, far over on the opposite side, wading into the shallows to collect their nets before the tide turned. They hauled quite a catch. Another man lit fires, and dampened the flames with green birch, until sweet smoke billowed out to cure the fish. With my baited hook and line sitting in the stream, I watched the men's skill as they filleted the fish and hung then on racks to dry. I almost wish I had braved the marshes to stay on the east shore. I could have traded for a flounder, maybe even a little salt if they had spare.

When the sun began its climb down to the hills, I gathered up my few crabs, bound their claws, and stowed them in my pouches. As I set off in search of fresh water for my pony, I saw the most magnificent sight of my life. A sailing ship of three times the length of any our tribe has ever made, came cruising up the river. It had the head of a horse, and a tail of a dolphin. This vast boat had more than a clan's worth of oars to each side. It sliced through the water with the aid of the widest sail I have ever seen. Each of the stitched white panels of cloth, had a colour between them of which I had never before seen dyed into fabric. I had to know how they came about such a vibrant shade. I have only ever seen purple that rich on butterflies' wings in spring.

My initial shock, that it could be invaders did not last, for in the bow, was my handsome nephew, Tallack. His golden locks of hair swept back by the wind, his hand shielding the sun's rays from his eyes. I chuckled to myself. Only a son of Cryda could return home, with a better ship than when he left port. I wondered what other riches lay in the hull of that great wooden beast, and set off at a jaunty pace back to camp. No matter how much I urged speed, my pony would not oblige me, for my brave nephew and much of his crew, arrived long before me.

Row boats ferried their goods from the great ship, upstream to the Chieftain's encampment. They were still unloading as I rode into the compound, since the ship was too enormous to risk its belly on the shallow mud flats. I could see from Tallack's face, that he had many tales to tell, and much to boast about come the evening. His mother fussed about his torn tunic and length of his beard, until he scooped her up into his arms and spun her around as though she were a child. It's good to see her happy, as short lived as that might be. Eseld will be brewing up another plot to raise Paega's standing in the tribe, above the favoured Tallack, or Blydh, for that matter. More feasting tonight. I shall look like a roasted boar if I eat any more pig.

I napped until darkness fell, rising to check my goats and strain a few of my tinctures. With such a joyous evening ahead, I wore my best tunic, and secured my hair with the pin that Tallack brought back from his last travels. I admit to a little excitement. He never forgets about his old aunt, and I wondered what trinket might have found its way home for me.

Before I headed over to the Long Hut, I went to see if the slave I entrusted with my crabs, had put them in water. He looked up at me with panic in his eyes. There had been a crab for each finger on my hand. Now there was one fewer. He tried to tell me that it must have walked away when he turned his back. I knew differently, of course. For a few moments I was torn between handing him over to my nephew for a thrashing with a willow stick, or giving him the rest to eat. He looked so ill; the man was more skin than flesh. And there was me, tiring of fatty pig dinners. All things said, I left his punishment hanging until the dawn. I could not decide his fate on an empty stomach.

Word must have reached Cryda long before her son reached camp. As I walked across the planks towards the Long Hut, I saw a massive number of new slaves. Their matted hair and open sores, showed me just how malnourished these poor creatures were. Some of my nephew's crew, were whipping them into submission. I charged over there and gave them such a tongue lashing. They each turned around and, upon seeing me, apologised. Their explanation was simple. These were slaves from Frynk. One man claimed that their discipline aboard ship on their crossing was dreadful. None of the slaves could speak our language. This seemed to give Tallack's men an excuse to beat them brutally, whenever they failed to understand their commands.

One young boy, had painted skin. It was brown like the mud from the salt flats in the estuary. I had never seen someone so dark before. As they dragged him out of the cage, I noticed his foot at an odd angle to his leg. It was clearly broken in two. Still the warrior sailors dragged him by his rags towards the Long Hut. I could see him writhing in agony as they leaned him up against the cold walls, and rebound him at the wrists.

"You are too soft hearted, Fur Benyn, these slaves don’t deserve your time. They’re savages from the coast lands of Frynk.

It was Lorden, a particular favourite of mine when he was a child. Now he had grown into a severe adult. I stood between the warriors and slaves, inspecting their health under the guttering flames of our torches. The first, in the long line was no more than a child. She was fair of hair and pretty, underneath the filth. If Tallack’s dogs had not yet ravaged the poor girl, they would soon enough. Grabbing her hands, I turned them over to see a small woven bracelet of hair and clay beads. Each one painted with a flower. I pointed to the workmanship, and then at her, trying to make her understand my question.
“

“Did you make this, girl?” I said, repeating my gestures. She looked terrified. I tried again. “You, make…this?”

A stream of nonsense tumbled from her mouth. I assumed that she was speaking in the tongue of her people. As I was about to give up, the brown skinned boy leaned forwards and spoke.

“Yes, great lady. She did make that bracelet.”

For his troubles, the young lad received a back hander from Lorden. I hobbled closer, swiping the brute with my stick. “Get out of it.” I growled, threatening to clonk him on his fat head. I approached the boy. “Where did you learn our speech? And don’t lie to me, boy, or I’ll have you skinned.”

“Lying is a sin, great lady. I learned a little from a traveller, who came to our lands far from here.”

“In Frynk? They have dark skinned people like you there?”

"I am from beyond Frynk. Where the sun cooks our food and dries our soils. Where the sand stretches farther than the sky, and rain is a blessing." He tried to stand upright, forgetting the state of his foot. The moment it connected with the ground, he whimpered in pain. Lorden rushed towards him, His fist raised at the ready.

I held my stick up across his path, blocking the blow. "You will not beat him. Who do these slaves belong to?"

"They are Tallack's, Fur Benyn." He backed down. Not even Lorden would dare to strike me. Aebba would have his head on a pike at the gates before the sun's waking. More warriors unloaded traded goods and raided spoils to the side of the Long Hut.

I left the slaves, and went in search of my nephew. I knew his talent for spectacle. He loved to be at the centre of fun and frolics wherever he went. That is not to say, that he lacks the courage of the toughest of our fighters. He could slice the ears from an invading tribesman while swinging from the sails of his new ship, such is his swordsmanship. No, I am talking of his love for the finer things. Of woollens and jewels, exotic furs and wines and oils from the sunny hills of Frynk and the seas that lie beyond. I only had to wait until he had taken his fill of the foods and drink of home, and he would grant his old aunt anything I wanted.

I took my seat next to little Derwa, and her chatty friend from one of the Alchemist Clan's families. I wriggled my toes next to the fire pits, and waited for the dishes to arrive at my table. Aebba was in fine form. He ate with one hand resting on Cryda's thigh, guarding her against any attention from the visiting Ordos. As Tallack made his grand entrance, wrapped in a massive black bear fur, all the families and slaves cheered for his return.

Aebba stood to greet his favourite son, grappling his shoulders and touching their foreheads together. "Thank our Lady of the Seas, you are back. You have been gone a long time, my boy, and what is this I hear about a mighty ship the size of a whale, with a wolf's head?"

"A horse head, but good enough, father. It is good to be home." Tallack skirted around the Chieftain, and kissed his mother's cheek. "Look what I bring you…" He swung the bear fur from his back, wrapping Cryda in the soft folds of skin. "And there is much more to come. I have my men outside guarding the gifts and tokens."

His sulky half-brother, Paega, piped up. "Did you trade our tin for copper or gold? And where are the grain and oils you promised to deliver?"

"I did better than that. How do you think I secured the largest ship in our lands? I traded my boat full of tin, for the finest vessel from the Phoenicians. You must let me row you downstream to see it, mother."

Cryda preened and fluttered at her eldest twin.

Paega stood up from his seat next to Aebba. His neck flushed red and his nose flared. "You traded all our tin, for a pretty boat? No grain, no copper, no gold. You are a disgrace to this tribe. You are not fit to be Dumnonii."

Tallack and Paega squared up to one another, both snorting and posturing, ready for a fight.

Aebba slapped Paega around the back of the head. "Stop your whining boy. I don't see you out on the seas, exploring new lands and arranging trading partners. You sit on your arse, counting tin nuggets all day. Now shift, and let your brother sit down. I want to hear about his adventures."

I knew that this snub, would rile young Paega. He has a similar disposition to his mother. She was the one I kept an eye on. I anticipated another scene. At the very least, I expected raised voices proclaiming Paega's rights to sit at the Chieftain's side as the eldest heir to the tribe. Much to my surprise, Eseld did not react. Instead, she poured herself more ale, and drank as though she had not a care in the world. I thought again about her message to her father in the Priest Sect, sent via her cousin. Was this 'easing' of the way, a direct threat to Aebba, or his sons? I resolved to speak with the Chieftain at the earliest opportunity. He should know that his wife is plotting against him.

The food was plentiful and delicious. The tunes played were a welcome change from our usual piper. Many of Tallack's crew were musical. Some had brought drums from other lands, while others plucked strings stretched across hollowed out shells of wood. Their choice of melodies was a bit mournful for my tastes. I prefer a merry jig with my ale.

When all the dishes were eaten, or picked at, Tallack ordered the crew to carry in the traded goods. He explained to the Chieftain, that after the exchange of ships was made, he returned to port near Lands' End, and collected more tin ingots, before their first major voyage began. When Cryda heard this, she narrowed her eyes at the boy Paega, muttering under her breath. If I did not know her better, I would have sworn that she was summoning a curse on the young man.

Lorden entered the Long Hut first, carrying a wooden cask, filled with beads and bangles, fibulas and torques. As he approached the top bench, Tallack reached over and plucked the golden necklace from the pile, and handed this to Cryda. She almost purred with delight. As Lorden set the box down in front of Aebba, Tallack dug deep into the tangle of metal and clay beads, and extracted a fine set of bangles.

He called over to his half-sister, seated by my side. "And for the stunning Derwa, beautiful adornments. Come…" He beckoned her towards the top table. "Come. Let us see how good they look upon your strong arms."

Her confidence seemed less shaken with this summons. Tallack had a soothing tone, unlike his father. Derwa hopped from her bench, and took the wide bangles from her brother, slipping them over her delicate hands onto her forearms.

"There…" Tallack admired. "Don't you look fine?" He turned all about him, encouraging others to agree with his declaration. Some of the elders laughed with awkwardness. Many of the younger women jeered, until Eseld shot them with a scalding glare.

Before long, Tallack had distributed all his gifts, and displayed the traded goods for the entire tribe to behold. It was a bounty like no other. Aebba beamed from his lofty seat at the head of the Long Hut, with Cryda to his right, and Tallack to his left. Only then, did Tallack order the slaves to be dragged in, each of them bound to a long length of twisted hemp to stop them from running.

It was the first time Eseld looked animated all evening. She stood and walked over to the first, examining her teeth and strength of muscles. "We should make another offering to the Lady of Lakes and Seas for our good fortune. One of the strongest must be chosen." She made her way along the line, peering at each of them in turn.

"We need all the slaves we can get for the mines. Tallack will take them along the coast to Bentewyn." Aebba announced. His word was final. Eseld did not seem beaten. It looked to me, as though she favoured the pretty blond girl for the bloody knife. I could guess as to her motives. Why put temptation in Aebba's path, when it could be sacrificed at the source? The string of slaves were still shuffling into the hut. As Eseld neared the end of the line, the dark-skinned boy heaved himself and his damaged foot into the centre of the space.

"What about this one?" Eseld queried, grappling the torn material of the boy's rags.

Tallack looked up from his cup. "If you like. He's broken anyway. No use to anyone." He rose from his seat and unsheathed the blade from his scabbard. "I'll do it for you now if you want to say the words?"

Eseld took a breath and raised her arms in the air. She paused, formulating the chants in her mind. Tallack reached around the boy's neck, drawing him in close with the blade's edge.

CHAPTER FIVE

The boy struggled for a moment, and then with pitiful resignation, slackened his grip of Tallack's tunic and closed his eyes, awaiting oblivion.

"Wait!" I yelled, struggling to my feet. "Nephew, I have need of this boy."

Tallack grinned. "A little young for your tastes, surely, Aunt?" His sneer provoked my temper. I blundered over to where they stood, and slapped his arm away from the boy's throat.

"You'll do well to mind your tongue. If I am to continue healing your warriors, and tending to all your women folk and children, I need more help. I am not as young as I was. If you have any fondness for your old aunt, you'll grant me this boy… and that grubby girl over there too."

Eseld's mouth dropped open. "You cannot make demands, Meliora. These slaves belong to Aebba, not you." She turned to the Chieftain for his support. He leaned to his right, listening to a conspiratorial whisper from his first wife. When she had finished her private discussion, Aebba waved Eseld away. "Let her have them. They are no use to us." I could see him watching the blond Frynkish girl move. It pleased him to keep her at the compound.

"I am indebted to you, Aebba. You will not regret the decision."

He grunted, muttering something to Cryda. She grinned and twirled a braid of her hair about a finger. Nothing amused her so much as victory over Eseld and her faith. Her being with child had a softening effect on our leader. With a quick glance about the room, it seemed that others looked to attempt the same manoeuvre, sizing up the slaves and approaching Aebba and Tallack with reasons to take them into their homes.

I could not afford to wait for the Chief to change his mind. I took the knife from Tallack and cut the filthy girl, and hobbled boy, loose from the tether. With a jab of my thumb, I told them both to follow me. As we left the Long Hut, I peered back through the haze of smoke. Eseld looked positively murderous. I vowed to speak with the Chieftain about my fears, at first light.

What a pathetic sight we were, me clinging to my long stick, and the slave girl hooked beneath the dark boy's arm. We all staggered across the board walks towards my hut. As they entered inside, I realised how little thought I had put into the arrangement. My other slaves were not really mine. They belonged to Aebba, who granted me permission to order them about whenever I required assistance. These were the first that were claimed as my own. My hut was too small to accommodate us all.

As late as it was, I knew that without medicines and treatments, this boy would die a long and agonising death. I stuck my head through the doorway and called to one of Aebba's warriors, one whom I knew would help me, whatever I asked of him. It did not take him long, to return with all that I needed to repair the break in the boy's leg.

With split hazel wood, and twisted hemp, I prepared the splint and lay it to one side. The boy guessed what had to come next.

"I beg of you no." He squealed, as I took hold of his swollen foot. He wriggled, attempting an escape. That was when I required the warrior's assistance again. As he held down his shoulders against my bunk, I yanked the bones in his ankle until all lined up as they should. He screamed loud enough to send the crows skyward from the neighbouring forest, and then lost consciousness.

When he came to, his leg was bound and supported by the splint. It was fortunate that the bone did not break the skin, for that presents a whole new raft of problems. I stewed some dried willow bark in hot water and told him to drink as much as he could manage, but he drifted off once again. My warrior friend lifted his skinny body from my bunk and onto the rushes near the fire. If I'd been kinder, I would have left him to sleep off the worst of the pain in my bed, but the thought of a draughty night on the ground, filled me with horror. Still, he had the warmth of the girl alongside him and one of my furs. It's more than many slaves are given.

Come the dawn, I felt strangely relieved to see him awake, and smiling. The guardsman told me that the girl tried to make a run for it in the middle of the night, but she could not scale the fences, nor make it through the compound gates. After a brief struggle, the warrior told me, he cuffed her around the face and delivered her back to my hut. I had slept through the entire escape.

Grabbing the girl by the wrist, I took her out to my goats and presented her with a beaker and a log on which to sit. I mimed the actions of milking the udders into the pot. She pretended not to understand. Folding her arms across her chest and shaking her head. There is a limit to my patience, and I was hungry and thirsty. I pointed to the goat, pushed her down on the log and thrust the beaker at her. "Milk!" I bellowed. That did the job. I watched her for a few moments. This was not her first-time grappling goat's teats. When she was done, I sprinkled a handful of crushed barley into the milk and rested the pot into the hot embers.

Her clothing smelled foul. She was covered in her own kawgh, her hair crawled with lice. Steering her with my stick, I marched her out of the compound gates, through the thickets at the start of the woodland, and down towards the river. There is a tributary to the Exe, that runs clean and cold. I ripped the rags from her back, leaving only the wrappings about her loins, and before she could complain, I pushed her in. I figured that she would either thrash about until she smelled better or would swim away.

Again, I mimed the actions for her to scrub the muck from herself, but the icy waters made her scramble towards the bank. I held her off with my stick, until she made an attempt to rub the filth from her skin. Only then would I let her back to shore.

Screaming at me in her native tongue, she snatched her rags from my hands and tried to put them on. I shook my head, wrestling them back from her in order that they too could be washed, but it was not to be. With dripping hair and a scowl that could frighten Morrighan herself, she stomped back towards the compound, with me snapping at her heels. She was not as daft as she looked. Rather than run from me, she hurried into my hut to warm herself by my fire.

I lingered by my small herd, for I could see Eseld speaking with the taller man from the Ordo Tribe. He was making his way into little Derwa's hut, until Eseld pulled on his arm to stop him. I harvested some herbs from my plot, and wandered closer to hear their exchange. It did not take much to work out why he was there.

Aebba had, after all, promised his remaining daughter to the heir of the Ordoviches. They must have packed their things in readiness to leave. I skirted behind Derwa's hut, bending low to pick at the roots close by in pretence. Through the doorway, I could hear their raised voices. They had entered the hut. Derwa was crying great sobs of distress.

Eseld's nasal whine was unmistakable. She pleaded with the Ordo not to take her daughter away. When this failed, I heard her say, "You don't have to leave right now. Stay until the next full moon, and I will reward your kindness with a share in the foreign trade goods. You will have more gold and silver than you ever dreamed possible."

His response was rapid. "You don't have the authority to give me anything. That plunder belongs to your Chieftain, or his son. And anyway, what makes you think that I will deal with you?"

Her voice reduced to a rasping whisper. I had to strain to hear her. She said, "There is a great change coming, one that will strengthen my standing in the tribe. I will give you all that you desire, so long as you give up your claim on my daughter."

I heard nothing but the end of Derwa's tears. They must have reached an accord, for the next I saw, was the Ordo warrior stomping from the hut, all alone. I stayed as long as I dared, not wanting to risk discovery. Eseld comforted her child, shushing and soothing her, the way only a mother can.

I admit, I forgot all about tending to the training of my new slaves. Scurrying off to the Long Hut, I dropped my gathered herbs into the mud. As I bustled in, Aebba kicked out at a woman dressing his erupting toes. He saw me enter, and wailed at me.

"Call yourself a healer. I am in a worse state than before. All these potions and poultices do nothing but stink out the place. Can't you give me something else, Fur Benyn? He used the phrase in a sarcastic tone.

I retaliated in kind. "I can, nephew. I can cut off your festering toes and seal them shut with a hot poker. How would that suit you?"

He grumbled, bested.

"Send your slaves away, I need to speak with you about an urgent matter." I watched as the servants took away the soiled bandages and his third wife, Brea, brought in fresh hot water in a bowl.

"There, we're alone. Say what you have to say, then get me some willow bark. I have a sore head to match my feet."

I raised a brow at the presence of Brea.

"Oh, she won't say anything, will you woman?"

She lowered his foot by the ankle into the hot water.

He yelped and kicked out, sending her flying backwards into the bench struts. "Too hot. What are you trying to do, cook me?"

Brea picked herself up, straightened her linens and cooled his bowl with a few splashes of cold water from a jug. Aebba glared up at me as she continued his treatment.

"I think Eseld is plotting against you." I scanned the hut again, making sure that no one lurked about us.

"Ha! Tell me something I don't know. That scrag end is always plotting. Forget about it, Aunt. Focus your concern on my poor toes."

"I mean it, Aebba. I heard her give her cousin a message for the priests. She told her father to make his move by the next full moon." I landed my hand on his shoulder to lend weight to my words.

He grinned up at me. "That rabble. What are they going to do, curse me or pray for me? They can't even hold their own lands and ponies from the Duro's raids. They have even less chance of taking mine." He wriggled his red and purple toes in the warm water bowl. "Don't worry yourself over it. My boys have everything under control."

Brea dropped a few crushed birch shavings into the steaming foot bath, and let them soak. I wandered from the hut, dismissed as an old fool, but I could not help but feel an omen whipping the leaves and branches of the elms and beech trees surrounding the camp. There will be dire trouble here before too long.

I returned to my hut to discover my breakfast gone, and drips of my porridge spilled down the slave girl's front. My tolerance snapped. I cuffed her around the head, and demanded that she make more, warning her that I would feed her to the dogs if she ever crossed me. Again, she pretended not to understand. I gestured to the dark-skinned boy, laying in his weakened state by my fire. "Tell her my orders, or by the Lady, I will sacrifice her myself."

I swear that I saw him hide a grin. I just knew that he had wits, and I will make sure that I use them to their fullest. By high sun, my new slave knew her duties and looked suitably sorry for her behaviour. Not that I will turn my back to her when she prepares the meat for my supper. A Frynk slave with a blade is a tricky beast.

Checking that the bindings on his splint were not cutting off the flowing humours, I asked the dark boy his name. His response both puzzled and distressed me.

"Which name would the great lady, prefer, the one my mother gave to me, my Frynkish slave name, or the many shameful names used aboard your nephew's ship?"

"You were taken by the Frynks?" I knew his answer before I posed my question.

"I was taken from my family in the Berbers, by a raiding party of Celtiberians. I served them, as we sailed through the roughest seas you could ever imagine. Waves higher than the tallest trees. Dips lower than mountain valleys. We lost some of my closest friends overboard. They whipped and tied us to the masts, left us to starve or drown, until finally we made it to the Urnfield Cultures of the Frynks.

"I was sold to work the fields and tend the goats. It was there that I met with the traveller. He spoke many languages, told me about different lands and people. I listened well, and learned much."

"And that was when my nephew took you?"

He nodded. I knew how Tallack's crew treated slaves. Brutality is their life's work. "Which of them did this?" I re-tied the braces around his leg.

The boy lowered his eyes. "The one they call Lorden."

I figured as much, a Dumnoni nickname for a clown. He was such a joy as a child. I would dearly love to know what made him change so drastically into the man he is now. "What name shall I know you?" I asked of my young charge.

"If this is to be my new life, I should have a new name. One that pleases you, Fur Benyn."

I chuckled. He had already picked up on how others refer to me. "I will call you, Jago."

He responded with a half-smile and a single nod. I handed him some day-old bread, and a little ale I had stashed for later. He will heal better with some meat on his bones. As he tucked into my food, I was distracted by loud voices and dogs barking near to the Long Hut. With my suspicions already on high alert, I went in search of the source of rumpus.

I was barely two board planks away from my hut, when I saw the first fist thrown. Paega jabbed at Tallack, missing his mark by some distance. He is brave or foolhardy. Tallack will not stand for a petulant outburst such as this. The reasons for their falling out became clear as I drew closer. Paega appeared to be making off with a trunk of Tallack's traded goods. Gold, silver, clay beads and more, all spilled out into the mud.

"It's not for me…" Paega offered, feebly. "These are tributes to the Chieftain. How else can we trade for grain, or copper from the Ordos?"

Tallack would not be appeased. "You expect me to believe that? We have ample tin for barter. These goods belong to me. I know your greed. You will bury these with your mother's other secret troves."

"Lies, all of it lies. Our father put me in charge of trade goods. This will ensure a stockpile of grain for next winter."

"Giss on… you're full of kawgh! Winter grain… do you think I'm addled?" Tallack swept the precious metals back into the trunk with his foot, then stooped to pick it up. Paega grabbed at the box. They struggled, Paega head butt Tallack in the face, splitting his nose open. I rushed over to break them up, but was beaten to the spot by Eseld. She is, by every reckoning, of a higher standing to me. I stopped to see how she would settle the affair, hoping, rather than expecting for a fair outcome.

Eseld laid her hand on her son's shoulder, forcing him to take a step back. Tallack was not so easy to calm. His fair face was cracked like an egg. Blood spouted in big globs from both nose holes.

"You little kyjya!" Tallack lurched at Paega, his fists whirling just a breath away from Eseld's head. She pushed him by the chest backwards, skidding her neat shoes in the ground against his strength. I had to step in before they murdered one another.

"Tallack." I yelled, hobbling closer. "It's not worth your efforts boy. Let me see your poor face." I stepped between the boys hoping my seniority would put an end to the standoff. I reached up to his nose, wiping away the blood and ill humours, allowing Eseld her chance to move out of their reach.

As I dabbed and took my time examining him, the guardsman at the gate called out. "Head Hunters! Blydh returns with his men!" The gates swung open, and thundering hooves sprayed filth as they galloped into the compound. Everyone cheered them, running from their huts to see the proud warriors stream in and around the houses. I saw a great many preserved heads swinging from their horses, marking their victories.

Tallack turned to Paega. "Now we will see how you fare…"

CHAPTER SIX

Paega has the same disposition as his mother. As soon as Blydh rode into the compound with his men, he slunk away from the argument without stopping to take the spoils. If that boy is to ever take the Chieftain role after Aebba, he will need to earn the respect of the whole tribe, something the twins have already achieved.

Blydh greeted his brother, younger to him by less than a sunset. He launched himself from his horse, and clasped Tallack by the back of the head, touching their foreheads together. It is a moving sight. They each beamed with an unspoken secret bond between them. In all their years, I have never once witnessed the merest hint of jealousy. Their strength is in unity. Each draws comfort from the fact that should one fall in battle or misstep, the other would protect and care for those left behind. That alone, gives them both courage where others might falter.

Leaving his horse to bear the heads of his enemies, Blydh entered the Long Hut to bring news to his parents. I knew what tidings he would deliver. It changed little each time. The great Chieftain's son and his clan of wild warriors, fought back those tribal factions daring to cross our borders and plunder our settlements. I cared not for the details. There is enough blood and entrails in my line of work, without adding to them.

A quick glance at his horsemen and I knew how busy I would be by eventide. These men bore the wounds of their labours, but took great care not to appear bothered by their discomfort. While the sun slept, each of them would appear in my doorway, asking me for herbs and tinctures for their pains. I hurried back to my hut to issue orders to the girl, with Jago's help. I really must find a name for her.

I spent much of my day, gathering, grinding and boiling my healing mixtures in readiness. How fortunate that I collected the willow bark. My stores will take a hefty beating this evening. The moon was high and nearing its fullest girth, when I finished swilling out and patching the last of the Head Hunters' cuts. I used up the last of my cattle-gut and blunted my best bone needle, stitching a gash that could easily take the life of one man. His open flesh stank of rot. I burned out what I could, but his skin stayed hot even after the pain died away. He is in the Goddess Brighid's hands now. Only she can decide if he should live to hunt heads again, or join his ancestors in the Summerlands.

When I washed the blood from my arms, I realised how famished I was. Exhaustion urged me towards the Long Hut in search of leftovers. There was more than my own mouth to feed now. The Frynkish girl and Jago had worked alongside me all evening. Jago has his own crutch now, cut from the elm beyond the camp fences. His progress is slow, but sure, and I am glad of his help. He has such a good-natured temperament, and he takes care of the girl. I think he might be a bit smitten by her, especially after a change of rags into a clean tunic.

The Long Hut was loud and bawdy, as you would expect with the return of the Hunter Clan. Many of the elders and their families paid their tributes, and retreated to their huts. I heaved my aching bones through the singing beasts, ignoring their shouts and jeers. Brea jumped up from her bench upon seeing me, eager to leave their boisterous antics.

"Can I be of service to you, Fur Benyn?" She said, following me to the rear portion of the Long Hut, where the slaves drooled over the roasted meat carcasses.

"Brea, you are Aebba's wife. You don't have to serve me. And call me Meliora. I feel neither wise nor womanly today."

She saw me scrape the bits from a wooden platter, and begin to stack the uneaten food high. From a lidded pot, she drew out a fresh loaf, baked for the morning. "Here, take this. I can get the slaves to make more."

I touched her cheek and smiled. "You are kindness itself, Brea. I thank you." With the loaf tucked beneath my cloak, and the scraps held aloft, I began my amble back through the rowdy men. Squinting up at the top bench, I noted Cryda missing from Aebba's side. She must have retired for the night. Eseld grimaced from her lowly seat beneath Aebba's table. I swear that woman is cooking up something foul. Before I made it to the door, Aebba bellowed at me.

"Stealing again, Aunt?" He, and the entire Hunter Clan, laughed at my expense.

"It's only stealing if you are unaware of my theft." I glared back at him, too tired to banter.

"Hark at her!" He chuckled. "She would take the ale from my cup given the chance." He thumped his chest, wearing the same screwed up face he makes whenever he has food stuck in his gullet. "You will have better pickings tomorrow, Aunt. I shall bring back the biggest stag you have ever seen."

"You are for the hunt, in the morn, nephew?"

"I am. And all will see me as the best hunter in the tribe."

The cheers were deafening. I took a long breath and waited for the noise to die down. "Then I will have to cut more willow bark for your aches and pains. I had better start now, if I am to harvest enough." I left during the roar of merriment, and before he could snipe back at me for my insolence.

At my hut, I ripped the loaf into three pieces and placed the platter of scraps next to the fire. Perched on the edge of my bunk, we each tore into the meats and bread, until our hunger was sated. Jago winced and moved his ankle beneath his injured one.

"You did well today." I told them both, urging them to finish up the rest of the food. I got to my feet and fetched my last sliver of willow, and handed it to Jago. He gave me a nod of appreciation as I patted his head. He's a good boy. He learns fast and keeps the Frynkish girl in check. Not that I trust her fully, yet.

I'll be glad when the warriors are on their way again. I cannot recall so many patients to treat in such a short time. They have a habit of stirring up the older folk who should not be taking such risks to prove themselves. Why men have to kill to prove their worth is beyond me.

Come morning, I set the girl to make our porridge, and wandered out to see the men gathering for the hunt. Aebba is starting to decline. He eats and drinks too much for good health. I watched him make several attempts to sling his leg about the horse's back. Each time, he grunted and moaned. He waved me closer, laying against his horse's neck.

"Meliora, can you look in on Cryda later? Make sure that she has what she needs."

"Did she say the pregnancy is troubling her? What shall I take to her?" My concern waned as he pulled a disquieted face.

"Make sure that she has female company…I don't want the Ordo's bothering her."

That made sense. Aebba's first day away from the Ruvane since the announcement of her impending child, and his thoughts immediately jump to her straying from camp with one of our visitors. I reassured him before he rode away, frowning and pounding his chest with digestive pain.

Armed with baskets, and my sharpest knives, my slaves and I went in search of fresh plants to restock my supplies. Jago is such a fast learner. Thus far, he can identify the plants of value as I teach him, but his ankle makes it difficult for him to reap them. Where possible, he sits on logs in the water meadows and harvests cress and mints, rushes and the like, other times he hooks the basket on his stick, while the girl picks plantain and nettle tips. I haven't had the courage to give them knives to help me with barks and twigs. Maybe that will come in time.

It is such a blessing that the rains have finally stopped. We are now two full days without it pouring down and swelling the rivers. Every now and then, the sun peeks out from behind clouds to warm our faces. It must have made the wildlife giddy too, for I was able to snag a squirrel near the woods as it settled by my feet. That will do us well in a stew with a few of those fresh nettles and a bit of barley.

We headed back to camp to find that the Chieftain had returned before us. His horse wandered about the compound untethered, chewing on my herb patch. There appeared to be no other hunters with him. I sent Jago and the girl after the pony, and hurried into the Long

Hut. Aebba was lying on the top table, with Eseld and Cryda screaming over his loud groans.

"Meliora, thank the Lady. Where have you been?" Cryda cried. "He's in such pain."

Eseld shoved Cryda's hands away, sprinkling a blue powder on the wound site and chanting nonsense while she rattled a stick with bones and feathers bound to its end.

I stepped up to their level and looked at the narrow cut above his hip. I could see the fat in yellow swathes under his skin. He was lucky that he is not a thin man. Anyone else would have died from such an injury. "An arrow?" I ventured, flicking the congealing blue powder from him and picking out globs of birch pitch from the gaping hole. "Move." I bleated at his wives. "I can't work with you under my feet." Cryda and Eseld did as I commanded, but no doubt I will pay later for my gruff manner. "Do you think maybe it's time for you to admit that you are not a young man anymore, nephew?"

"An accident. My age has nothing to do with it. A bow snapped flinging the arrow towards me." He shifted his position, allowing me better access.

"You did this yourself?" I could not keep the surprise out of my voice.

"No, daft old woman. Of course not. It was Lorden's bowstring which gave way. He said he'd restrung it only recently. Can't imagine how it failed."

Cryda narrowed her eyes at Eseld. "Unless someone tampered with it."

"Now, now. Cryda. No one could have predicted this outcome. Don't go stirring up trouble without cause."

While they bickered, I sloshed heated water over him, flushing out the bits of dirt and powder. Without any cattle-gut to stitch him up, I made a temporary poultice of ground plantain and boar grease and covered him with leaves. Sweat poured from his neck and face. Leaving Eseld and Cryda to fuss over him, I went in search of Brea. She was keeping a watchful eye over the slaves as they prepared their food. I gave her a handful of willow and a bunch of plantain for later, and made my way back to the front of the Long Hut.

Jago stood in front of Paega attempting to enter. The nearer I drew, the more I could discern his anguish.

"As if we'd let the likes of you in our Chieftain's hut. What are you…some sort of cursed animal?" Paega shoved Jago's shoulder, making him stagger to stay upright on his crutch.

Jago spotted my approach. "Ah, great lady. The others talk of an arrow piercing the Chieftain. I brought you some catgut I found in one of your jars. You'll need it to stitch him, yes?"

"That's right, Jago. I thought I had used up the last of it. Well done." I took the dried length from him and headed for the door. Jago swivelled on his stick to follow me.

Paega lurched forwards, catching his fist with the back of Jago's head. "And where do you think you're going?"

Jago lost his balance, toppling to the floor and smashing his head against a rock embedded in the ground next to the walls. He bled like a sacrificial lamb, his body jerked and spasmed against the soft mud as he thrashed about.

I stooped low to protect his face against further harm. "That'd be right. Pick on crippled slaves, never on anyone bigger than yourself. You're a disgrace, boy." I sat on the rock with Jago's head on my lap until the fitting stopped. The inside blackness of his eye went to a pinprick in size, the other as wide as can be. That cannot be a good sign. Before the fit let up, he babbled such a string of things in a tongue I have never heard uttered before. I can only assume that this was the language of his homeland. It nearly frightened Paega into messing his leggings.

"He's got bad spirits protecting him; cursed by the Morrighan. She will rise through him and kill us all in our sleep." His trembling arm pointed at Jago's shuddering body as he lay in my arms.

"Ah giss on. Don't talk such rot." I chided, but I have to admit, I was enjoying his terror.

"I'm going to tell mother. She will know what to do." He turned tails and ran into the Long Hut in search of Eseld and her feathered stick. I waited until I could see the Frynkish girl leaving my house in the distance and called her over. With a great many gestures and attempts to make her understand me, I ordered her to help Jago back to my hut, and make him comfortable in his groggy state. After I had stitched and bound Aebba, I returned to find Eseld in my hut performing some ridiculous ritual over the poor boy.

Her prancing and dancing I can cope with. Even her chanting is tolerable and relatively harmless, but when she whips out a knife, it can only mean one thing. She's about to make another sacrifice to be certain that the God of the Underworld is banished from the camp.

"Put that knife away. He is my slave and I will decide what happens to him." I held her wrist at bay, and removed the blade from her grasp.

She wrestled her arm from me and spat on my rushes. "This boy is cursed. You risk all our lives keeping him here. There is only one safe course of action, and you know that."

I picked up Jago's stick and swiped it across her calves. "Get out, you pitiful wretch. Touch him again, and a good cursing will be the least of your worries." I waved the crutch at her again, poised to smack her in the shins if she did not leave. She chose the latter.

"Aebba will hear of this. This is not the end of this matter, Meliora. Just you wait and see." She screamed the last of the threat through the doorway as she stomped along the boardwalks away from my hut.

On reflection, hitting the Chieftain's second wife with a big stick was not my finest day's work, and it will probably come back to haunt me, but I had more pressing concerns to deal with. Jago drifted in and out of a daze for some time after I had tended the cut on his head.

I left him in my bunk, with the Frynkish girl watching over him, while I called upon the feverish warrior from the previous night. I removed his leaves and dressings, and the tissues oozed with a stinking greenish humour. He fretted in his sweaty furs, half awake, half addled. I tried to prepare his woman for the worst, but she would not stop crying to hear me. I've done all I can. The gods will decide his fate.

The sun grew as tired as I. It sank behind the trees in a celebration of rose and golden colours across the sky. It gladdened my heart to see. As I made my way back across camp, I noticed that the watch man climbed down the ladders and opened the main gate ajar. My curiosity piqued, I took the longer route over the boards to my hut, so that I could see what was occurring.

In the gloom, I could just make out the face of the horseman, as he handed something over to the guard. I adjusted my leggings, giving me time to confirm my suspicions. The man on the horse was Eseld's cousin from the Priests' Sect. I remembered him clearly from binding his leg wound in my hut.

With deep concern churning in the pit of my stomach, I called to the guard and waited for him to trudge through the sticky dirt to where I stood.

"What have you there?" I demanded of him.

"Forgive me, Fur Benyn. I am not permitted to say." The guardsman said, in his most imploring voice.

"Are you permitted to show me?" I gave him a stern glare, hoping to intimidate an answer from him.

Slowly, he held out his hand and opened his fist. Laying in the palm of his hand were two small crossed bones, tied in the centre with twine. I looked at the offering and then at the guard's face.

"And who are you to give this to?" I already knew, but confirmation removes all doubt.

"The Lady Eseld, Fur Benyn."

We exchanged a look of complete understanding. Both of us knew what this meant, and to what it could possibly lead. Eseld's father, leader of the Priest Sect, was no more than half a day's walk from our compound.

CHAPTER SEVEN

The knowledge that the Priest Sect were so close to our settlement made me uneasy. Eseld was not one to cower in a corner when her status was threatened. Even less so, when the elevation of her son to the position of Chieftain was in question. With two popular sons, and another child on the way, Cryda remained the favoured wife in all matters.

I kept my keen eyes trained on the comings and goings of the Long Hut all evening. The hunting party returned, laden with game and beasts, but I could tell from their squabbles and infighting, that they grew restless in camp. These were the wild warriors of the heath lands, nomadic in nature, and spoiling for war at the least provocation. They hunger for battle, taking as many heads from tribes invading our lands as possible.

In truth, there are plenty of resources for all to share, but our tin mines are precious. Many Chieftains have their eye on those, whether by taking small chunks of land at a time, or planning more ambitious and long-lasting raids. Those Head Hunters are our first line of defence. Without their patrols, the Duro's further east, or the Ordo's worst enemies, the Demetae, would have overrun us. It is only luck, that our tin is mainly on the southern coastline, where Tallack's men roam the seas.

By dawn, Jago had much recovered. I left the girl with the chores, and took Jago foraging, away from Eseld and her threats. At a steady gait, we wandered to the mud banks at the side of the Exe, in search of new leaves and shoots. I had a little tin ingot in my pocket, should any worthy trades present themselves.

With my old pony carrying the load, I could gather enough rushes and withies to last a quarter moon or more. I showed Jago how to split the reeds and weave them together until he could shape the material around his sore feet. Cushioned with a little dry moss, they will do him until I have enough squirrel skin for shoes. While he wove and plaited, I gathered razor clams and a fat crab. I was on the lookout for more samphire, but someone else must have beaten me to the spot.

The further into the salt waters we travelled, the more activity on the river we saw. Row boats of dried meats and mended sails, loaded from the river banks, were filling Tallack's new ship to its fullest. His men rigged the ropes, stacked the provisions and swept the decks. He was preparing for his next voyage. Smaller ships lay at anchor further downstream, each of them manned with crewmen of all ages from our tribe. He will take the remaining slaves to the mines and pick up enough tin to trade across the seas. I almost envy him. He gets the chance to see all the sights and sounds of far off places; the different people and their customs, new medicines and fresh thinking on curing old diseases and agues. How I wish I was young again, and a man. My life would have taken an entirely different course, but then it's doubtful that I would have made such old bones.

I was just reflecting on my journey, and pondering our return to the camp, when I heard muffled sounds and gentle splashing from the reed bed, nearly a hut's length away. I thought it might be a plump duck, and crept closer to my potential supper. The noises were more distinct the closer I sneaked. They were not of duck, but of man. A couple of Sea Warriors were at it like dogs. Disappointed, I turned away to find Jago had caught up with me, hobbling on his stick to lend a hand.

"Come away, boy. There is nothing there worth the hunt." As I faced him, his eyes widened along with a smile that cracked his face in half. "What?" I said, glancing back over my shoulder. There was Tallack, in all his naked glory, standing tall in the bow of a rowboat, hidden in the rushes. His playmate was on his knees in the hull. I grabbed Jago by the shoulder and spun him around, but it was too late. He saw it all and, by the sounds of the struggle and frenzied splashing, so had Tallack. Pushing Jago back towards my pony, I declared that it was time to return home. In the distance, I could see Tallack swimming across the wide waters back to his ship.

"It'd be in your best interests not to tell anyone what you saw today. As far as anyone knows, Tallack will take a wife when he is good and ready. Until then, he is free to do as he chooses." I did not know about the customs and practises in Jago's country of birth, but from his amusement, I doubted what he saw was commonplace. Had it been anyone but the Chieftain's son, no one would care a bit, but Tallack has a duty to continue the tribal line, laying with his crewmen, will not help that along.

With my pony burdened with willow and rushes, I could not hasten our return by hoisting Jago onto the beast. I could have cut loose our pickings, but that would have wasted our day. There was no other choice, but to hobble and dawdle until we reached the main gate. It was late when we arrived at my hut. The girl had disappeared, and the fire gone out. I knew that she had to be nearby, since none of the watchmen would allow her to leave the compound, unless she used her charms to corrupt their minds. You cannot be too guarded where pretty young Frynks are concerned.

Leaving Jago to unload our takings and relight the fire, I went in search of my slave. She was not at the river bank, for all the washing was done before the failing light of the sun. I tried the fire pits behind the Long Hut, but Aebba's slaves claim not to have seen her. Neither was she with the woman folk, weaving and stitching around the hearthstones. Tired, and desperate, I poked my head through the Long Hut doors and found her sitting on Aebba's lap with her rags up around her neck. What is it about the full moon that raises everyone's dander for tupping?

I would have yelled at her, but since she has no given name, I had to make do with shaming my nephew instead. "Aebba! Unhand my slave. She has left my fire to burn out and I have no supper." This did not dampen his ardour.

"You can have her back when I am finished with her, Aunt. It'll make up for all the liberties you take around here."

"The least you could do, would be to take her to somewhere quiet. If Eseld sees what you are up to, she will sacrifice her and I will need a new slave."

"She already knows. Caught us earlier. She doesn't seem to care anymore."

Those were the words which troubled me the most. Eseld no longer cared. That did not bode well. Despite my exhaustion, I instructed Jago to cook our seafoods, and save a little for the girl on her return. I can't punish her, if she was taken against her will from her chores. Until I know otherwise, she is safe from my wrath. Eseld, is a wholly different matter. Whatever she has planned with her cousin, it can only spell disaster.

By nightfall, I entered the Long Hut once more, and sat in my usual spot next to my young niece. Her face was filled with joy. When I asked what had prompted her happiness, she said that Tallack had made her a gift. She held the necklace aloft for me to have a closer look. The pearls strung with woven cow hair was far finer than anything Tallack could have made. I kept the falsehood to myself. It pleased her to think that her half-brother had taken the time and effort to craft it for her. I suspect that he either traded or stole the item with her in mind. That is not to say that all mischief eludes me.

"When are you to leave with the Ordo's for your binding ceremony?" I asked her, hoping that she might divulge Eseld's plots in passing.

Derwa looked up at me, filled with calm confidence. "I'm not going now. Mother says that isn't necessary. I'm to wed someone else instead."

"Is that so? And who shall you be bound to instead?" I tried to keep the shock from my voice, but it was not easy.

"She didn't say. But whoever it is, I'm to have the finest metals and jewels you ever did see, so it will be a clansman of enormous wealth."

I bit my lip, keeping my thoughts to myself. That could only mean one thing. Eseld has arranged a more profitable trade behind Aebba's back. One that will secure the status of her bloodline, and gives Paega a greater chance of succeeding as Chieftain. While I churned over the possibilities, I kept one eye on the dishes served to Aebba's table, particularly those offered by Eseld. He seemed less ravenous than usual, picking at his plate and sipping his ale, rather than guzzling like he would on most occasions.

A few times when I turned around to view those on the top table, I noticed him rubbing his chest, and pulling a face. The same face he pulled before his hunting trip. I stood up and stretched my legs, wandering closer to him. "Is your gut troubling you again?" I muttered in a hushed tone, so few would hear me.

"A burning in my gullet, Aunt. It's nothing." He kicked out at Brea sitting beneath his table. "Get me some chalk and plantain. That'll put out the fires." She scurried off to mix his tincture.

Eseld filled her stomach with the rich pickings of Frynk and beyond. "You must try these blackened olives. They dry your teeth but fill your mouth with such flavour. Here…" She stood up and held the bowl out to me. I glared at her, suspicious of anything that woman had to offer, shaking my head. Clambering up to Aebba's level, she picked up an olive and shoved it between his lips. "You never know, it might help." She said, hopping back down to her own seat. My heart froze, expecting him to keel over where he sat. He chewed, pulling a different face, and swallowed. Before I could get him to spit out the offending article, I saw Eseld take another olive for herself. "Hmm, I could get used to these. Do you think they'd grow here?"

I was not sure that my poor mind could take anymore worry. She fed him all sorts of items, some he took gladly, others with an air of annoyance, but all without a second glance. I could barely keep up with her.

As the evening wore on, and much ale and Frynkish wine was taken, I started to relax. Apart from his normal digestive aches, he sang and bellowed through the evening in much the same way as any other night.

Long after sundown, a rider came galloping into the compound. Known by us all, as the brother of Lorden, this trusted warrior warned of a scouting party of Duro's heading into the moorlands. Word reached him, that settlements were raided and their homes lit by torches.

We listened to his accounts, of screaming mother's, terrified children and slain menfolk, as their livestock were slaughtered before their eyes, and ponies driven across into their territories.

When the rider finished his account, he stood before the top table, panting and awaiting Aebba's decision. Every eye in the hut looked in his direction, as the Chieftain struggled to focus.

When the silence had deafened us for a time, Blydh spoke out. "Let us ride out, father. We will make them pay for their crimes. They will kawgh their leggings when they see us chasing after them. Our bronze weapons will slice their necks and we will add their heads to our horses." A great roar filled the Long Hut rafters. All were in agreement. The Duro's would pay with their lives. Aebba took some time to catch up with events. He agreed with a smile and a slap to his knee, but said nothing.

Taking their cue, the Head Hunter's gathered up their swords and pikes, finished off their ale and left the hut in search of fresh torches and their horses. Before too long, their thundering hooves rumbled and shook the ground, as they poured out of the compound hollering and wailing their battle cries. Many stood out to watch them leave, others tutted and moaned, having spent a great deal of time soothing youngsters to sleep, only to have them woken again.

I stood in the doorway of the Long Hut, and stared up at the full moon. This is a time when good and evil fight over the pale light, when the spirits of Inglond are at large. Some say, on a clear night, when the moon is its fattest, you can see the gods Cernonnus and Lugh, fighting in the sky. If Cernonnus wins this night, evil will triumph. The compound was eerie and still without the horsemen or Tallack's sailors at camp. We are undefended and under a fateful sky. Few remained in the Long Hut to drink to the health of our young warriors. I returned to my seat, to find that Derwa had gone. Eseld had sent her to bed. Cryda waved off her son, and slunk away, I know not where. I hoped that she had returned to her hut to sleep, but with the taller of the Ordo Tribesmen missing, I suspect our Chieftain's fears are founded in fact.

Aebba sat still, slipping in his chair from too much wine and ale, and still complaining about his guts aching. Brea flitted here and there, fetching and carrying and doing his bidding in general. As soon as I could see Eseld retiring for the night, I made my way home too. There were few nods of sleep left to the night before dawn. Aebba was in safe hands until then. With my furs tucked about me, and the fire loaded with logs, I drifted away to dream of the Summerlands, where no one is hungry and there is no word for pain.

Come the morning, I awoke with such a fearful knot in my stomach. A wail worthy of the Morrighan tugged at my senses, until I opened my eyes with a start. My heart rate quickened. At first, I thought a burning log had fallen from the fire onto the rushes, but the reason behind the scream was far worse. I hastened to my door, and saw the gathering crowds about the Long Hut.

Many of the elders pushed to the front, leaving the women to guess as to the cause of distress. Wrapped in my bedding, I struggled through the clans and forced my passage into the hut. Two guards held the door, but upon seeing me, permitted my entrance. Wives, children and slaves huddled around the top table, blocking my view.

"What is it? What's all the fuss and noise?" I had to shout above the clamour and hysterical women. They moved apart, allowing me to see our Chieftain, slumped in his chair. His skin waxy and pallid, his eyes black as soot. As I moved closer, Cryda began pawing at his chest, trying to rouse him. Even with my poor sight, it was clear he was dead. No tonic or potion could awaken his final slumber. I flicked my wrists at those clinging to hope. "Stand aside, let me look at him." There was nothing I could do, but I needed to see what signs could be taken from his body. I held my hand to his forehead. It was icy cold. The stiffness had already taken hold.

"Can he be saved, Meliora?" Cryda cried, clinging to my furs. I said nothing, watching the reactions of Eseld and Paega closely. She was cooler than the Exe in midwinter. Not a hint of expression gave her away. Brea fetched warm ale for Cryda's faints and stood apart from us all.

Only Paega seemed shocked by it all. "I should tell my sister." He started to walk towards the door, but Eseld grabbed hold of him, securing his waist with her arm.

"Let her sleep a little longer. She will be overcome when she finds out."

"There may be something Meliora can do yet. Don't give up hope." Cryda sobbed.

I shook my head, stepping back a pace. "I am sorry, Cryda. He is gone. There is nothing to be done for him."

For a moment, I thought I saw a glimmer of shock in Eseld's eyes, but I was mistaken, for the first words from her mouth were, "And now Paega is to be

Chieftain." Pride swelled within her. It filled her chest and spilled from her venomous face.

I reached over and pulled Aebba's chin until his mouth opened. A black stain trailed down his face to his neck. There were red spots inside his mouth and a rash on his throat. Taking a deep sniff, I could smell unripe fruit, slightly bitter. I was rapidly forming an opinion of the manner in which he died. If it is what I think, he suffered a frightening ordeal, lasting a good long while. It begins with wide eyes and a mild rash, until unsteadiness takes hold. In the final stages, the pounding headache is joined by hallucinations and loss of voice, before breathing becomes impossible. If Aebba was lucky, the last stage came quickly, with fitting until the heart fails.

I turned to the grieving widows and looked at each of them in turn. With anger boiling inside, I said to them, "Aebba was murdered."

CHAPTER EIGHT

My declaration took a while to sink into their thoughts. Eseld reacted first, reaching for her feathered stick and chanting odd sounds over his body. In between her gestures, she stopped and said, "This is what happens when you mock the gods. I warned him often enough. Our Lady of Lakes and Seas has taken her revenge." Thrusting her arms in the air, she invoked a protection spell over her son, warding off any potential threats. I must say, her performance was most convincing. I almost believed that she played no part in Aebba's death.

Cryda wept openly, falling into her seat as though her strength had fully left her. Brea rushed to her side, offering support and comfort, and brushing Cryda's hair back from her face. I called the servants to bring ale.

"We should drink to his spirit quickly, to send it into the Summerlands. Any delay and I feared that he would linger, and seek retribution." I said this to Eseld without giving much thought to her reaction.

Paega jumped on the idea. "It's your dark slave's fault. My mother was right to offer him in sacrifice. You have brought a curse down upon us all. See what your insolence leads to, old woman?"

Eseld stopped her chanting to lend weight to Paega's argument. "We must banish the evil sprite this day." She turned to one of the slaves. "Have a pyre built before nightfall. His body is to burn. See that it is fit for a Chieftain, at least five trees must fall, no fewer."

"You will not burn him. He is my Chieftain. I am the Ruvane, and I will decide how we see him into the Summerlands. Meliora, will you prepare him? I trust no other." Cryda looked at me with those puffed and bloodshot eyes and I crumbled. He was my nephew. I was there at his birth, and missed his death by a whistle.

"You ask a lot from me, child." There was place in my heart for him too. I knew what she wanted of me, and I found myself overcome. On the one hand, I would get the chance to examine any signs to support my claim. On the other, I knew that washing and scraping the flesh from his bones would take me to the edge of ruin.

"Please, Fur Benyn." Cryda said, in deference to my aged state. She knew how to get around my steely resolve. "He must be preserved in a clay pot, and taken with us to a stone circle for full funeral rites at midsummer. We shall have offerings like no other. A barrow all to himself and marked by the largest stone around for miles."

"That's a foolish idea." Eseld chided. "Any delay will see us all overrun with bad spirits. He is to burn. No one buries in barrows anymore." She shooed the slave away to begin preparations. Cryda stood up and gave Eseld such a glare, but she would not back down. "Do you want us all killed in our sleep?"

I stood between them. "This is not the work of evil spirits or curses; do you hear me? Someone…a person from our camp, has murdered our Chieftain. There must be a reckoning."

"Nonsense. I was with him the whole time." Eseld bayed. "How could anyone have stopped his heart in front of us?"

"You were not with him at all times, Eseld, for I saw you leave a little before I did last night. This is the work of poison." I admit, she riled my temper. My fury built something terrible.

Cryda wrung her hands together and then cradled her growing belly. "Are you sure about this, Meliora? Aebba complained about his guts hurting for quite a while. Could it be a build-up of bad humours that took him away while we slept?"

I thought about her suggestion. I suppose the dried black residue could have been regurgitated food, but there are few black berries in this season, and the rash was all too familiar. "I will look further into this, even if you will not. Blydh and Tallack will want a full investigation into their father's death, even if you don't." I glared pointedly at Paega, who showed no remorse for losing Aebba one bit.

Eseld snorted. "Just as you like, but the cremation will not wait. He will burn at nightfall."

Cryda looked to me to break the dead lock. I had no choice but to agree to Cryda's terms. "Actually, law of our lands state that the Ruvane has the right to take possession of her Chieftain after death. Aebba's bones belong to Cryda."

Eseld screwed up her face, contemplating her next angle. "Fine, but my father will perform the rituals and rites, and he should be here during the preparations too." Eseld stood her ground, slipping her arm beneath Paega's elbow, anchoring him to the spot.

Cryda was still giving me imploring looks. "So, you will do this for me, Meliora?"

I sighed. “I will.” And to the slaves, I ordered that they set up all that I needed on the rough grass behind my hut. I beckoned the warriors guarding the door, and instructed them to carry Aebba out to the riverside, reminding them of their duty of care. They handled his body with great reverence, taking two of his furs on which to lay him. Returning to my hut, I changed into my oldest tunic and told Jago to stay inside until the fuss had died down. He had plenty of work to be done, drying and preserving the plants harvested from our trip. He looked relieved when I told him this. In his current state, he is not able to defend himself against attack, especially from a weasel like Paega.

“Can I trust you with my knives?” I asked him.

Jago nodded. “Yes, Fur Benyn. What do you need?”

“I want you to sharpen all my blades. Get the girl to drag my whet stone in here. Don’t let her take them. I still don’t trust her.”

“If it pleases you, great lady, her name is Morgan.” He dipped his head, in respect, waiting to see my reaction.

“Is it now? That seems a noble name for a slave girl.” I swapped my turn-shoes for wooden pattens, and then rummaged for cleaning cloths.

“She was no slave in her homeland, Fur Benyn. Her village was raided. She was swept up along with the spoils and traded for tin with your kin.” I watched him take my leather knife wrap and unravel it onto my bunk in readiness.

“That would explain her attitude. Still, could be worse. She could be on her way to the mining pits along the coast.”

“Or made sacrifice to your gods.” he said. Clearly, the incident weighed on his thoughts.

"You might want to remind the girl of that, in case she gets any other mad ideas in her head." As I bustled back out of my hut, I heard him shout after me.

"I will, Fur Benyn. Morgan will not trouble you again."

I made a stop at a round house at the edge of the compound. This I knew to be the home of an old friend who weaves the finest threads into cloth like no other. With a handful of tin in exchange, I chose a length of woollen fibres of the lushest blue. Aebba deserved nothing less. With it folded to one side, I tasked the warriors to place Aebba on a length of wood, and carry him to the riverbank. I looked all about, expecting to find at least one of his widows to accompany me, but I found myself all alone with him.

As I knelt and dipped a bowl into the running waters, I saw Paega gallop off through the main gates on Aebba's fastest horse. I have no doubt that he will return in the same haste, with his grandfather and the rest of the Priest Sect in tow. I have little time left to me to make my investigations. If I cannot find the cause of death and culprit before Paega's return, his kin will most likely accuse me of harbouring a demon within. I have seen their powerful acts of persuasion before. I am in danger of ending my days burned as an evil spirit alongside Aebba's remains.

Before I began the ritual cleanse, I sought out my warrior friend and asked him a favour which may cost me dearly. Somehow, I had to get word to Blydh and Tallack before they were too far from our compound to reach. With no other heirs to challenge Paega, he and the priests will take command, and may the Lady have mercy on us all. With good grace, my warrior fellow assured me that he would himself, ride after the Head Hunters. He too, saw the storm brewing in our little community. With so few able men left to ask, he saddled his elderly father and sent him along the coastal path to signal Tallack's ships in warning. We are now without protection. Those who remain are too feeble or too young to defend our camp. Should attack befall us now, we would crumble in a matter of moments.

Stripped of his soiled finery, Aebba's body showed no sign of injury, barring the arrow wound to his side. I removed the leaves and sealing resin, flushed the stitched area, and examined the humours for bad odours or discharge. There were none. This was not the cause of his death. The rash covered patches of his chest as well as his neck and mouth. My last experience of tiny red bumps like these, were when I caught one of Aebba's dogs chewing a patch of Nightshade berries. The dose affected the mutt quickly. The rash appeared on its belly as it writhed around the ground in fits and starts, it wheezed and staggered for a time, appearing to choke, until death came and took it to the Underworld.

Every child in the tribe is taught which berries to avoid. This was no accident, but neither was it proof. I washed Aebba down and allowed the bile and black humours to drain into the river waters. With a young boy paid to stand watch over him, I sneaked along the outskirts of the compound, over rough grass and furrow by the tall fence, and found the slave girls who wait upon the top table. Two of the more buxom women, prepare and cook the meals for Aebba and his wives Word had reached them, for they took one look at me and scurried away like scalded rats.

I followed them into the storage huts. "I have no desire to accuse any of you. You have no reason to want to harm the Chief. Please though, will you tell me about last night? I can solemnly promise; no one will punish you for speaking with me."

At first, they glanced to one another, fright clamping their tongues. It did not take much of a mistake to feel the wrath of Eseld. A lashing or two with a leather strap, might be the least of the outcomes. Their newest friend was used to appease the Lady of Lakes and Seas during the last moon. Their faces told me that a knife to the throat was uppermost in their thoughts.

"Good and gentle woman." I approached the one with strongest forearms. "Can you tell me if you saw anyone lurking about the cooking pots? Did you see anyone add anything to your dishes and stews?"

She shook her head with vigour until I thought it might fly from her neck.

I tried to word it another way. "Who came out to this area last night, perhaps to see the moon after so much rain, or ask you to fetch more ale?"

"Please, Fur Benyn. It was a night like any other. The Lady Brea gave us our orders as she does every night. The Lady Eseld beat poor Gwyn, for sneezing on the olives, and Ruvane Cryda asked for cooked eggs." She shrugged as though Gwyn took a beating every night. Each of them stood staring at the ground, hoping that it would mark an end to the matter. As far as I was concerned, this was just the beginning. It was obvious that whatever they saw, it would not be divulged in such a public place.

I leaned in close to them. "If either of you would like to speak with me later instead, I am sure that I can reward bravery with a nugget or so of tin." As I leaned back, I saw that Gwyn held back her mousy locks with a carved bone comb. "That's very fine. It's a dolphin, is it not?"

She reeled back from me, placing her hand over the ornament in her hair. "I did not steal it, Fur Benyn, I swear by the gods, I didn't. Your dark slave made it for me."

My surprise turned into a howling laugh. They both smiled at me, until Eseld wandered into view over my shoulder.

"You find my husband's death a laughing matter, do you?" She scowled at the women, who fled from the hut and hid well from her vengeance. To me, she said, "Aren't you supposed to be tending to Aebba?"

"Each stage has a process; every process has a stage. He dries in the strengthening rays of the sun." I trotted my excuses out as though they were as important as what came next. She knows little about our ways. The priests have their own ungodly methods.

"Well, mind you wait until my father gets here before you remove his guts. He must have the portents read for his oldest son, and the next Chieftain of this great tribe. You can wrap him and begin the tribute collection. Have him surrounded by furs and his metals on the top table, maybe some flowers too. That should mask the smell a little."

I returned to my duties, trimming his hair, plaiting his beard, and wrapping his body in the blue fabric. With the chilly rains banished, and the heat returning to our days, it would not be long before the rot set in. I pondered on the wisdom of waiting for the priests to arrive before removing the fetid innards. What retribution would I incur by ignoring the Lady Eseld's commands? With the subtle shift of power gaining momentum in her favour, I declare myself too weak to resist her.

Aebba's bear fur from across the seas, encased the blue shroud. He was a majestic sight. His strong brow, wind tanned and scarred from a thousand battles, or so the tales will tell. It was such a sordid way to go. Aebba deserved to end his days swinging a great axe, or bronze sword in a fight with the Duro's, or sailing across the ocean to seek out new lands and spoils. Now his life will be sung without an end, for who could create songs of shameful murder at the hands of one of his tribe? At the very least, Cryda will insist on full burial rites at the solstice. All the tribes will unite to see him sent to the Summerlands. That will be a spectacular event, one worthy of singing.

I only hope that I can prove which of them caused his death, so that Blydh and Tallack can send the guilty into the Underworld, without ingots or fur to bribe the demons. May they burn for all time.

It took four of the elders to help me take him back into the Long Hut. Brea picked some primroses and bluebells from the woodland outside the compound, and arranged them with sprigs of yew and fir around the body. The newly cut branches filled the air with a fresh pine scent. Cryda directed me to the stash of metals and weapons she wanted laid at his feet. His ceremonial bronze sword was polished to a deep shine. I wrestled it into place, and crossed it with his favourite axe. Lastly, I rested a torque of gold around his neck. With the torches lit, he was ready to receive the elders and their wives. Each of them wanted to pay tributes.

The baskets laid beneath the top table filled quickly. Families from outside the compound walked for near half the day to pay their dues and ask the gods to take care of their fallen leader.

As the daylight began to fail, I remembered my equipment left at the riverbank. Weary, and with a heavy heart, I rinsed my shears and cleaning cloths in the waters, knowing that I would need my sharpest knife, and a strong stomach for the next phase of Aebba's preparation. Resting my aching back, I stretched my spine and wandered up the bank towards the Long Hut. With my tools wrapped and stowed in a pocket of my tunic, I headed back towards home.

From my position, I spotted Eseld wagging her finger at the slave who butchers our carcasses. He nodded at her, as contrite and servile as one of my herd. Curious, I dried my hands on my clothes and wandered closer to listen, but by the time I was close enough to hear, Eseld had marched away. The poor slave looked beaten.

"Ho there." I called to him. "What ails the lady?"

He looked at me with a frustrated air about him. I could see that he thought her request a poor idea by his pinched expression. "She demanded that all the meats and stews be thrown to the dogs. She said they are spoiled. We are to butcher more animals for a feast."

"A feast? You mean in mourning rites for Aebba's passing? But is it not too late in the day for that?"

"No, Fur Benyn. A feast in celebration for the new Chieftain. Paega is to be pronounced this night."

CHAPTER NINE

And thus, it begins. Poor Aebba barely cold, and the infighting and clan manoeuvring begins. The Priest Sect cannot be as far away as I first thought, if Paega can reach them on horseback and still return for his feast this eve. Their clan leader must have recovered quickly from the Duro's raid on their camp. They must have barely had time to mourn for the loss of Eseld's mother, before setting out for our compound. I must be more vigilant than ever, if I am to discover the murderer among such villains.

I changed direction and crossed the boardwalks to Cryda's hut. She saw my approach from the open doorway, and burst into fitful tears. The closer I got, the clearer my view of the person comforting her. Sitting beside Cryda on her large bunk, was the taller of the Ordo visitors. His arm draped casually over her shoulder while he shushed her. As I entered, Cryda shrugged his arm away, but my opinion had already formed.

"Cryda, I must speak with you alone." I straightened up and glared at the Ordo. He took my meaning, patted her back and left her house. I waited until he was far enough away so that he could not hear me before I turned back to her. The tears were all noise and no substance. She felt little for her Chieftain's death. "You cannot hide away in here. Eseld plans to announce Paega as Chieftain tonight. You must go and put a stop to this, or your sons will have no claim on the title."

"What does it matter? Let her play her silly games. Blydh has always wanted to hang Paega's head from his horse. The moment he returns, he will kill him and take the tribe for himself."

"He will not get the chance. Paega has ridden off to fetch his grandfather. When their entire sect makes camp here, do you think you will survive long enough to see Blydh and Tallack's return?" That made her sit up and think. "You must act now." I urged, grabbing her arm to pull her to her feet.

"What do you suggest I do? I cannot stop the priests from coming here, they are still Dumnoni even if they choose to roam our lands and not settle." The full enormity of the situation was, at last, starting to crystallise in her mind. With Eseld's son named tribal Metern, and with the guidance of the powerful leader of the priests behind him, both she and Brea would find themselves banished at best, or sacrificed in the most brutal manner. Anyone opposing their views, would follow shortly after, and that would include me. I trawled through my memories in search of a solution.

"You must confront Eseld before her father arrives, and challenge the claim Paega has on the title. Don't let them proclaim him undisputed Metern, or Eseld will claim a higher status as his mother, and your influence will vanish along with it. While Aebba's body is above ground and unburned, you are still the most powerful woman in all of our lands."

She paced the floor, allowing my suggestion to sink in. "Can I do that? Is it part of our custom for the mother of younger sons to make the challenge in their absence?"

"No one remembers the old ways. It pays to be a fur benyn, at times like these. I will back your claim, with every muscle and sinew. It's fortunate that the priests know little of our laws. I have sent word to your boys to speed their return, but I fear that without this plan, they will lose their claim." I slumped down on her bunk, exhausted and fretful.

"But both boys cannot become Metern. Who shall I put forward in challenge?"

I looked into those fair eyes and did not expect the genuine conflict. I thought that she and Aebba always favoured Tallack, but her knotted brow and panicked look, told me otherwise.

"I have a potential solution in mind."

I told her my plan, leaving out much of the detail, for I judged her to be only half listening to my words at best. Before I left, I had one last piece of advice. "I know not whether the child you carry is Aebba's, or that fat calved Ordo's, but you'd do well to distance yourself from him. He schemes with Eseld, and we all know her motives and designs." I walked from her hut before she could respond. One thing I drew from our discussion which swelled my spirits higher was that she would not have placed herself or her boys in peril by murdering Aebba. Her life would have continued to flourish under his power. While I cannot rule her out entirely, it is in my best interests to see that Paega does not rise to Metern.

I dragged myself back to my hut to check up on Jago and the girl. Smoke billowed into the sky from the rendered fats as the slaves of the Long Hut yielded to Eseld's new instructions. The Frynkish girl brought me a bowl of hot water to scrub myself of muck from Aebba's ritual cleanse, and help me to dress in my best tunic. Jago laid out my knives for inspection. He made a fine job of the blades. He even added fresh binding and birch pitch to better secure the handles.

"I saw the bone comb you made for Gwyn over at the roasting pits." I watched him flutter his lashes and bow his head. "You're a sly one." I grinned at his show of innocence. "How many other slave girls have finely carved dolphin pieces from you?"

He hopped backwards, dipping his injured ankle to the floor to regain his balance. "Only her, Fur Benyn. I didn't think you would mind."

I passed him his crutch. "You have a fancy to tempt Gwyn under your furs?"

His face took on quite a glow, his rich dark skin shone in the light from my fires. "I heard that she makes the tastiest squirrel broth of all the slaves."

I could not help but cackle. His interest in her stemmed from his stomach, and not his pintel. At the time, I thought how unusual for a young man, that is, until I saw the way he stared at the Frynkish girl. She was shapelier and far prettier than Gwyn, and her bedding much closer to his. That's all I need, a pair of rutting slaves a few feet from my bunk while I try to sleep. I will have to think up a new arrangement for them, and soon.

"You have great skill with a knife. Makes me fearful to sleep in the same hut as you." I squinted at him, assessing his reaction.

His face fell into one of shock. "I would never hurt you, great lady, you must know that? You saved me from a far worse fate, and could still send me to the mines or have me killed." I deemed him sincere, although I have little trust for the girl. I will sleep with my knife wrap beneath my fleece bedding from now on.

"You liked the razor clams you had for supper last eve?"

He nodded.

"Does the big crab still live?" I asked of him.

"Just, he sits in the water I gave him and no longer struggles."

"Then boil him up for your supper. Get the girl to pick you some fresh leaves to go with it. Should make you both a fair meal. I will take my fill at the Long Hut this night." With my cloak wrapped tightly about me, I trudged the boards over to the feast. Fighting through the last of the elders making tribute, I squeezed in and slipped around the benches until I neared the top table. In all my distraction, I had failed to notice Paega's return.

There he was, sitting in Aebba's seat, in his best leather tunic and bronze plate, as though ready for war. Eseld gloated from one side, his grandfather flanking the other. I scanned the crowds, looking for a sign of Cryda. She was late as usual, and this was one time when she really ought not to be. I could not make a stand without her authority.

Flushed with fury, I approached the top table to listen to their discussion. Paega sat looking over the corpse of his dead father, holding Aebba's massive bronze sword across his lap. I wanted to scratch out his eyes and feed him to the pigs, but calm I remained.

Fixing my attention on their mouths, I was able to hear most of their words. The priest made comments about the quantity of metal adorning the women in camp, calling it a waste of resources.

Eseld agreed with him. "We should send word to the Alchemists down at the mine to step up extraction and processing."

Her father grunted. "And you should order bigger boats to be built, and more of them, if you expect to trade further afield. That is how you build an empire. Not like that addled Metern you called a husband, he pissed away more wealth than he made."

"I'll see to it, father." I watched her pull the beads of silver from her hair and tuck them into her robes.

His shaved head, speckled with coloured daubs and raised scarring gave him quite the look of a mangy dog, except for his hooked nose. Altogether, he was a terrifying sight. Stories of his protracted sacrificial rituals were told at the bedsides of every child in the tribe. His father before him, was even more savage. Eseld came from brutal stock. I slipped closer.

"And another thing, your brother should lead the horse warriors from now on. We will need to think of a way to stymie young Blydh. He grows too popular among the distant settlements. Families throughout our route here had nothing but praise for the boy. You must think of something to put him in his place."

"Yes father."

I had heard more than I could stomach. Pushing back through the wailing woman of the elders, past Brea and the slaves, I went in search of the Ruvane. Before I could make my way through the doorway, a tap on my shoulder made me spin about. Gwyn carried a pot of stew in a long route about the space, taking the opportunity to speak with me.

"Fur Benyn, I did see something last eve. If it please you, I shall come to your hut later, when the moon is past peak and tell you all." She hurried away before I could thank her for the bravery she had shown. That was when I saw the narrow-eyed snarl of Eseld, glaring at us. It wouldn't do at all to go after Gwyn and warn her to take care. I guessed that she would already know the dangers, but had need for my inducement of tin ingots.

Distracted from my mission, I began my search anew. As I heaved and shoved to get through the doorway, the crowd parted, allowing the Ruvane Cryda her spectacular entrance. Dressed head to toe in a new tunic and cloak, dyed the deepest blue to match Aebba's shroud, she floated into the Long Hut and took flowers and clay bead tributes from her tribesmen. Her beauty was arresting, and fair dazzled the eyes of the elders who looked upon her, their love for her undiminished.

She took the longest route imaginable to the top table, allowing her followers to express their sorrow for her loss, and the young girls to touch her braided hair as she swept past. Finally, she reached Aebba's chair, and stood before the upstart Paega.

"You sit in my husband's chair before his death rites are even begun? You insult our Metern and the gods." She said, with an army of elders at her shoulders and back.

Paega glanced up at his mother, who looked at her feet, and then at his grandfather who nodded with resigned affectation. Still the stubborn child refused to budge.

"Get up, child, or fear the wrath of your father curse you for all time." Cryda was remarkably forceful in her rebuke. Paega shot out of the chair and stood against his mother for support. Cryda was not done mocking him. "The sword, child. Return it to its rightful place."

"But…" Paega began.

Eseld had the sense to shush him and urge his cooperation. Paega clanged the weapon across the great axe and huffed a disgruntled sigh.

"We will observe the death customs for now, Cryda." Eseld piped up. "But Paega will be named Metern thereafter."

"You assume too much. My sons have equal right to the Chieftain title over the Dumnonii, more so perhaps, since my blood is that of the Canti's Metern. Your lowly birth should pitch Paega from the claim entirely." She turned and smiled at the elders and their families. Each of them murmured in support, but would not make eye contact with the priest, for fear of his powerful connections with the Underworld.

"Your sons are not here to make their claim, if they even had a right to do so. By all our laws, they are forfeit, and Paega shall rule, and rule well, for he is the true heir."

Cryda looked to me to wade in and save her. I took a breath, and stood forward. "That is not our law at all." I gestured to the elders around us. "Had you been born among the fine families here, you would know that, Eseld. Our customs go back to a time before your priests came to these lands, with their new rituals and barbarous ways. Not only is it a right of the Ruvane to put forward her children in succession of their father, she bears the responsibilities of the entire tribe until the next Metern is found. While Aebba remains above ground, our Ruvane leads the tribe." I heard the old priest scoff, until he was fixed with the bravest of the elders' stares. It gave me courage to go on with my ruse. "My mother's mother, told me of a time when the Metern died leaving many heirs, just like this day. In such a case, those who have a claim on the title, must prove themselves worthy. At Beltane equinox, each of them will undertake a challenge of endurance. I will set it out to all three young men, when each of them returns and are together."

There was a chorus of elders behind me, muttering among themselves, until one voice shouted above the rest. “Yes, I confirm that was the case.”

And another said, “Aye, I heard that tale too.”

Others began to speak out with, “Me too…” and several muttering, “And me.”

It was enough to gain all their support against Eseld and her lethal kin. They could not put all of us to death, although I am sure the old devil thought it a possibility. The priest’s black look near turned my innards to water, but I held firm against his unspoken threats. In the moments of silence, while Eseld considered her options, I caught sight of the Ordo’s grinning from the guest seats at the side of the top table. I threw them a wicked glare and wished them both far from here, with their knack for stirring up trouble.

Eseld stepped down from the high benches and approached the Ruvane. “You think you are so smart, don’t you? You get a couple of wrinkled old-timers to fight your battles and you think you have won. Paega will be Metern, and then you’ll be sorry. He will wipe the floor with your boys. He brought down the biggest Auroch the world has ever seen, when he came of age.”

“My boys were there at the time and told me all about it. Your son cheated. Tallack injured the beast and Paega took the credit for finishing him off. Hardly a fair trial, Eseld. We all know the boy to be weaker than the ale he sups. Especially since everyone knows that you still water it down for him.”

There was an unfettered roar of laughter, so loud in fact, that it nearly shook the rafters. Eseld inflated her chest, pursing her lips in wild fury. With her arm crossing her body, she swung the back of her fist clean into Cryda’s face. The sound of bones crunching, and blood spattering shocked everyone into silence. For that frozen moment in time, Cryda recoiled grasping at her broken nose and gasping in breaths. In all our long history, no one has ever had cause or courage to strike out at a Ruvane. A collective gasp unified the tribe. Barring the smirk on Paega and the priest's faces, all who looked on, were horrified and powerless to help.

Cryda came to her senses. Her fists balled up, her right foot slid back, and with one colossal lurch, she delivered a punch to Eseld's jaw that would fell an ox. By the time the crowds had caught up with events, Cryda and Eseld were tearing at each other's hair, scratching, biting and kicking out in a scrap that look set to go on all night. A chant rippled out from the back of the hall in support of the Ruvane, her name yelled over and over in a mesmeric rhythm. Elders pushed back their wives and offspring to make space on the floor, as tangled limbs flew out in all directions.

Cryda was tall and wiry, but Eseld had the greater muscle mass. As Cryda wrapped her arm about Eseld's neck and held her in a headlock, she checked her with a powerful blow to the small of the back. Cryda groaned, doubling over in terrible pain and loosening her grip. Eseld wriggled free, and bent low to scoop up the material of her long skirt. Strapped to her leg was a dagger suspended in a scabbard. With lightning reactions, she grabbed Cryda by the hair and yanked her head backwards to reveal the length of unguarded neck. In slow and deliberate movements, Eseld revelled in her victory, drawing the blade ever closer to Cryda's throat.

CHAPTER TEN

The gasps in the Long Hut were accompanied by a frozen look of horror from all tribal elders and their families. Only Paega and his grandfather seemed to enjoy the turn of affairs. Eseld held Cryda at her mercy, poised to deliver her to the Underworld, kicking and gurgling in her own spilled blood.

"Don't do it, Eseld." I took a step closer to them, trying to get close enough to take a firm hold of Eseld's blade. "You will begin a war of revenge that you cannot win. Every clan in our tribe loves and respects Cryda. Do you want to bring about such infighting that it marks the end of the Dumnonii?"

She looked to be considering my statement, her hand moving further from Cryda's neck as she glanced at each of the elders in turn.

I tried again. "You know that Tallack and Blydh would make sure that their mother was avenged, and the warriors would stay loyal to their cause." That seemed to shift her stance, but if she did not carry out her threat, she would lose face with the tribesmen.

The priest knew best how to handle her. "Stand down, daughter. This is a time of mourning and reflection." He approached her and took the knife. From her other hand, he untangled Cryda's hair from Eseld's fingers. Finally, he turned to the rest of us. "She is upset at the loss of Aebba. Her reactions are to be understood. Forgive her, dear Ruvane, she is not herself."

Choose your battles, I thought to myself. He is wilier than I gave him credit for. The level of Eseld's popularity was in no doubt. They would not win tribal favour by killing Cryda. The Priest Sect could not take full control of the tribe without securing the backing of all the clans and elders.

"She started it, father." Eseld spat blood and humours from the build-up in her smashed nose. "She needs to pay for what she has done." She cuffed her sleeve across her face.

He also knew how to diffuse the tension. "I will make an offering to the gods and perform a cleansing ritual over this meeting place. The Long Hut is plagued with evil spirits. It is they who stoke the fires of conflict this day. Paega, take your mother to her hut. She is tired and in need of rest."

"But I am to be pronounced Chieftain this eve." The boy whined. The priest gave him a curdling look, sending Paega scampering away from the hut along with his bloodied mother.

He moved towards the top table, where Aebba laid among wilting flowers and pine brush. A cursory glance at the distended belly was all the knowledge he sought. His cloudy eyes sought me out. "You are the one they call, Fur Benyn?"

"I am." I stuck my nose in the air, awaiting his attack, but it did not come.

"Then I would be honoured if you would join me come morn for Aebba's preparation. From the look of him, it cannot wait any longer." His manner took me unawares. He smiled, showing me the few blackened teeth he had left to him. Whatever he and the priests chew to gain the sight, it softens their teeth something wicked. It made me shudder.

"I agree. Aebba must undergo the next stage as soon as dawn. The Ruvane has declared full burial rites, following our old ways."

"Then it shall be so."

Brea beckoned the slaves to enter with the dishes prepared with fresh butchered meat. My hunger faded fast. I took some bread, and wandered from the Long Hut, my heart filled with worry for the new day. With all that awaited me come morn, I needed a full night of sleep to gain my strength.

As I wandered into my house, I could hear the girl giggling beneath the furs on the rush floor. From the light of the fire, I could see the lumpy mass of animal hair moving. Then I heard the soft moans of Jago's deeper voice. "Stop that, or I'll have you gelded. If you must be rutting, you can go down by the river, where my sleep won't be disturbed." I heard them gathering up the bedding and sneaking out. "And mind you don't get her with child. I have enough trouble finding food, without having another mouth under my roof."

When they were fully out of the door, I remembered my wrapped knives. Picking my way across the rushes in the dark, I found them in a hollow at the far side of my hut. I took them to the fireside and unrolled the material. One of the sewn slots was empty. My best knife was missing.

***

It was not the orange glow of the sun that woke me, but the sound of the entire Priest Sect entering the compound. They must have walked through the night to arrive in readiness for the rituals. It made my innards roil and grind all the more for seeing them. Their menfolk were all shaved, with tattoos covering their scalps and hands. Their chalked faces carried blue symbols and the finger bones of their ancestors swung from their pierced ears.

One of the largest men, wore a headpiece of raven feathers stitched to the skull of a wolf. With charcoal lining his eyes, he struck fear into our young ones, who scampered back into their huts to hide beneath their bedding. This man led the way on horseback, along with Eseld's cousin. I assumed that he must be her brother, the man earmarked to take Blydh's place leading the Hunter Clan. I wondered if her father intended Tallack's ships and Sea Warriors for her cousin too.

As the sun rose, I watched Eseld's father order a couple from his clan, to fetch Aebba's body and carry it towards a large platform erected in the centre of the compound. I had slept through too much. He had begun without me. This I could not endure. I grabbed my knife wrap, threw on a tunic and my wooden pattens and hurried to catch up with them. This was a command made of me by our Ruvane. I had to find a way to re-establish her authority over the clans.

Two great trench circles now surrounded Aebba's central altar, one of crackling fire, the other of water. Eseld must have whipped the slaves all night preparing this elaborate stage, for our earth is too sandy to retain water without first lining the channel with clay. To allow passage to the altar, a raised bridge of no more than a foot's width, spanned the flame. I hurried over the licking flames to the central circle. Eseld's father stood over the corpse. In a closed basket, I could hear the panicked quacks of his sacrificial creatures. Several earthenware beakers surrounded Aebba on the platform, awaiting his organs and bones.

A part of me recoiled at the job before me. I wanted nothing more than to allow this power-hungry clan leader to complete the ritual without me, but the rest of me knew that path invited trouble. His clan gathered around the circle, with the youngest at the front. His son and nephew dismounted their horses and stood either side of the narrow passageway, barring entry to the bridge with crossed spears.

Eseld's father approached me. "Would you prefer that I opened his gut, Fur Benyn? It would save you the anguish of performing such a deed on a much-loved relative."

"I can manage. Ruvane Cryda wanted me to perform this rite, not you." I shoved past him and laid out my knives on the small patch left open to me on the altar. Others from the compound houses, tried to join the crowd, but were blocked from view by the close shoulders of the priest's menfolk.

I could not see whether Cryda or Brea were even present, we were so overrun by the sect. Eseld appeared between her brother and cousin. Her expression of victory was marred by her bruised face. She scaled the bridge, and was followed by Paega, her brother and then her cousin. Each of them took up positions in the circle. Paega stood at the western point facing east. Eseld moved in position opposite him. Her brother and cousin, each took their places at the southern and northern aspects of the circle. The priest's preparations were complete.

I looked for my sharpest and best knife, and then remembered it was gone. Selecting the largest in its place, I stood over Aebba's naked body and felt for the end of his ribcage among the bloating. With a trembling hand, I made my first incision. Drums thundered all around me, taking me out of my concentration. Where had they come from? The result was that my hand jabbed further into the flesh than I had intended. Clotted blood and noxious humours oozed out, along with the fetid stench of death.

"And with the blood of the first, we make ourselves known to the four elements." The priest chanted, pushing me aside from my work. He stuck his finger into the bloody mess and drew the swirls of the Triskellion on the altar stone. With one of my knives, he sliced at the flesh, taking a good chunk of Aebba's fat along with it, and placed it into a copper bowl. "My daughter, if you would…" He urged her to pick up a flaming branch and use it to ignite the fatty skin. The priest must have slipped some powder or a little oil over the flesh when our attention was diverted to Eseld, for it burst into fire so readily, and reduced it to ash in no time at all. The drummers beat out a rhythmic thrum, as the conniving old man began his invocations.

"Elemental fire, giver of the spark of life, of courage and wisdom, light and passion…" He trailed off, awaiting the collective worship.

Every one of his sect knew of this ritual. Each of them chanted in return. "I call to thee."

With the charred remains extinguished by a little puff from his lungs, he reached in to bowl and took a pinch of the hot ashes, and placed them onto one swirled arm of the Triskellion. This he repeated twice more, until three little piles of Aebba's ash sat on the symbol drawn in blood.

Next, he picked up a jug of water, and poured a little into the copper bowl, adding back one of the ash heaps and stirring with his finger. "Elemental water, giver of the drink of life, of creativity and love, patience and understanding…"

"I call to thee." The sect trotted out in unison.

Another pinch of Aebba, he placed into his palm, blowing the ash to the west and his grandson. "Elemental air, giver of the breath of life, of faith and mystery, hope and song…"

"I call to thee."

With the last pinch of ash, he crouched low, dug a hole in the ground and sprinkled Aebba inside, before covering the remains with more soil. "Elemental earth, giver of the food of life, of knowledge and wisdom, strength and abundance…"

"I call to thee."

I thought that might be the end to his tedious ritual, but he had just started. As I moved towards him to take over, he raised a hand up to stop me. What could I do? Surrounded by four of his kin, and with him so close to my knives, I had no choice but to let him continue. I almost put out my neck, trying to look above the crowds for signs of Brea and Cryda, but they were nowhere to be found. All I could do was retreat and let them butcher the Chieftain's remains however they wished.

With my knife in hand once again, the priest sliced off, another chunk of Aebba's flesh. This time, he divided the piece into four smaller sections, each no bigger than my thumbnail. These he also placed onto the Triskellion, one for each swirl, and the last one in the centre of the symbol.

"We call upon the Morrighan now, to oversee the rightful son rise to be the greatest Metern of all time, ruler of all the clans of the Dumnoni people. May she protect him in all the battles to come, and bless him with many strong sons and daughters." As he said this, three large ravens shot into the sky from behind a nearby hut.

Each of them cawed and flapped and made a general fuss in their ascent. Every member of the tribe fell silent and still, in awe of the priest's power. The Morrighan must have chosen him, or why else would her emissary birds respond to his call, and with such precise timing?

Some of our elders fell to their knees, learning the new words and incantations from the sect members around them.

"Washer at the ford, oh powerful warrior goddess, see our offerings and our gratitude." Eseld said, moving towards the wicker crate of ducks, grabbing each one by the neck to deliver to her kin. When the four birds swung and flapped from the hands of each of her kin at the north, south, east and west positions, they drew out daggers and sliced off their heads. With their bloodied hands, they daubed red marks onto their foreheads, and tossed the bodies into the fire trench. The smell of burning feathers overwhelmed us all, black smoke and hot embers shot into the air, obscuring the crowds from our inner circle.

The priest was not about to have his performance ruined by thick fumes. He ordered the sect members to fling chalk powder and dirt onto the flames to tame them. This they did rapidly, causing such a scene, that no one noticed the man carrying another wicker crate away from where the ravens had flown. It was all organised and staged to perfection.

When the audience could see once again, the ritual continued. The four pieces of Aebba still lay on the Triskellion. The priest stabbed the first with the point of my blade, and walking over to his nephew, thrust it into the man's mouth. I almost spilled the contents of my stomach over my feet. As quick as lightning, he retrieved the second piece and fed his son with a mouthful of Aebba. The third went to the eager widow,

Eseld. Each of them chewed and swallowed as though it was a gift from the Summerlands.

"We take into ourselves the strength and courage of our great leader. His life is now our life. His memories, are now our memories. His spirit is now our spirit." He went back for the final piece. He stabbed it with a pathetic jab of the knife. It fell from the blade, making him handle it while he forced it in place. I watched him move towards Paega, holding the folded meat towards his face.

"This most sacred flesh, from the centre of the Triskellion, will show us the true leader and next Metern. Eseld, son, nephew, open your mouths and let us see your tongues." They each did as the old man commanded. Their mouths were empty and clean of Aebba's flesh, and rosy in colour. "Paega, take in your father's spirit, and let him show us a sign of his faith in you."

The boy opened wide and accepted the flesh of his father into his mouth. A brief chew and swallow, and his grandfather pushed his chin down, revealing the blue coating across his tongue. The crowds gasped; this man was truly without limits. He must have hidden a pinch of Eseld's powdered woad in the fold of the meat.

"There we have proof, that his father marks him as heir to the tribe, but only you elders can grant this. We of the Priest Sect respect your old and outdated ways as well as our own. You must decide if Aebba speaks through these signs and warnings." To lend weight to his words, he paraded his grandson around the circle by the chin, like an obstinate goat.

As repulsed as I was by these obscene rituals, I could see why the old man would invent them. This played into the superstitions and tales of the old ways, using their gullible natures to garner support for Paega's rule.

I swallowed back erupting bile, and stepped forwards once again.

"Forgive me, Fur Benyn," he said, still clutching one of my knives. "But I have not yet read the portents. Surely you would not waste this opportunity to gain an insight into our future?" He said it loud enough for the elders to hear above the heads of the priest warriors. He had won the support of more than I had anticipated, for some of them yelled, "Let him read the signs," and "We need to know the future, Meliora. Let him finish."

I knew what this meant. He would steer the portents to warn them against the old ways, and to embrace their religion for all its worth. That would mark the end of me and Cryda. There was nothing that I could do. I stood back from the altar and watched him take all the attention.

With the sleeves of his tunic rolled above his elbows, he sliced the cut I had made, wide open. Aebba's gassy innards slid through the gap without aid. All drums and muttering fell silent.

"Great Cernonnus, God of wild forest and of death itself. Give us the courage we seek. Oh, great Cerridwen, crone and mother, keeper of the cauldron of knowledge, tell us what is to come." The old man dropped the knife down, and dug both his hands into the stinking innards of Aebba's belly. He closed his eyes tight, and mouthed some strange words, unknown to any of us. He made such a show as to make all who watched believe that the gods had taken full possession of his body. They moved and spoke through him now.

The tribe were utterly transfixed. His arms slithered about in the dead man's guts until he grasped the organ for which he searched. With a viscous slopping sound, he yanked out the heart, still attached to all its cords and tethers, and opening his eyes, pulled a horrified face.

The priest stared at the dark and congealed lump. “This cannot be… please Goddess Cerridwen, say it isn’t so…”

CHAPTER ELEVEN

The priest held the whole tribe on the verge of despair. With his audience captivated by every word, every movement, he slashed the heart free from the innards and laid it down on the alter stones. I looked at the elders and their wives, their faces contorted in concern.

"What is it father?" Eseld cried, buying into his performance. "What fate awaits our noble tribe?"

With the separated organ lying flat next to Aebba's head, he cleaved the heart in two and examined the chambers inside. With his hand covered in rotting offal and thick dark blood, he streaked his fingers over the top of his scalp, leaving huge red stripes about his person. The jabbering began again, as he stalled for time and built the terror within the crowd. Throwing the knife down, he shook his fist in the air and tipped his head right back, rolling his eyes to great effect.

"Father! Tell us…" Eseld yelled, running and throwing herself at his feet.

"It is worse than I feared, child." He reached down and grabbed her shoulders, raising her to her feet so that the crowds could see. "The goddess has spoken to me. The portents are indeed heavy, and filled with woe. She told me that a terrible illness… a plague, will ravage our mine workers and elders of the Alchemy Clan to the west. Many lives will be lost. Without tin, our tribe will not be able to trade, and our grain stores will run dry during the winter. People will starve. No matter how many attempts to grow grain, it will rot in the boggy soils. With so many menfolk sick and dying, we will fall prey to stronger tribes, who will invade and take our mines from us."

"But what can be done, father? Are we to die, or is there another way for us all to survive?" Eseld was word perfect. She had rehearsed her lines beforehand, that much was clear.

The old man dug back inside Aebba's distended belly, taking out the liver and kidneys and slopping them down on top of the heart. With a few prods and some faked muttering with the goddess, he raised his hand high to silence the murmurs from this disquieted and frightened crowd.

"There is one thing that can be done, my child. We must all go to the mines, and give offerings to Cerridwen, and to the Morrighan, and hope that they will take pity on us all. With a high enough sacrifice to each of the goddesses, they might protect us all, and favour us with their choice of Metern."

I snorted, a little too loudly, for it drew scowls and stares from each of Eseld's kin. I knew what game he played and saw him for a cheap fraud. He meant to gather us all in a settlement too small to house us comfortably, so that we may all be infected with the ague. That would give him licence to offer the widows of Aebba up for sacrifice. The elders would have no other option but to agree, leaving Paega and the Lady Eseld to manage affairs from the compound next to the River Exe. I had no proof of course. All I could do was grumble my discord and hope that I would receive no punishment for my disloyalty.

How did Aebba ever let the Priest Sect gain so much control? They had to be stopped, but for the life of me, I could not work out how.

The old man squinted in my direction. He must have noticed my reluctance to submit to his elegant performance. "I can see that you are overwrought, Fur Benyn. It is a harrowing sight, for someone you loved to be so disgorged. Shall I complete the defleshing, so that you may rest in your sorrow?"

Cryda had asked me to undertake this stage of the preparation to assure that Aebba was treated with respect and honour. After the priest's disgraceful intrusions, respect could never be regained. I looked into the crowds. Cryda was nowhere to be found. My temper got the better of me, for I bundled up the rest of my knives and stomped from the inner circle towards the Long Hut.

"Do as you please…" I shouted over my shoulder. "You will anyway." I made no attempt to hide my outrage, as I pushed through the sect members and elders of our camp. My anger seemed enough to remind one or two of their earlier support, but not enough to make a difference. The show was sufficient to turn the heads of the sternest of Cryda's friends.

Some of the more delicate women of the camp, fled from the gore of the old man's butchery. Others stayed to watch until the bitter end. That rogue kept my knife. That is the second to be lost to me this day.

I marched past the Long Hut and made my way to Cryda's house. It was here that I saw the reason for her non-attendance. Two large men, covered with scalp tattoos and symbols scored into their skin, stood at the entrance. "Step aside." I growled at them, letting myself into her hut. Cryda was sitting on her bunk, with Brea banking up the fire with logs. "So, this is where they have you imprisoned.""

"Meliora, thank the gods." Cryda gushed. "Tell us all that has happened."

Her request left me bereft of words. How could I tell her that our Chieftain had succumbed to the priest's brutality, his body desecrated and spoiled? I thought about her unborn child and the likelihood of her endangering its life by stirring the sect into anger. I sucked in my lips, constructing how I should tell her about the ritual. "The priests have taken control of everything. I was not able to stop them." I hung my head, feeling the shame, although I spoke the truth. I edged onto the bunk at Cryda's side and rubbed at my eyes. Too many springs have passed me by, each one leaving their mark on my tired old frame.

She stood, barging Brea out of her path. "Oh, get out of my way, girl. Why they sent you to attend me is a mystery. Fetch me some ale, it might calm my nerves."

Brea scuttled from the house without an utterance. I gave Cryda a scornful stare.

"What? She's always under my feet." She preened in front of a polished copper covered shield, fixing her hair and admiring her blurred reflection. "What are we to do? There is no telling how long it will take for my boys to return to camp. If Eseld and her father have taken possession of Aebba's bones, we have nothing with which to bargain." She looked to me for all the answers, but I had none. Age doesn't always confer wisdom. Our hopes lay with the return of the Head Hunters and Tallack's crewmen. Together, they would stamp out any notion of rebellion from the priests.

I did my best to soothe her frayed temper and assure her that her sons would move mountains to see justice done by their parents. With my best placatory phrases worn from use, I left her to offer prayers to the gods and set about my work. Leaving her hut, I could see that the priest still held the majority of the tribe in awe as he set about the tedious and messy job of removing all flesh from Aebba's bones. Bile rose in my throat, as I wondered what he might do with the excess meat and organs.

There was not a moment to waste. I dipped in and out of as many huts as I could. To those who were present, I made up some lame excuse about a cleansing ritual, holding a bunch of smouldering sage leaves aloft, and wafting them about as I invoked the gods' help in clearing the compound of evil spirits. If the priests can get away with such a ruse, then I can too. For empty huts, I was free to poke about as I liked, in the hope of finding something which might lead me to the poisoner.

Checking the show was still pulling the crowds, I sneaked into Eseld's hut and found precisely what I thought I might find. A bowl containing the black berries of nightshade. Some of them were crushed, others had already turned and smelled of the rot, but some were ripe enough. These had to be what I saw staining Eseld's bag when we met on the road back to camp. My problem was, that I had also found plenty of poisonous items in other huts, from slave quarters to high ranking elders' houses. We all used such poisons to dose food scraps at the perimeters, in order to kill off the rats. That was how I saw that poor dog die from picking up a morsel by mistake.

It was not enough evidence to convince the elders that she was responsible for the crime, especially since she was so involved in celebrating his life, however gruesome those rituals might be. All I could do, was to wait for her to make mistakes. If I confronted her with my findings now, she had the backing of all the priests behind her. Right now, she was invincible.

I went in search of young Brea, to discuss her options now that she was a widow. Rounding the edge of the Long Hut, I felt sure that she would be giving the usual instructions to the slaves at the roasting pits. There was the lad who did most of the butchery, and the beefier of the cooks, but I could not see Brea.

Dawdling towards them, I thought about my next move, when I remembered that the prettier cook, of the famed squirrel broth had not met me during the night to tell me of her sightings. Taking the remaining cook aside into the storage hut, I asked her where the slave girl, Gwyn had got to, explaining that I had wished to give her instructions for a meal.

"No one's seen her, Fur Benyn. She was supposed to help me gather roots at dawn. I ended up carting the lot back here and doing it myself. If she's done a runner with your dark cripple, they'll catch her and flog her till she's just bones."

That was extremely unsettling. Gwyn was never the most obedient slave, but she cooks well. I knew for a fact that Jago's interest in her was purely culinary. He would not risk fleeing with Gwyn, and leaving the Frynkish girl behind. "When did you last see her?" I asked, fearing the worst.

"It was when you collared her in the Long Hut last night, and had a word. I guessed that you and she had made some sort of arrangement. Either way, I'll be in the kawgh with Lady Eseld, if I don't get all this prep done." It was a thinly veiled snub, to get me to leave so that she could finish her chores. I thanked her, and did as she suggested. From the looks of things, most of the dishes were already prepared. She simply didn't want to be seen speaking with me.

With the compound overrun with jubilant priests and bedazzled elders, I slunk back to my hut with despair taking hold of my heart. Jago appeared much brighter, his ankle is healing well, and he can use his crutch to speed almost anywhere since I bound the end with fleece and dry grasses. Before, it would rub his underarm sore. It won't be long until it is fully healed. He greeted me at the entrance and offered to make me some refreshing water mint tea, but I really needed ale to fix my black mood. I helped myself to a cup from a jar near to the fire, its warm bitterness, chased away a few fears for a moment or two.

"What do they drink in your homeland?" I asked him, eager for distraction. I patted the bunk beside me, expecting him to sit at my side. Instead, he lowered himself down his stick to the rushes on the floor, and did his best to fold his legs.

"We have ale too. The wines were for the wealthy, or very special occasions. I had a sip from my father's cup once. I complained that it tasted sour, but he laughed at me, and said that it was supposed to taste that way. I'd much rather have honey water. Do they have that here?"

I nodded. "That's if you can get hold of the honey. Nests are few and far between, and once you spot one, you got to get to it smartish, or someone else will beat you to the treats inside."

"It is always cold and raining in this part of the world. The sun is so weak. I have to feed the fire with wood all day long."

"That's true enough. Lady Eseld would have you believe that it is our fault for not blessing the gods, or converting to her faith. She seems to think that if you shave your head and tattoo the Triskellion into your skin, then the sun will warm us all through the seasons."

"You do not believe in the gods, Fur Benyn?" His sweet face beamed up at me, with those high cheek bones and glorious smile, I'd almost forgotten that he'd been stolen away by slavers.

"All I know, child, is that all this rain rots our attempts to grow anything. If there are gods controlling the weather, they are cruel indeed." I finished my cup of ale and poured another. Tempted as I was to offer some to my young and interesting friend, I knew that might spark a riot with the other slaves, and I did not want the Frynkish girl helping herself to my ale.

"You do not drain the fields with irrigation channels here?"

"With what?" I put my cup down and concentrated my attention. "What are irrigation channels?"

"Where I am from, saltless water is precious. Our sun is strong. It dries everything out and kills our plants and cattle. Where you struggle with too much, we have too little. Farmers take great care to collect whatever water we can. We dig channels so that it will run down to our crops. If we do have rain, it drains through the sandy soils and collects in the lowlands. Not a drop is wasted."

I looked at him, half puzzled, half amazed. This foreign slave might have just hit upon the solution to our problem. I tucked the information away inside my mind, with the intention of speaking to the elders at a later time. Taking three small grains of tin from my pouch, I handed them to Jago. "Go and see if you can fetch two loaves of bread, a jug of ale and some fish for later." He held out his palm to receive the metal pieces.

His face lit up. It was enough tin to buy his own freedom, but I needed to know that I could trust him. "If you can barter three loaves, and two fish, you and the girl can have a whole loaf to yourself." I added as an extra lure. As he hobbled from the hut, he did not take his eyes from the metal lumps in his hand. It was a risky test, but worth losing the tin to discover his loyalties.

Preserving and drying my plants and herbs calms me. Despite feeling the effects of warm ale on an empty stomach, I set about my business in a blind daze. I have mixed the same tinctures and ground the same powders for so long, I could do so in my sleep. Jago's information about his homeland swam about in my head. Common sense told me that we should be working together as a community to drain the soils about the compound ready for sowing what little seed we had left. With all hands tilling the earth, we could start to settle in one place, instead of roaming about Dumnonium between springs.

Jago was gone for less time than it takes to burn a thin log. He staggered into the hut, with the jug of ale, but no food. I looked at him with a scolding frown. Poor mite looked to be frightened from his wits.

"Forgive me, Fur Benyn, but a terrible thing has happened." He slid the jug down his side to the rushes, steadying its descent with his stick. As I drew closer, I could see him trembling.

"Spit it out, boy. What is it?"

"I came back by the riverside from where I bartered for the ale. As I crossed the rough grass and shrubs at the back of your hut, I saw her laying there…"

"Who, child?" I grabbed him by the shoulders, shaking some sense into him.

"The slave girl, Gwyn. She's dead."

So many wicked thoughts trickled into my brain. A dead slave girl, who was last seen speaking to me in front of tribal elders and wives alike, at the back of my hut. "Show me." I grunted, pushing him out of the door.

We shuffled and scurried back to where Jago had found the dead girl. We were not the first back to the scene. Eseld and Derwa arrived before us, along with a few other curious onlookers.

"There he is… the dark one has killed her. Gwyn was my slave. He must be sacrificed and you must pay me what I am owed for her life." Eseld commanded, her voice shrill and loud.

I straightened my spine and approached Eseld, thumping my stick down close to her feet and making her jump back from me. "Hold fast. He is not to blame and you were not her owner. Gwyn was Aebba's property. Now move your scrawny arse out of the way and let me see the body."

I leaned over the half-naked slave and took a long look at her. Her neck was slashed with such violence, I could see her wind pipe poking out from her throat. The hair clip that Jago had carved and gifted was gone from her brown locks, and my knife rested on the ground by her side, drenched in blood.

CHAPTER TWELVE

Gwyn would not have suffered for long. After the initial slash at her throat, she would not have lasted more than a moment. The missing dolphin comb confused me for a while. I chose not to mention it to Jago, for fear that it should render him under further suspicion of the crime. Having my knife used as the murder weapon disturbed me most, especially since she lay right behind my hut. Eseld was not prepared to let the matter drop.

"I tell you that heathen you took in, was sent by evil spirits. He killed the girl. Now who will make my favourite stews? He must be punished." Eseld made so much noise in her protestations that she drew the crowd from her father's butchery show. The more she stamped her feet and snorted, the more tribesmen and women gathered. Jago tried to back away, but slipping through a great throng of people with a crutch is a tricky feat. The more he tried to disappear, the more they pushed him towards the centre of attention.

"How is it that you got here before me, Eseld?" I enquired, peering down at the muddy footprints for a clue as to the size and bearing of the killer from any tracks left behind.

"I could see her body from the main boardwalk over there." She huffed at my insolence, tramping her massive feet about in the mud, ruining any chance I had of seeing the killer's imprints.

"That's a lie. This grass is too long, her body too well hidden." I rebuked. It did nothing to quell her anger.

"How dare you call me a liar. It is you who should be under suspicion. Did I not hear the girl say that she would come and visit you in the dead of night, and now here she lies, behind *your* hut with her throat hanging out by *your* knife."

I had to admit; it was a clever gambit. My knives were well known to all in the tribe, and worth a tremendous amount in metal. Aebba had been generous with me over the years, making sure that I had the very best equipment to tend to his kinsmen and warriors. Now they looked to frame me as the killer. I should have been more careful in my dealings with the Long Hut slaves. It was my enquiries which put poor Gwyn in danger. The killer must have heard her admit that she saw who had poisoned Aebba.

Was Eseld playing a two-sided game with me, admitting that she'd overheard our conversation? Most would think her foolish to admit to knowing of my plans with the slave, and yet she had done just that, in front of everyone. Such openness did not assure me of her innocence, even if it went a long way to persuade the elders. With any potential evidence spoiled, there was nothing to be gleaned at the victim's side. I grasped Jago by the elbow and led him back towards my hut, leaving Eseld to deal with the body.

At least he still had the tin nuggets about his person. He offered to leave the compound in search of ducks for my meal, but I could not see that being a successful expedition while he hopped about on one leg. I was, however, inclined to trust him a little more than before. Perhaps when he has healed, I can send him out for errands alone. As for the Frynkish girl, I would not trust her as far as I can spit without supervision.

With the tin back in my pouch, I went in search of food with which to barter. I know that this is indulgent, and that with Aebba gone, my supply of metal will dry up, but I am getting too old to hunt my supper these days. I wandered along the central planks, looking for any huts with loaves left from the morning's baking. This late in the day, there was not much on offer, and I had to bargain hard for my food. In uncertain times, people often get meaner and reluctant to share. Hoarding becomes the way of tribe's folk, until the summer can replenish their stores.

On my return, Paega crossed my path. He wore his father's belt and scabbard, fixed at his waist by a bronze fibula, fashioned in the shape of a curled snake. This, another item from his father's trove, taken without the permission of the Ruvane. His swagger was comical for someone so gangling.

"Meliora." He shouted, which irked me for some reason. His half-brothers were a full cycle younger than he, calling me both by my name and as their aunt. Why did it bother me so when Paega addressed me thus? He waited until I shuffled closer before he said his piece. "You are to attend the Long Hut this evening. My mother has great concerns about the murder of one of our slaves. She would like to discuss this with you further and in the presence of my grandfather's wise counsel." He postured for a bit, adjusting the angle at which his sword dangled from his hip, and sniffing back the loose humours from his cold nose. I let him wait for my answer, sizing up the arrogant little brat and giving him my most suspicious glare. He buckled in moments, his shoulders slumping, his manner pleading. "You'll come tonight, won't you, Aunt?" That was the respect for which I was looking. This boy is not ready to assume the duties of a Chieftain. He can barely hold up his leggings, let alone lead our warriors into a skirmish.

"Maybe…" I muttered, pushing past him on the planks and carrying my loaves back towards my hut.

The fire had burned low when I got back inside. I sensed that Jago was too frightened of what the tribe's folk might do to him if he ventured out for more wood.

"Where's the girl?" I barked. She was more than able to fetch logs from a little pile stacked outside. Jago shrugged. I thought that he might try to keep her in line. The last thing I needed was a slave escape with all that had happened. I threw down my loaves in a temper, and stormed back outside to search for the Frynkish creature. As I passed my herb patch and rounded the side of the hut, I spotted her approaching me, the sun at her back and low in the sky.

"Where in the name of the goddess, have you been?" I shook my stick in her direction. She paid me no heed whatsoever, since she hadn't understood a single word from my lips. Towering over me in height, she stopped, swung her arm down from her shoulder and revealed a plump goose hanging from its neck.

She trotted out a string of words in her own tongue, smiled and then called to Jago. He appeared in the doorway with my knives, ready to pluck and gut. I felt wretched. For all my mistrust and anger, these two youngsters, taken from their families and homes and treated like vermin, were busy taking care of my needs. I wandered back inside and collapsed down on the bunk. I must think of a way to extend our living quarters. We cannot go on squashed together under my small roof. If she is a good hunter, perhaps she can catch more for us to eke out my tin.

I sat for some time, trying to decide what to do. The summons to the Long Hut by Paega and Eseld irritated me. While they are higher in the tribe than I am, their pushy manner following Aebba's death lends weight to my suspicions. I cannot accuse Eseld of murder without angering the priests. I have no evidence on which to base my theories. As much as I hate their company, missing the evening in the Long Hut would make it look to the elders as if I had something to hide. Jago, I am sure, is not to blame for the slave girl's death. My decision was made. I had to attend the gathering, and hope that Eseld and Paega would make a mistake that pointed out their crimes. At the very least, I would be there to defend myself and my slave.

I banked up the fire, and told Jago to save me some of the goose. The feathers would fill out my bedding too. By the time I trundled across the boardwalks towards the Long Hut, I saw some of the slaves lowering Gwyn's body into a burial hole. Her rags stripped from her body, her head hung from the bone and sinews left attached at the neck. I sent a belated prayer to Cernonnus, begging him to forgive Gwyn for her humble offering. She has only flesh to take with her into the Underworld. Slaves cannot take material offerings as all they have, belongs to their owners. They crumpled her legs up as they lowered her into the narrow pit. Her buxom friend threw down a few flowers, while the butcher backfilled the hole with sodden mud.

I could not get the image out of my mind. She died trying to tell me what she had seen the night of Aebba's death. I am partly to blame. She may be just a slave, but she was someone's child before being taken. She was once loved, and certainly admired for her squirrel stew.

I shook off my mood, and girded myself as I entered the Long Hut. Eseld and her kin would make it their sport to take me down. I'm a thorn in her side, a champion for Cryda, and too well respected among the elders to be of use to the priests.

Paega was sitting once again in Aebba's seat at the top table, overseeing all the families. His mother sat at his side. Cryda was relegated to the tier below, sitting chastened and red eyed on Eseld's old bench. I took in the relative positions of the rest of the tribesmen. Both the main entrance, and the doorway to the cooking pits, were guarded by warriors from the Priest Sect. Their leader took great pains to welcome me into the hut, as though it was his, and he the host. I nodded at him, taking care not to diminish his status. He is a dangerous man, and I have few friends left to protect me.

I moved towards my usual seat, noting that all of Aebba's furs, including the ones he would always lend to me, were gone. Eseld, no doubt, had hidden them away for her own selfish ends. Edging closer to the fire for warmth, I waited for the rest of the elders to take their places, expecting another well executed performance to begin shortly. I didn't have to wait long. As I predicted, the old man strutted around the Long Hut, throwing grits and powders into the fire, making the flames shoot up and sparks fly in a whole rainbow of colours. The elders were amazed. I was nearly singed. Moving further away, I reasoned that it was better to be cold, than have my tunic set ablaze.

The courses were sparse, compared to those ordered by Aebba. It looks as though we are all in for a time of poverty and abstention. Eseld had but one roasted meat, divided up into smaller portions and delivered to our tables already cut. Gone are the days of reaching over for a whole leg of duck, or a chunk of boar the size of my fist. An odd smelling gruel was served next to the meat, along with a paltry amount of roots. No one would go hungry, neither would they get fat on these offerings.

Eseld saw me turn up my nose at the meal. "Not to your liking, Meliora? Brea, get my son's aunt some squirrel stew."

I tried to protest. "No need. I am content with this food. I am neither precious nor special. Pay no heed, Brea." I shouted after her, who turned to Eseld for confirmation.

Eseld waved her along. "Don't dawdle, girl. Get the stew at once." With such a fuss made on my behalf, I had no other choice but to accept with good grace. Before any food could pass our lips, we all had to thank the gods and goddesses in yet another protracted display from the leader of the priests. By the time he had finished his prancing, feathered stick waving and speaking in gibberish, my stew was nearly cold. Nevertheless, I persevered, sipping the broth and chewing the gristly squirrel, and washing it down with plenty of ale. I have to say; I miss Gwyn already. The stew was fatty, with a strange sweetness mixed into the gravy.

Brea looked to be the most uncomfortable of all Aebba's widows. Poor thing sat next to Cryda as silent as the grave. She barely touched her food. Every time Cryda whimpered or made noises about the baby giving her discomfort, Brea jumped out of her chair to assist, only to feel the lash of Cryda's cruel tongue for her troubles. I guessed that's another of Eseld's suggestions, to pair the widow's together, knowing full well how they grated on each other.

The Ordo visitors seemed as awkward as Brea, in my view. Having enjoyed the favour of Cryda since their arrival, they now found themselves paying dues to the priests. I know not what beliefs they have in their mountainous wilderness, but I doubt they align with that of Eseld's father. The taller of the two, looked most put out. He tried his best to gain Cryda's attention during the meal, but she would not cooperate. I tried to persevere with the broth, but the more of it I ate, the queasier I felt.

Young Derwa at my side, watched me pushed the bowl away and offered me her bread instead. She has a sweet disposition for an offspring of Eseld. Her elder sister was wild. Aebba was quick to find her a husband within the Duro Tribe, further east. He meant for it to pull our two tribes together. For a time, we entered into talks about how each of our tribal elders and clansmen could gather at the Seven Sisters circle at solstices, but it never came about. Their Chieftain saw Aebba's advances more as a threat than reconciliation. He took Derwa's sister, Wenna, under his wing, and married her himself. Aebba wanted his first son to wed her, but she was young and pretty, and their leader knew that it would annoy Aebba. Some say that she is wilder than ever. Others hear tales of her ruthlessness. However she began life, she is now a Duro through and through. I would not stand with my back to her, if I should meet her again, for fear of a knife embedding in my ribs.

I nibbled on the bread for a time, but it did little to ease my discomfort. Shifting in my seat, the Long Hut walls blurred and moved around me. I pushed my ale over to the abandoned broth.

"Are you unwell, Fur Benyn?" Little Derwa commented, although I did not want any more attention drawn towards me. I patted her hand and smiled at her.

"Just tired, child." A few deep breaths steadied me for a while, long enough to see Paega thump his cup to the table and stand up from Aebba's chair.

"As per the former Ruvane's instructions, I have decided to allow the full burial rites of my father, to be performed at the midsummer solstice. We will all gather there to pay tribute to a great leader." There were general cheers and stamping of good-humoured feet from all the elders. Each of them drank in celebration of his life. Paega did not sit down. He had more to say. "As my father is no longer here to arrange things, I've decided that my youngest sister shall be bound to the eldest son of the Alchemy Clan leader to the west. She will meet her husband at midsummer and we shall make the journey to the mines later in the season for her binding ceremony." Paega raised his cup to his sister, but the room fell silent. All eyes fell upon the Ordo visitors, awaiting their reaction.

It took a short time for the news to sink into their ale addled brains. Everyone around them understood the enormity of Eseld's snub. They had been passed over in favour of bringing the wealthy Alchemists into their family. All arranged ties to the mountain tribe thrown asunder, along with the fortunate alliance with their copper and gold miners. I could see the power play for what it was, but the priests cared little for our wider tribal reputation. They were used to raiding and taking precisely what they desired. Aebba was seen as weak for forging trade relationships instead of waging war.

The taller of the Ordo visitors slammed down his cup. He snorted a great exhalation and shoved his tribesman in the shoulder, prompting him to move.

As they filed from the Long Hut, Eseld's father approached them in the doorway. "There is no need for disharmony, my friend. There are others in the tribe of an age who may be suited to your clime. My granddaughter would not fare well in the rainy mountains. You do understand…?"

The shorter Ordo snarled at him, throwing his ale to the ground. “Know this. We are not your friends, and that…that, child…” he pointed directly at Paega. “Is not fit to call himself son of Aebba. You’ll not see a single ingot of our copper. Mark my words, old man, and wait till the rest of our tribe hear of this deceit. You have made powerful enemies this day.”

CHAPTER THIRTEEN

Every eye focused on the Ordos' backs as they marched out from the Long Hut. All but Paega could guess the significance of his announcement. Conflict would not be far away.

Paega sat back down and ordered a slave to refill his cup with Tallack's fine imported wine. "Now that they have left, we need to discuss tribal business." He cleared his throat and spoke louder to silence the growing murmurs from the elders closer to the entrance. "We will save that of the murdered slave girl for last. In the first instance, we have decided that all tributes will now be dealt with centrally. Elders are to collect the offerings and bring them directly to my mother's hut. From there, all widows and orphans will receive sustenance, the rest will go towards building costs of more ships." He paused, waiting for the noise to die down. When it looked as though the elders were selecting a spokesperson to object, some of the priest warriors stepped closer to them, bearing their sharpened spears across their chests in readiness. The muttering silenced.

Paega continued. "Further to this, production in the mines will increase. We expect them to double the tin trades within one season. This will require more slave workers, therefore, as soon as Tallack returns, he will be sent to Frynk with a raiding party."

Cryda shrieked. "You cannot make such sweeping changes without my sons being present. They challenge you directly to the position of Chieftain. Aebba is still above ground, and will be until midsummer. That puts me higher than Paega. I will decide what happens until our new leader is decided."

Despite my head spinning and sickness gurgling in my throat, I had to stand behind Cryda's assertions. "She speaks the truth. That is our way, and has been since the beginning of time." I tried to stand, but toppled sideways against Derwa. She grabbed my shoulders, steadying my descent back onto my bench. I connected with a thud. The flames from the fire enlarged in my eyes. All was loud and dazzling. "Cryda is the Ruvane. She is still in charge." I yelled, but felt the floor rising to meet me.

"Fur Benyn is sick. Take her to her hut." It sounded like Eseld's voice, but I could not be sure. All I know is that I could feel strong arms either side of me, lifting my body and carrying me across the boardwalks. My skull bumped against a hard chest as the cool night air rushed into my senses and sent me reeling. One moment I was listening to Paega making his ill-advised proclamations, the next I was laying in my bunk with dancing sprites circling my vision.

A dark hand crossed my sight and clamped onto my head, while my body thrashed about without control. My legs kicked, my arms flailed, and no matter what will power I could summon, I swear that they had life of their own. When the spasms lessened, I heard Jago calling to me. During the brief lull in convulsions, he managed to make me hear him.

"Fur Benyn, your mouth is blackened, just like the Chieftain."

Trying to raise my head and focus on his worried face, I replied, "Do I have the rash too?"

He nodded, touching my arms and face where the raised bumps bloomed.

There was not a moment to lose. "You must feed me water infused with crushed charcoal. Do you hear me? I have to purge." As he nodded his understanding, another fit took me over. His garbled words were like boiled tree sap in my ears. Whatever was said made the Frynkish girl go running. Jago stayed by my side, cradling my head from harm.

When I next came to, he was pouring grey sludge down my throat. I tried not to fight him, but the urge was overwhelming. My arms flew to his face, clawing and hitting out, until the Frynkish girl climbed over my body and locked me down with her muscular legs. No matter how I rattled and shook, she held on for dear life.

With a belly full of black water, Jago lifted my upper half and rested a bowl on my knees. He rubbed my back, but it would not regurgitate. The girl saw the urgency of my plight. She scrambled forwards on my bunk, tipped back my head and shoved her fingers right down my throat. That did the trick. The entire contents of my innards erupted in a plume of foul-smelling humours. Jago managed to catch the majority, but a lot escaped over them and myself.

Even with a purge, it did not assure recovery. My meddling had put me in the killer's way. Either I was drawing close to proving my suspicions, or my outspoken manner of tribal laws had to be stopped. The ordeal was exhausting, and frightening. Between the two slaves, they subjected me to three bouts of forced drinking and purging of cooled embers. My bunk was as black as my tunic. I collapsed into my feathered bedding and tried to sleep.

That was when I felt the girl man-handling me. I was too spent to fight her. She stripped off my tunic and bedding, washed me down with clean, warmed water and slipped their fur beneath my limp body, wrapping me in the comforting folds. So much kindness, from those who themselves had received so little.

I slept, or was unconscious for a while, I know not which, but when I was next aware of my surroundings, daylight streamed through the open doorway. As my eyes flickered open, the girl was sitting on the edge of my bunk, holding a beaker of something. She pushed one hand under my neck and coaxed me to lift my head. The taste of the hot nettle broth enlivened my spirits. There was a measure of hope in my recovery at last. My gratitude towards these young people was immense. How could I ever hope to repay them?

Peeling off the fur covers, I looked at my body. I was once again clothed in a clean and dry tunic. Puzzled, I called to the girl, pointing to the garment. She nodded, and to my eyes, looked relieved. Sticking her head through the doorway, she called to Jago. I heard the dropping of logs, making their odd hollow noise as they impacted with the ground, and then saw him poke his head into my hut.

"Ah, great lady, you are back with us. You had us all so worried." He came closer and clasped his hands together in front of him. "Thank the gods."

"I have much to be grateful for too. You and the girl have done more for me than I could have ever hoped for. How do I say thank you, in her tongue?" I leaned up on an elbow, while he translated my words. Her face broke into the most terrific smile, followed by a blush. Her embarrassment led her to bundle up more bedding and cloths, and scurry away outside.

"It must have been a rough night for you and…"

"Morgan." He offered, bestowing a further kindness upon me. "More than one, Fur Benyn. You have suffered day and night for almost three dawns. We feared that we had lost you during the second night. The rash spread everywhere. Morgan covered you in a paste made from goose grease and plantain. It seemed to help a bit."

Weak, and pained in the gut, I tried to sit up. Jago saw my distress and hobbled over to assist me, bundling furs behind my head. "You both could have left me to die. Slipped out of the compound and gained your freedom. Why did you save me?"

He looked coy, unable to put together the words he wanted to express. "We have both had other masters. Some beat us or starved us, others far worse, especially for Morgan. You are not like others." He looked down at his broken ankle.

"That still doesn't explain why you stayed."

"Does it not, Fur Benyn? If we ran, where could we go? My black face and her Frynkish voice, we would be run down as deserters and sacrificed to your gods in less than a turn of the moon." We exchanged looks. He was right, of course. They would have freedom for a couple of nights at best. He pulled my furs higher up my body. "Anyway, you needed us, and now you are better." I watched him stand and shuffle outside to retrieve the fallen logs.

When the fire was banked up with a fresh supply of fuel, I bid him to return to my side. "Tell me, Jago. What have I missed? Are Paega and Eseld still in charge? Are the priests still in camp?"

His face drooped from cheery to concern. "They are, Fur Benyn. All is not well in the Long Hut, from what I have heard."

"Tell me all that you know, Jago. Leave out no details."

Reticent at first, the lad took a while to warm to the subject, but seeing my eagerness for news, he soon found his voice. He told me that the first night I was taken ill, Ruvane Cryda, tried to argue her case against the Lady Eseld. Their discussion got heated, to the point where Cryda lashed out at Eseld, screaming at her in hysteria. In so doing, the priests declared that she was possessed by the same evil that had killed Aebba and resulted in my sickness. This gave Paega greater power with which to order the elders about.

He demanded tributes of vast quantities of metal from every family, telling them that it was their duty to support the Chieftain and to pay for his burial and cist stones at midsummer. I queried this, knowing that the elders had already given all that they could afford, but it seems that was still not sufficient for Paega.

Next, he doubled the guard on each of the lookout towers, by adding warriors from the Priest Sect to each watch. Over the span of two nights, three more of our able men died in mysterious circumstances. Paega announced that they had fallen from the towers as a result of too much ale. There are only a handful of warriors left who support Cryda, and the challenge on her sons' behalf.

"What else?" I rushed him, through his account, desperate to understand the extent of their treachery.

"This morning, I heard by the river from others, that Paega has ordered the priest warriors to go to each hut and take one slave per family in donation to the mine efforts." He ladled more nettle broth into my bowl and encouraged me to drink. “You must be strong when they come, or I fear Morgan and I will both be sent under the ground.”

“Not while I have breath left in my body.” I pushed the bowl away. “Help me up. I want to be on my feet when they get here.”

“You are not yet strong enough. You need to rest and eat.”

His actions did not mirror his words, for he heaved me up by the elbows and set my shoes before me. I felt bowled over by the time I was fully dressed. I sat on the edge of the bunk, ready to pull myself up the moment they appeared. As it happens, they did not approach my hut all day. Whether they expected a fight on their hands, or truly believed me to be taken by evil, both Jago and Morgan were safe for the time being.

I dozed and ate a little, gaining strength and vitality throughout the day. My illness made me miss more than Long Hut gossip. While I was unconscious, Morgan and Jago had managed my affairs better than I could have done. Resting against the back wall of the hut was a stunning new long bow and fletched arrows sitting in a quiver woven from reeds. Two more geese hung from the rafters. When I enquired of their origins, Jago simply shrugged and pointed to the girl.

I heaved myself upright and took out my roll of knives. One gap remained in the leather case, from the knife which Eseld’s father had retained from Aebba’s preparation. The knife used to slice Gwyn’s throat, was returned to my hut by slaves during the clean-up process. I removed the blade and checked for signs of misuse. All the blood was washed from its antler handle, the edge made keen again on a whetstone. With careful consideration, I turned to Morgan, and presented it to her, handle end first.

She took it from me, and from her tone of voice, I realised that she was asking me for instructions.

Jago confirmed my initial thoughts. "She asks what you want her to do with the knife."

"Tell her, that I am giving it to her. This will be her blade for hunting." I looked to him to convey my message. He relayed it, with eyebrows raised to the sky. She did the same, her surprise apparent and gushing. Her response was to grab my wrist and take me outside, next to my herb plot. There, stretched over a stick frame, was a badger hide. The dried blood below it, along with flint fragments, told me that she had been stretching and scraping the pelt for some time. She turned to Jago with a string of rapid Frynkish words.

He grinned. "She says that she will make you a um…" He gestured to cloth circling my neck.

"Collar?"

"Yes, she will make you a collar in return." He could not stop smiling, his pride swelling with her skill.

"Tell her to make you both shoes first. You'll be needing them soon enough, but tell her I appreciate the offer." I left them to their plans and hides and curing, and went back inside. There is much to think about, and few opportunities to outwit Eseld and her dangerous clan.

By sunset, I heard the galloping hooves of Blydh and his clan returning through the main gates. My heart pounded with relief. His Head Hunters swarmed through the compound whooping and hollering until all the families ran out of their huts to greet them. I did the same. I wanted to assess his emotional state following news of his father's death.

Blydh sat tall on his mount. His teeth bared as he swooped in on his massive stallion. Young and old cheered and waved. The Priest Sect members slithered away into the darkest corners of the camp. Our numbers against the sect are hopeful. I sent a word of prayer up to Cerridwen, goddess, crone, mother and keeper of knowledge, asking her to send Tallack back to us on speedy waves. Weak as I was, I needed to see Cryda for myself. I needed reassurance that her unborn child was well, and that Eseld had not taken leave of her senses and poisoned her too.

I reached for my stick, wrapped myself in my cloak and staggered the short distance across the boards to the Long Hut. Blydh's men were already inside, taking ale and meat and chasing away the warrior priest guards from the door. In times of upheaval, gathering a mighty number of allies is crucial. It pleased me no end to see them, despite their noise and raucous ways. Scanning the room, I soon realised that neither Blydh nor the Ruvane were present. I wondered if Eseld was holding Cryda prisoner in her own hut.

Dipping back outside, I took a shortcut across the muddy grass. Here, I saw the long lines of slaves taken from the elders' houses ready for transport to the mines in the south-west. Another hut was filled with priest warriors in various states of intoxication, their eyes wild with fevered herbal concoctions, said to bring about blissful states, enabling them to talk directly to the gods. Others were scraping blades over their scalps, removing any hair which would spoil the sight of their tattoos and scars.

I got to Cryda's house just in time to see Blydh draw his great bronze sword from its scabbard. Despite his youth, Blydh is a big lad, taller than most. He waved the tip of the blade beneath the nose of the priest warrior standing guard over the entrance. Without a single exchange of words, the priest backed down, walking away from his post with his hands held high in submission. I lingered for a moment, allowing mother and son time to greet and grieve alone, before intruding on their privacy.

A part of me wanted to leave the entire business in their hands; to allow the younger folk a chance to develop their community skills, but this was too important to leave to the headstrong and war hungry. This required a clear head and patience, neither of which they possessed.

My sensitivity over their grief was short lived, for as I waited, I could see Eseld bearing down on Cryda's hut. In my feeble state, I hurried towards her to head her off. I failed. She bundled into Cryda's house uninvited and unwelcome. I could hear the shrieks of disgust from quite a distance away. Pushing myself on, I entered into the squabble, just as Cryda flew at her. Blydh did nothing to prevent his mother from tearing at Eseld's face. What could I do? I may be their so called, wise woman, but they were unlikely to listen to me. I stood by and watched as Eseld took control of the situation, grabbing Cryda's clawing hands and wrenching them up behind her back.

Who knew that Eseld was able to use such tactics? There is much we still have to learn about her, and all that the priests taught her as a child. With Cryda restrained, Blydh loomed up towards Eseld. His intimidating stance did nothing to throw Eseld off balance.

"Your mother is out of control. Clearly, Aebba's death has affected us all in different ways." She said, assessing the likelihood of further attack from the volatile Ruvane. As Cryda's arms slackened in defeat, Eseld released her. "It is good that you are back, Blydh. There is much to be done." Assuming she had mastery of the situation, she rounded on us all. “Glad to see you up and about, Meliora.”

I could have scratched out her eyes myself, but I reined my anger in. “No thanks to you.” I couldn’t help myself. I felt so bitter from the experience that I was not able to let the matter drop.

“What can you mean? Surely you do not think I have anything to do with your illness? If you did not welcome evil into your household, like that boy, for instance, you would not fall prey to the black humours.”

“Black humours, my arse. I was poisoned, and by the same hand who did for Aebba.” I yelled at her, my bile and vengeance boiling to the surface.

Blydh’s expression was murderous. “Are you saying that she killed my father?”

CHAPTER FOURTEEN

The veins in Blydh's forehead pulsed and bulged. I feared that he might snap and in one swing of his sword, take another head to mount on his horse. The repercussions of such an act of violence would spark a war within the tribal clans that few would survive. Reason tempered my accusations. I needed to diffuse the building tensions between the widows and siblings, not stoke the fires.

"All I am saying," I announced, "is that Aebba's death was deeply suspicious. Whoever slipped poison into his food, also killed the cook, and tried to silence me too."

Blydh turned to me. His eyes narrowed in fury. "So, you don't know if Eseld killed my father, only that he was murdered?"

I nodded. "That's right. Black drool in his mouth and signs of the nightshade rash."

"Then what has been done to find the killer?" His voice rose to the same shrill pitch as his mother's. He looked to me for the answers. I turned our attentions to Eseld. We stared at her for a good long while, watching her squirm and twitch.

"Why are you all looking at me? I did nothing, I tell you. Why would I kill my own husband?"

Cryda piped up. “You keep saying that, but it’s no defence at all. You have made it clear that you will do anything to push your addled lump of a son into leadership. Power is what you crave. That’s why you killed him, and then sent for your father to cover it all up. There’s no flesh to examine now that butcher has stripped his bones clean. That’s why you were so desperate for a pyre, to burn all traces of poison before my sons returned.” Her passion took her over, leaving her sobbing into her son’s embrace. His glare was beyond threatening. Another word from Eseld and he was likely to boil over into action. I took her by the arm and dragged her from the hut.

“You cannot go throwing your weight around now that Blydh is back. You must respect the Ruvane’s wish to do things the old way. Until the Chieftain challenge is resolved, she must be the one to speak directly to the elders, not Paega.” I tried to get through to her, but in her eyes, I’m just a meddling old woman.

“Stay out of this, Meliora. You’ve done enough damage.” She yanked her arm away from my grip, and marched towards the Long Hut. She will find little support in there now that the Hunter Clan has taken up residence. Some have wives and families, but most stay inside, feasting, drinking and passing out next to the great fire within. Paega will not hold sway over them.

My rush to intercept Eseld paid its toll on my strength. I leaned on my stick and took my time to return to my bunk. Rest was essential, if I was to set out the trials that lay before them, and be heard. As I neared the entrance, I heard rustling and the sound of sticks snapping. With the thatched slopes of my house supporting me, I edged towards the rear, and saw Morgan. She let go of a bundle of willow slung over her shoulder, and began sorting the withies into lengths for weaving. In the soft ground, a circle of hazel uprights mapped out the dimensions for a new hut. That girl amazes me. If I had half her energy, I would be unstoppable.

With a brief wave commending her efforts, I staggered back to my bunk. Jago prepared water mint tea to settle my gut. It helped a little, as did the porridge he made for me. What I really needed was someone to keep an eye on what was happening across the compound. Someone trustworthy and astute. I looked at my young friend and wondered if I dare send him as my spy. With barely half the suggestion passing my lips, he butted in.

"Yes, Yes, Fur Benyn. I will do this for you. No one pays any heed to slaves. I will hear and see all for you."

I've never seen such keenness to perform a task. He made me comfortable, refilled my beaker, and then took his stick beneath his arm. The dazzling smile made me chuckle. I am fortunate indeed to have found such slaves. They care more than family.

While I slept and shifted restlessly, the fire burned low. My bladder was fit to burst. I pissed in my pot, and took it outside to empty. It was later than I realised. Morgan had the walls hurdled to knee-height, and the sun flickered behind the tree line. Scanning the compound, I looked out for signs of my young spy. I tossed the pot contents and placed it back in the doorway to my hut. Venturing further afield, I saw him behind the Long Hut, talking to the butcher slave. All seemed to be well, until Brea appeared. She approached the slaves, her face puckering into a sneer. With a vicious swipe, she cuffed Jago about the ear and sent him scurrying away at top speed. That was a surprise. I didn't think her capable of such malice.

Jago spotted me lurking, and changed his course to meet up with me. "There is not much to report yet." He whispered. "Only that Blydh has sent all the slaves gathered for the mines back to their families. Lady Eseld was furious. I watched her stamping her feet at him, making nasty threats about curses and the gods."

It took all my will power not to laugh. "I think you should come with me to the Long Hut this eve, Jago. I will need your support."

"But that is not allowed. I will be beaten for daring to enter." He looked so pained, I almost caved in to his plea.

"I will make sure that you are not hurt, Jago. The poison still burns inside me. I shall need you to bring me bread and meat from our hut. No point giving the killer another chance to finish me off." I could see from his face that he understood my reasoning, but still he seemed frightened by the prospect. His last encounter inside had almost ended with a blade through his windpipe. I patted his shoulder. "Get along now and tell the girl of my plans." I watched him go for a little while, and then called to him. "Was it your idea to build the new hut?"

He turned back to me that grin spreading once again. "Yes, but I suggested that we waited until my ankle was better so that I could help. She ignored me and started anyway."

I rolled my eyes. She's certainly a headstrong character. "Help her tomorrow, Jago. We have much to do this night."

With a little more porridge in my belly and some rest, I was revived enough to take a stroll about the compound. One or two of the elders met me at their doors to remark how glad they were to see me recovered. That cheered my old heart somewhat. The priests were clustered in three or four huts close to the riverbank. Most were addled with bad herbs, but the warriors among them stood sober and alert around fires. Each of them was daubed in fresh whitened grease, and held spears at their sides as though permanently ready for battle. It put me on edge. I stooped at the riverbank and rinsed my hands in the water, glancing about me for anything worthy of harvest.

In the dim light of the setting sun, I caught sight of a familiar silhouette. A small boat drifted towards me, with room for two sets of oars. Tallack stood at the bow, readying himself to jump onto the bank side and make fast their vessel. My joy at seeing his return overwhelmed me. My arms stretched out to him, my relief filling my eyes with grateful tears.

"Gods be praised, you have returned."

Tallack vaulted the gap between bow and bank, and took his old aunt into his arms. He near squeezed the life out of me. "Now, Aunt Mel." He released me, tucking my shoulder under his arm and walking back towards my hut. "Tell me all that has happened. I am overcome with sorrow."

His manner was depressed. I never saw him so low. It gladdened my spirits to know that he still valued my words. On our short walk, I knew that this would be my chance to secure his support for my plans. I just needed him alone for a while to set him straight on tribal business.

My luck held. Barring a few priests, and a couple of slaves, no one else saw him arrive. Encouraging him to step inside my house, he met face to face with Jago.

"You kept this broken slave?" Tallack jeered, looking down at his bound leg.

"Mind your tongue. He's a good lad, and brighter than most of your crew. Leave him be. If it were not for him and that Frynkish girl you bartered for, you would not have an Aunt Mel to give you a shot at Chieftain. Then we'd all be stuck with Paega and Eseld ruling the tribe."

He snorted his derision, and then nodded his praise to Jago. That was more than I expected of him. Over the course of a couple of cups of ale, I filled my nephew's head with all that had occurred in his absence, and all that I required of him during the evening at the Long Hut. With Tallack's support, we may just be able to pull this tribe into shape.

With the crewmen and Head Hunters back together, the Long Hut was crammed. Pipers and drummers added to the general roar of good cheer and rowdy banter. Tallack slipped out of my hut to speak with his mother and brother, prior to my arrival. Jago finished preparing our food, promising to deliver it to me as soon as it was fit to eat.

Apprehension brewed inside me. I layered my woollens and trudged over the boards to the Long Hut. There were no guards at the door, and few priests inside. Taking my time, I surveyed the opposition. Eseld's father sat at the far end of the long table. Two of his men perched a little further away, ready to leap to his defence, no doubt. With Cryda's boys and their clans in abundance, Paega sat next to Aebba's seat. The Chieftain bench lay empty, as is the custom of the old ways. The Ruvane was back in her usual chaise, with her sons to her right, where the Ordo visitors once sat.

Derwa patted the bench next to her, holding a fur high to cover my shoulders. All was back how it should be. With us both settled and warm, she leaned into me and whispered. "Mother wants to mark my skin with the Triskellion, before my binding ceremony. She said it is to show everyone in the Alchemy Clan where I am from. Won't that hurt a lot?"

I looked into the fright filled eyes of my niece, and nodded slowly. What could I say to her? Her mother had, or intended to sell her to the miners and Alchemists. Her life would never be her own. “Have you tried telling your mother what you want?” I ventured.

“Once. I got thrashed for my outburst.” She looked down into her lap.

“Then let us hope that you wed a reasonable man.” I pushed my cup of ale over to her, and encouraged her to drink. Perhaps acquiring a taste for beer might render her life more bearable.

When the first dishes arrived, I sat back and let Derwa tuck into the meats, fish and roots. No one seemed to notice my reluctance to eat, at least, no one pointed it out. Tallack had the floor, telling the top table all about his adventures. Sea monsters and mermaids, were his general theme. What an imagination that boy has. Derwa was captivated, digesting his every word and gesture, while stuffing the best part of a duck leg into her mouth.

By the second set of dishes, Tallack’s hunger took hold, forcing him to sit and sate his appetite. “Aunt Mel…” He shouted above the hubbub and piping. “Tell us about the ancient ways. What trials do we men face in the challenge to find the next Metern?”

This was my cue. The pipers stopped piping; the drummers ceased their pounding. A hush fell upon the Long Hut, just as I had anticipated. I took a sip of ale and rose to my feet.

“It was in my grandfather’s day, when two sons had claim to the position of Chieftain. He knew the ways of old. This is how the matter was settled, and how it should always be.” I cleared my throat, and took in the attentive faces of those around me. Only those of the Priest Sect failed to show me that they were listening.

"Their Metern was celebrated and interred inside a cist on Hawk's Tor, in the middle of the moor. Three days and three nights, they feasted and sang of his victories and troves. His offerings to the Morrighan were plentiful; jewels from across the seas, fine metals and beakers and a pelt from the largest Auroch the tribe had ever seen.

"From there, the clans travelled to the end of the land, where the sea goes on forever. They waited out the winter near to the mines, working together to forge new tools and weapons for the next season. When the spring rains came, so too did the peregrines. These mighty falcons nested on the cliffs at the side of the bay, high into the sky. Their eggs were protected by razor sharp talons at the end of muscular limbs. Their ferocious beaks could peck out a man's eyes from a flying start. Their speed and agility have no comparison. Brave is the warrior who would disturb the mother in her nest."

I viewed the occupants around the room. I had them captivated. On I went with my tale. "Yet a warrior must prove his worth, if he is to be Metern of such a noble and courageous tribe as the Dumnonii - his arm strong, his justice swift, his cunning heroic. All those who dare to set themselves this challenge, should have all those qualities and more. He must be kind too, especially towards those under his protection. He should earn the love and respect of his clans. Aebba was such a man. He will be hard to replace." At this stage of my story, Tallack started a rapturous round of cheering and stomping. His crewmen were joined by the Head Hunters in a hearty guzzle of their ale.

When all had settled, I continued. "When first the eggs are spotted, the quest will begin. Each warrior must climb down the far side cliffs into the swirling currents of the never-ending sea. Here, he will battle the swell, and swim the span of the bay to the cliff face bearing the falcon's nest. The climb up to the eggs will be perilous, with rough waves crashing their icy waters over sharp rocks. On they must scramble, ever higher without alarming the Peregrines, or suffer their attacks." I caught sight of Paega's face. His face was ashen. Still I laid on the mortal peril, recounting my grandfather's story.

"Each warrior must secure an egg, without losing it to the ire of the falcons. This he will stow in a pouch about his person, before beginning the return journey. Down the rock face, across the bay, and an exhausting climb to deliver the egg to the Ruvane. All this, before his opponent can beat him to the end." I sighed my relief, having reached the end of my tale without rancour or dispute. Tallack began another series of cheers and table banging, until Blydh called out.

"What happens if they are killed in the attempt?" Blydh looked directly at Paega, his eyes reduced to slits.

"Then there are fewer opponents for the role of Metern." I answered, thinking that it was a redundant question. That it might be, but the exchange of looks it afforded was not. Blydh was giving Paega an advanced warning. Fair play was a foreign concept in this Chieftain challenge. It certainly had the effect for which Blydh was hoping. Paega's throat bump bobbed about, as he gulped back his fear.

I wondered at the time, would Blydh be as eager to kill his own twin? Would the terms of honour extend to his closest kin? It was my turn to swallow back my anxious thoughts. As much as I wanted Paega and Eseld defeated, I did not want to see the brothers descend to such murderous antics.

"Think you can take us on, brother?" Tallack sneered at Paega. His crewmen took the hint and shouted their own taunts and jeers. Blydh and his clan were more reserved, but no less lethal. While the sailors boasted and caroused, the Head Hunters preferred a stealthy approach. When his men attacked, they rarely gave any indication or prior warning. That made Blydh's taunt all the stranger, since it was not his usual way.

Paega did not respond. He knew when he was bested, and when to withdraw. There was nothing to be achieved in baiting the twins further. Eseld's father had more confidence. He chose a natural lull in the commotion before launching his rebuttal.

"Do you think the gods favour you, young Blydh? You who scoff at the faith just as your father did. See what that brought him."

Blydh got to his feet and unsheathed his sword.

Tallack jumped up and pushed him by the shoulders until he was seated. "Not now. Can't you see what he is doing? He will provoke us all into turning on each other until there is no one left but Paega." His voice came out in a low growl, filled with menace. Blydh returned the blade to its scabbard, and pushed Tallack aside.

The priest was not content. "You should all convert and give yourself completely to the faith. Every member of this tribe should bear the mark, and make a sacrifice to honour our gods. If you don't, you risk the evil spreading further among the clans."

At that moment, Jago chose to appear, carrying my bowl of food. He leaned in the doorway, craning to catch a glimpse of me. The priest made good use of the timing.

"See now, what devilry lurks in this camp. See how your disdain sets the bad spirits free. This slave reeks of base wickedness." The old man gestured towards his two men. “Take him now, and bind his hands. He must not be allowed the chance to infect us all with his ways. We will sacrifice him at dawn to be safe.”

Jago’s eyes darted from one looming priest to the other, in a blind panic. His eyelids fluttered for a moment, his arms trembled and shook. The bowl slipped from his grasp and tumbled to the rushes beneath his feet. As the priests reached him, Jago lost his balance and sensibilities. His body slackened, and then buckled in the middle, until he fell in an awkward pile on the floor. Jerking in random spasms, the priests backed away, truly frightened. I rushed to his side and protected his head.

From the depths of his innards, a great spout of strange words poured from his mouth, and would not stop. His arms thrashed, his head jerked, but still the speech came out fluently. To us, it was unintelligible. To him, it was his mother tongue.

Every one of the tribes’ folk present, gasped. It was as though the old priest had foreseen this event. I had to act fast, or the sacrifice would not wait until morning.

CHAPTER FIFTEEN

Kneeling by Jago's side, with my hands cradling his shaking head, I shouted above the clamour. "He speaks with the Gods, and they hear him." I slipped one cupped hand over his mouth as he jabbered on in his birth language. The old priest loomed over me, staring at the boy having a seizure on the rushes. He drew his knife from the waistband of his leggings. It wasn't enough to persuade him. I had to exaggerate my claim.

"The words travel into my body through my hand, and I can understand what he says…" Some of the closer elders stepped forwards, crowding out the priests and Eseld's father. I continued with my ruse. "Cernonnus speaks through this painted child. He warns of rotted seeds and more rain to wash away our efforts in the fields. He insists that we dig drains to channel away the flood, use the slopes in our grain fields to keep the rot at bay." I peeked up at their faces. Each of them silent and still, taking on board all I had to convey. "He tells us that Aebba now sits at his table in the place between worlds, and seethes over the manner of his death. He commands that his burial is fit for a warrior, to make up for the shameful act of poisoning."

The elders gasped, buying into my story. One shouted, “What else is he telling him?”

I couldn’t think of any other sage phrases or warnings. My mind was a blank. As luck would have it, Jago pulled himself out of his fit, and rubbed the froth from his chin. It was a critical moment. Would they accuse him of carrying the curse of the Morrighan, or believe that he was the messenger from Cernonnus? All eyes fell on Eseld’s father. His blade still rested in his tight palm. As he lumbered forwards through those gathered, I shifted my body to guard that of poor Jago on the ground. The elders cleared a path, expecting bloodshed. Holding my arm aloft to plead for his mercy, the man fell to his knees alongside me, his knife to the floor.

“Gods be praised. We are sent a herald.” He blustered, bowing his head in the direction of my slave. His two flanking priest warriors copied him, kneeling and muttering their acknowledgement of their faith. I sat there, stunned. No one could have predicted this fortuitous outcome. Still I did not trust them. I maintained my guard, anticipating further showmanship and priestly antics. I make a point of never turning my back to one, for fear of becoming their next offering. The old man, shuffled closer on his haunches, grabbing at Jago’s hand. “What did he show you, child? Speak.”

I could hear Eseld’s distinctive scoff from the back of the hut. She never has liked competition for attention, least of all her father’s precious favour.

Jago sat up, and upon seeing my bowl of food scattered across the rushes, he was upset and vexed with himself. “Fur Benyn. I am deeply sorry. I don’t know what happened. I will fetch more for you. Forgive me.” He tried to stand, but his wits failed him, his eyes rolled about in their sockets and he fell back to earth with a thud.

“Ease yourself, lad. That was quite a turn you had. Anyone would be woozy having the gods take them over like that.” I cackled, grabbing his arm. Leaning on each other for support, we got to our feet and mooched out of the building.

“Wait…” The old priest bellowed. “There may be more to hear.” He seemed genuine. Had I really duped the old goat?

“Don’t bother the boy. He needs to rest.” I chided, chivvying Jago along and out of harm’s way. We were barely halfway across the boards towards home, when I glanced back at the line of people in our wake. Each stood with their mouths hanging open, hoping for more from the chosen one. It wasn’t until we were safely inside my house and out of hearing, that I explained his brush with the faithful.

I kept my eye on the boy. Despite my quick thinking and the boy’s good humour, a seizure like that one is no laughing matter. I’ve seen them before. They mostly happen after a whack to the head.

“How is it that they believed us, great lady?” Jago asked of me, lowering himself down to the rushes by the fireside, allowing Morgan to cover him with their shared fur.

“No one around these parts has ever heard of the speech from your homeland. I doubt even Tallack and his men have. That made it easier to convince them. A few tall tales and a spot of wisdom, that’s all it took. It seems that the priests are not the only ones to put on a good show.”

“Do you think they will still want me for sacrifice?” The panic in his eyes was undiminished. What could I tell him? Had I made him a more appealing target or secured him a long and fruitful life? I helped myself to more of the roasted goose, some plump grains simmered in nettle water, and sat on my bunk. He still looked to me for an answer.

I shook my head. "I don't know. Best to keep out of sight for a few days. Let things die down a bit."

The night passed in fretful stages. At first, I couldn't sleep at all, listening to his breathing and squinting at him by the low firelight. Later, I jumped at every imagined and real noise from within and without. I owed him my life, and that is a heavy burden to carry. Worrying myself into a deep slumber, I did not hear Jago nor Morgan rise to rekindle the fire and make our porridge come dawn. They crept out of the hut at first light, so that when at last I did wake, I fretted about his life all the more.

With my piss pot emptied, I went in search of them. Morgan was already waist high in willow withies and working up a sweat in the early sunshine. Calling to her, I asked where the boy had got to, but all she could do was shrug. I took that to mean that she hadn't understood me. I must get Jago to teach her a few of our words. It would make life a lot easier. Passing most of the elders' huts, I wandered towards the river, anxious that he had met his fate among the priests. I found him standing on the bank side wearing nothing more than a tiny cloth about his loins. His beautiful dark skin smeared in a mixture of blue woad and chalk grease, from head to toe. He saw me approach. His expression reached out to me, pleading for rescue. More than ten women from the sect held him captive, daubing more of the brightly coloured grease over his face.

"What in the name of Cernonnus are you doing with my slave?" I squawked at them, glaring at each of their nasty little pinched faces. I thought one of them may well be Eseld. Dressed in their ceremonial robes, with half their faces shielded in those ridiculous masks and animal skulls, it's hard to tell them apart. As it is, she was not among them. Just as I was gearing up to give them a tongue lashing, and tell poor Jago to jump in the river and clean off all the muck, Eseld's father appeared from a nearby hut.

In his arms, he carried a huge headdress. The majority of feathers, were crow and raven, but the ones closest to the carved wooden beak were blue, from a jaybird. It was a magnificent piece, but I was determined that none should see my admiration of their craft skills. I have to admit, the effect was stunning, and more than a little alarming. It looked to me like they were preparing him for slaughter. It may have been another of their mysterious rituals, but I feared it might end in the letting of all his blood.

"That's enough of all that. I need my slave. He has work to do." I sounded as crotchety as I felt. The priest waved the women away leaving us alone with the boy. He gave me an odd look. I couldn't figure its meaning. "What were you planning on doing with him?" I asked tentatively, bringing my stick to the front of my body in case I needed to defend myself.

He dipped his head closer to my ear. "This boy is special; the gods have favoured him. Would you be willing to trade for his life? I can offer gold, if that's what it must take?" His sickly words, revolted me, as did his foul stinking breath. Why the sect members insist on smoking that disgusting hemp, I'll never know.

"I won't trade for him, no. He was a gift to me from Aebba, and I shall keep him."

"I can get hold of more gold than you could ever need. You could have dozens of slaves for the price of one."

"What, and let you carve him up and serve him to your warriors as the main course? No fear. You leave him be, or I'll have to ask my nephews to step in on my behalf." I gave him a sour look and beckoned Jago. We limped away together, looking such a sorry state between us.

Morgan roared with laughter on our return. Suffice to say that this was her first encounter with the sect's faith and rituals. From What Jago tells me, things are simpler across the seas. Time and effort are poured into new settlements and improving harvests. There is little time for savage rituals and offering up food to the gods is a waste. I removed his headdress, and sent it back to the priest with the girl. Leaving Jago to rinse himself down, I took stock of the situation in my hut. It would be better all-round if we were away from camp and all threats to his life for a few days, particularly with Tallack and Blydh's men keeping the sect warriors outnumbered.

For once, the compound was relatively calm. That's when boredom and mischief breed. My stock of salt was almost out. We would need to dry and cure a whole load of meat for our journey to the solstice burial. With the sun beating down on our heads, it was the perfect excuse to go to the coast for more. With a plan churning in my head, I ambled across the boardwalks to the Long Hut. Most of the clansmen were still coping with the aching heads and sickness from the night's revelry. They reclined along benches and on the rushes, according to their state of drunkenness.

Blydh and Tallack were up at the top table. They sat with their heads together in quiet discussion. It's times like this when you can see how alike they are. Strangers may not recognise them as sharing a womb at the same time, what with Tallack's braided hair and tin studs in his ears, compared to Blydh's short crop and bearded face, but I see their likeness. It's more than similar noses or eye colour. There are times when they share the same tone of voice or walk in a particular way. Both are fierce warriors, despite their young years, but Tallack has a gentle side to him that is harder to find in Blydh. Seeing them next to their father's great chair, I cannot help but think of them as little boys.

They saw me come through the door. Their secret conversation shelved for another time, Tallack rose to greet me.

"That went well last night, Aunt. Don't you think?" His arm crept around my shoulders the moment he drew near. He gives an old lady much comfort in these uncertain times.

"Well as I could've expected, Nephew. The challenge is set down. Now we'll have to keep the peace right through the next winter." He helped me round the benches to sit at Blydh's side in his place.

"You couldn't think of a quest we could have done this summer, Aunt?" Blydh grumbled. "Eseld will have murdered us all in our sleep before next spring."

"Aye, I know you think me a foolish old woman, but I did not make up those stories. True as my word, that is what my grandfather told me of the old ways."

Tallack poured me a cup of ale. "Nevertheless, Aunt Mel, it's a fearsome long time to wait before declaring a new Metern. Can't see Eseld sitting back and leaving all tribal business to our mother." He had a point. If she could poison me so brazenly, during a Long Hut feast, what was she cooking up for poor Cryda and her unborn child?

"Might be wise to stick about as much as possible." I gestured to Blydh, hoping that he would remain in camp to keep Paega and his mother in check.

Tallack toyed with the stud in his earlobe, thinking about my suggestion. "If we stay to man the compound, we cannot patrol the borderlands or sail to trade our tin.

If we leave, we cannot protect our mother or the tribal affairs."

Blydh sat upright in his chair. "No, but we can make sure that at least one of us is at camp, or in the area, until father's burial."

"Take it in turns? Makes sense. What say you, Aunt Mel?" Tallack still held me by the shoulder.

I looked up at him. Those twinkling eyes spell mischief. "Work it out between you. I'm going to the coast for a few days."

"What for? Have you got a new man tucked away in a hut on the cliffs, pining for you?" Tallack roared with laughter. Even Blydh cracked a smile.

"Ever the butt of your jokes. I'm going to get salt and gather what I can for our travels. It'll do me the world of good to be rid of those blasted priests for a while." As I finished my sentence, I could see Blydh wince at something behind me. I turned swiftly to see Eseld with her hands resting on her hips. She could be as miffed as she liked. There was no way I was going to apologise for speaking my mind about her relatives.

"Why don't you take father's cart down to the sea? Then you can sleep in the back and fill it with all that you need." Blydh offered. It was a kind thought.

Tallack offered one better. "How about I sail you down the river and help you to collect what you need? A few of my men and I can row us all there and back again. It'd be nice to get fresh shellfish and a bit of samphire. What do you say, Aunt Mel? Up for it?"

Before I could get a word in edge ways, Eseld shoved her oar in. "If you are going to the beach, then Derwa and I'd like to come too. I'll go and tell her to gather her things." She bustled off before any of us could gain say her.

I pulled a face to Tallack. "Sorry. I wasn't expecting that."

Blydh held his hand over his mouth, chortling at his brother's misfortune. "You may as well take Mother while you're at it, brother. Make it a proper family affair."

Tallack growled at Blydh. "Then you should join us."

"Can't. One of us has to stay in the compound at all times, isn't that right, Aunt Mel?"

"Don't put me in the middle of your fights. I'll be back in the shake of a dog's tail. Don't sail without me." All appeared to be settled. There was no way to back out. The prospect of one day alone with Eseld was more than I could stand. There was every chance it would stretch out to much longer, if the tides were against us.

Returning to my hut, I found Jago, explained our journey and gave him instructions to inform Morgan about staying behind to continue building their roundhouse while we were away. It did occur to me that without us present, Morgan might fall prey to the unwanted advances from some of the priest warriors or even Blydh's men. I raised this thought to Jago, who assured me that she was able to defend herself, especially now that she owned one of my knives. He might be right, but if she were to injure or worse still, kill another in defence, it would most likely result in her own slaughter as punishment. I could not take up three spaces in Tallack's long boat, as this would spark more arguments, and could lead to a full accompaniment of Eseld's hand maidens and skivvies. No, she would simply have to fend for herself.

I bundled my knife wrap, a couple of jars and a ball of hemp string, plus my tinctures and ointments bag and secured them together in one of my bedding furs. With careful knots, I attached the bundle to the end of my walking stick and headed down to the riverbank. Jago offered to carry the load for me, but the poor lad could barely carry himself.

Tallack and his men lined the river bank, in their long dugout canoes. Eseld and Derwa were loaded into the first boat, their own belongings taking up much of the hull. A second boat sat idle in the middle awaiting the arrival of Cryda, who, true to form, was late. Tallack summoned me to his craft, chuckling at the spectacle of a half blue, crippled boy and an old woman trying to board a slippery boat.

"You wait till your joints harden like mine." I squawked at him. "You won't be laughing then, I can tell you." He helped me to stow my things and steadied the rocking motion with a foot on the bank, while Jago stumbled into the boat.

The sun was already high by the time Cryda wandered towards us, with poor Brea tripping up behind carrying more items than is decent for Aebba's widow. Cryda took a slow and indirect route to the central boat, making sure that she was seen by as many elders as she could muster. A child from one of the closer huts ran out to greet her, handing her a posy of meadow flowers. She bent low to receive them, kissing the little girl's cheek in thanks, an act which drew out more people from their huts to wish us well. My, she certainly knows how to work a crowd. Where Eseld elicits fear, Cryda exudes love. Both are powerful in their own way, but only one of those methods girds clan loyalty.

As we pushed off from the bank, I twisted around to see Eseld's father, wearing the blue jay headdress, smeared in dark ash and grease. He raised a goat child up by its young horns and slashed its neck through with a long blade. I could hear his chant long after we rounded the bend in the river and passed between the trees beyond. I swallowed back my fear, and sent a plea out to Cernonnus for protection. What sorcery had he invoked with this sacrifice? What curses has he conjured for our trip?

CHAPTER SIXTEEN

It was my only chance to rest. Tallack pulled in the oars and allowed the current to wash us down the Exe to the sea. The warmth of the sun thawed the chill in my spine and soaked into my face, but I could not rid myself of the feeling that something terrible would result from the old priest's chant. I whispered to Jago to keep his wits about him, while I lay back on my fur bundle and closed my eyes.

The swish of the waters lapping against the boat, the call of the gulls flapping and stealing fish from the nets near the shore, all drowned by the noise of Eseld bickering with her daughter. There was nothing restful about being downwind of the widows of Aebba. Their constant need for drama was exhausting. How poor Brea tolerates their nonsense I will never know.

The sun was well past its peak when we drew close to the mouth of the great river. Tallack called to his men in the other boats, issuing instructions to steer into the deepest channels as the tide rolled out, sweeping in a giant bend through the delta and past the jutting headland. There before us were the great lengths of sandy shores, stretching all the way to the rocky outcrop, where the land turned a sharp corner. It gladdens my heart to see the light glinting on the waves. There's something truly magical about the ocean. I can see why my nephew loves it so.

Tallack was all for putting in at the first beach, but I managed to convince him that I needed a particular plant from the grassy cliffs above Red Point. He grinned at me, recalling his fondness for the caves there, and shouted to his men to run the boats up to shore. I reined in my curiosity as to what he may have experienced in those caverns. He tends to save those tall tales for the evening suppers over the campfire.

When we reached the beach, the expertise of the sailors came into play, gauging the swell of the waves as they took the vessels up the sandy beach between the rocky patches to safety. Tallack's kindness, it seems, only extended to me, since he swooped to pick me up and carry me over the edge of the boat into the waiting arms of his crewman. As they set me down on the dry sand, I turned to see poor Jago struggling with his crutch and bandaged foot. He fell into the shallows and crawled for some distance on all fours to dry land.

With the boat ropes staked into the ground above the high-water mark, Tallack ordered his men to make camp, while he returned to the second boat for his mother. Cryda's exit from her craft was significantly more elegant than mine. Her flowing gown dipped into the sea giving her all the appearance of a goddess. Tallack's men were less kind towards Eseld, leaving her and little Derwa to wade to shore, carrying their own bundles of belongings with them.

Salt spray whipped across the headland and directly into our faces. Derwa whined to her mother, who grappled her arm and yanked her ashore. Pregnancy seems to have a demure effect on our Ruvane, who contented herself with a seat in the warm sand, oblivious of the breeze. The men set to collecting firewood and setting up camp, while I stretched my limbs and relieved myself in the shelter of the dunes. When I found my land legs once again, I called out to Jago that I needed my knives and my bag so that I could go foraging.

Young Brea, may Cerridwen bless her, took it upon herself to grab my things and run towards me. "I shall go with you, Fur Benyn." She hollered. I expect she had all she could take of Cryda's demands, and Eseld's shrill voice. I was glad of the company. We scrambled and climbed the dunes, picked sorrel and horse parsley, flea bane and scurvy grass, before returning to the beach to poke about in the rock pools. Brea caught a lovely fat crab, while I cut the threads from a clump of mussels ready for the pot.

In the distance, I could see Tallack's men gathering grasses and making shelters beyond the high tide line. At least Cryda would be warm and dry for the night. My old eyes may have deceived me, but it looked to me that the crewmen had been at the ale. I feared for Jago, in among their boisterous fighting and manners. As the light began to fade, I told Brea that I would continue my gatherings in the morning, and set off along the beach for the camp. She scurried to catch me, carrying my bag and knives to save my back.

Eseld stood next to the largest fire, wearing a face of stone. "Where in all the gods have you been?" She scolded Brea. "Ducking out of all the hard work again. I have never known anyone quite so lazy." She shoved Brea towards the cooking pots. "Are all the Ordo women as idle as you, or was it their plan to offload their shirkers on to us?"

Brea didn't respond. She passed me my bag and knife wrap and knelt beside the cauldron of stew bubbling away over the fire. I couldn't let that go without sticking in my oar to defend her. "That's enough of that, Eseld. Brea has done me a great service this day. I don't think I could have managed without her help." I swiped my stick in the sand and caught Eseld's ankle, making her pout and leap out of my way. I tried not to grin. "Sorry, my dear. Not as steady on my legs as I once was." I exaggerated my movements, arching my back and shuffling along in the shifting sands towards the caves.

As I drew near to one of the shelters, I could hear Cryda's high voice giggling. "You know she will get you back for that, Meliora." She said. It was almost an invitation into her temporary quarters.

I pulled back the woven windbreaker and smiled at the Ruvane. "I dare say you're right. I know it's foolish of me, but sometimes I just can't stop myself." Her dwelling was well furnished with dry grasses and a hot bowl of stew. "What's for supper?"

She pulled a face. "Fish broth."

"Not to your fancy?"

She stuck out her tongue and crossed her eyes. "If I wasn't sick from the child before, I certainly am now."

"I'll make you some mint tea to sooth your guts." I wandered away, and then turned back to her. "Have you seen my young slave lad?"

"You mean, The Chosen One?" She gave another snort and chuckle. "They're all talking about it. Can't shut them up. Tallack instructed him to make you somewhere warm to sleep. Last I saw of him, he was carrying great stacks of grass into that shelter over there."

I nodded to her, and returned to the fires. There were a few beakers resting in the embers to warm through. Each contained a flat ale, dark as midnight. "I need water to make the Ruvane some mint tea." The crewmen looked at me as though I was speaking Jago's foreign tongue. I kicked the leg of one, and raised my palms up to the sky. "Well?"

They looked at one another for a few moments, until one spoke out. "She'll have to drink ale, same as the rest of us." He handed me a jug and settled himself back against the rocks. There was little I could do about the lack of clean water this late in the day. I cuffed the lout about the ear and instructed him to take the jug to Cryda and explain the difficulties. A stern look from Tallack made him jump at my suggestion and scamper towards her sleeping quarters.

Jago sat apart from the main crowd. His fire was neat and tidy, like those he makes in my hut. Not twigs and branches sticking out haphazard in any fashion, but laid with care and consideration. He was bent over something resting at his feet. Intrigued I ventured closer.

"Have you enjoyed your day off?" I smirked, although he didn't seem to understand my humorous jab.

"Very much, Fur Benyn. The men taught me how to harvest the shine from the inside of shells. See?" He held up a handful of shards, sanded down from oysters. He was so proud of himself.

"And what are you going to do with all those bits?" I asked, but I knew what his answer was likely to be.

The coy look and diverted gaze told me everything.

"You're going to make a necklace for Morgan." I laughed. He frowned trying to understand my response. I didn't think it was worth explaining myself. Young men always think that a pretty girl's heart will be won over with trinkets and jewels. May Cerridwen bless them for their idiocy.

He looked affronted and then said, "But if you would like it instead…"

"Save your pretty baubles for the young ladies, Jago. You can't put a pig in a dress and call it a bride." That stumped him. His knowledge of our language extends to basic commands. He'll never get his head around some of our sayings. "Get some sleep now, boy. I have a job for you at sunrise." He pocketed his treasures and began arranging himself next to the fire.

Further along the beach, I could see Eseld arguing with her daughter again. From their demeanour, I guessed that Derwa was none too pleased about being sent to her bed for the night, when so many handsome warriors surrounded the main fire.

My gut rumbled like I'd been starved a week. The thought of fish broth brought painful eruptions up into my gullet. If anyone had something nice to eat, it would be my nephew. I edged closer to him, skirting the drunken sailors and raucous play fighting. A bowl lay beside Tallack, containing a few greasy smears and the chewed bones from a big fish.

I leaned over his bent legs and peered down at his bowl. "Any more where that came from?" I winked, pushing my luck.

One eyebrow flicked up, his mouth pursed and then flattened into a smile. He was as soft hearted as his dear father, which is fortunate for me at least. With a gruff command issued to one of his men, two juicy fishes were fetched from their catch and laid at Tallack's feet. With a swift slash from his blade, he gutted both and fanned out the flesh, securing either side on a forked stick over the fire.

"Did you get all that you needed today?" He asked, pouring ale for me from his own jug.

"Not quite. I still need to mount the cliffs in the morning. There should be plenty of juniper. I have run clean out." I rested my back against the rocks. "And of course, I still need salt."

"We can trade for that from the settlement in the next bay. I'll leave my men to smoke today's catch while we walk over the cliffs to get all that you need." He leaned forwards and adjusted my supper until it sizzled near the flames. He caught me smiling up at him. I was lost in those kind eyes of his.

"Someone has to look after the old folk." He grinned back at me.

I patted his arm and took a gulp of the ale. It was mighty strong. I thought of how lonely Jago must feel so far away from his family, in a foreign country whose ways must seem so barbaric to him. At least at the Chieftain's compound he has the Frynkish girl. I made the decision, there and then, that she should accompany us to the solstice burial. Perhaps if they see our rituals and practises, how we trade and barter between clans and tribes, they might feel that they could become a part of our world.

My fish was delicious. I was just grappling the second, ready to devour, when I thought about Cryda and the stinking stew. A woman carrying a child should never go hungry, especially the tribal Ruvane. I leaned on Tallack's shoulder and heaved myself to my feet, carrying the skewered mackerel. It steamed in the cool night air, wafting its fresh flakes towards her shelter.

"Cryda?" I called, giving her warning of my entry. "I have brought you something to eat." For the second time that evening, I pulled back the wind breaker and climbed inside. Her stew was cold and had formed an oily sheen on the surface.

She shook herself awake and took my offering. "Thank you, Fur Benyn."

It was the first time she had ever called me that. I was thrown, and filled with emotions that would not settle. I sat at her side on the grasses, and watched her digging into the fish. With that one simple reply, she had forged a new and loyal ally; one who would see her son's rise into leadership, a friend who would weather any storm in the protection of her unborn child. At length, the silence felt uncomfortable, but I was reluctant to leave her alone.

"I am surprised that you chose to come with us when you have such comfort in your own hut." My curiosity was genuine. For the life of me, I couldn't imagine why any of the widows would travel without cause.

"It was Brea's idea. She said that the sea breeze and a change of scene would be good for us." She took another bite and swallowed the hot flakes down. "In truth, I didn't know that Eseld was coming when I agreed. She is a walking nightmare, constantly shouting and screeching. If I was her daughter, I'd bind myself to the furthest tribe I could find." She sipped a little ale and wiped the juices from her chin. "Besides, the priests make me uneasy. I shall be glad when they have moved on."

"I know exactly what you mean. That was my main reason for this trip, although I am worried that they will follow Jago and I wherever we go, now that he is their Chosen One."

"You only have yourself to blame on that score. You should have let Tallack put the boy out of his misery when he arrived at the compound."

I heard her cold logic and wondered how she could be so loving and kind in one moment and so harsh the next. To hear her speak of Jago, you would think him a midden dog. Her company suddenly irked me. I looked around for an excuse to leave. The oily stew sat near to her feet. "I'll take this away or it's likely to make you feel ill again."

She nodded, thrusting the bones of her meal and the stick at me, as though I were to replace Brea as her hand maiden. I sighed my contempt, but she did not notice. Gathering the bowl and stick together, I left her to her furs and slumber, and hobbled away. In the darkness of the upper reaches, I could not bring myself to waste food. Rather than slopping it over the dunes, I rested the bowl down among the tufts of hardy plants, and returned to my own shelter. I figured that some poor creature might make use of it before sun rise.

With food in my belly and a mild giddiness from the ale, I slept as though I was with our warrior ancestors in the Summerlands. I had to be woken by Jago long after first light, such was my comfort. The sand moulds itself so ably against my old bones, that I have never felt so comfortable and warm. It is tempting to make my home by the shore, if I did not know how the waves beat and lash the beach in winter.

Jago had risen early and gathered clean water from a spring further in land. He must have struggled to bring the heavy jug back to camp without the use of his crutch. When I approached him, he was kneeling next to his neat fire, stirring the grains we brought with us into some hot milk.

"Where did you get that from?" I was truly puzzled. He must have walked farther than I could have guessed.

"I went in search of something for your breakfast, when I saw a woman milking her goats on the grassy banks inland. I asked to trade with her, but she fell down to the ground and scratched a symbol into the soil, begging me not to harm her."

He looked embarrassed, upset even that someone should react to him in this way. “Go on…” I urged, keen to hear the rest of his tale.

“I told her not to be frightened, that I was just looking for milk to feed my mistress. She told me to take the lot. I could not see her punished for giving me the milk, so I gave her the necklace I made for Morgan. I will have to make another now.”

I stood and looked at the porridge bubbling away in the beaker, and wondered how he had made such an impression on the woman. “What was the symbol she drew?”

He picked up the stick he used to stir the grains, and sketched the three-spiral shape of the Triskellion into the sand. “Hmm.” I grunted. Bloody priests get everywhere. Word has spread, young Jago. You are the painted Chosen One.” I looked about me for a bowl. I decided that Cryda might like some of the porridge. Then I remembered the fish broth I left at the foot of the dunes.

Scrambling over the sandy ridges to a private place, I emptied my bladder and returned to the spot where I had deposited the bowl. Night time creatures had indeed made use of the offering. A short distance from the spilled broth, lay two dead fox cubs, their swollen muzzles and mouths coated with foaming spit.

CHAPTER SEVENTEEN

The bowl was almost empty. Those cubs must have been in tremendous pain before their sudden death. Reaching down to pull open the swollen mouth of one fox, I checked for the blackened signs of nightshade. There were none, whichever poison this was, differed from that used on myself and Aebba. Nevertheless, Cryda was the target this time. Who would benefit from her death? Eseld most certainly would. She had access to the broth when Brea and I returned from foraging in the rock pools.

I sat in the dunes to think, holding the bowl at arm's length for fear of succumbing to the sickness. How could I prove that Eseld was to blame for ridding herself of competition? If I confided in Tallack, he would slice off her head without waiting for proof, and then where would we stand with the priests? No, I had to keep this to myself. I rinsed the bowl thoroughly in the sea and returned to my porridge. With the clean bowl half-filled, I took it to Cryda. I ate my meal and drank some of the milk and emptied my gathered haul onto the sand.

"Jago. You are to stay behind today. I want you to prepare the herbs for drying and to make all the Ruvane's meals and drinks. Is that clear? You are not to let anyone else give her food or ale. You must prepare everything she needs." He looked concerned, as if he had displeased me somehow.

"Fur Benyn, did I do something wrong? Are you giving me away to another?"

"No, Jago, quite the reverse. You are about the only one I can trust right now." I lowered my voice. "It is crucial that you protect the Ruvane. I think someone is trying to kill her, you know, like the great Chief Aebba?"

He inhaled sharply; his eyes widened. "No one will harm her, Fur Benyn. I give you my solemn word."

With one knife removed from my wrap and an empty bag, I left Jago in charge of the camp and joined Tallack. Brea was standing with him, giggling and wriggling as though he had told her one of his more salacious stories from his travels. "Are you coming with us?" I called to her, surprised that she had evaded Eseld's demands for a second time.

"I am, if that pleases you. The Lady Eseld is bathing with Derwa in the warm shallows so I sneaked away." She glanced up at my nephew, with fluttering lashes. I thought at the time how foolish her errand was, but who am I to curb her pursuit. The poor girl deserves a bit of fun in the wake of so much unpleasantness. It might take her a while to realise that Tallack is not her man.

"It's more than alright with me." I replied.

"They had better watch out, bathing in the warming waters." He said. "I spotted one or two larger blue sharks edging closer to the mainland just the other day. If they choose to attack…well…" Tallack sucked in his lips until dimples appeared in his cheeks. He may not have any love for Eseld, but he has great affection for his half-sister. It was touching to hear.

"Now then," I declared, keen to change the topic. "I hope that you don't mind a few prickles, I need to replenish my stock of juniper." I didn't wait for their replies as I began the trek over the dunes to the rock escarpment of Red Point. The climb up to the first ledge was hard going, but with Brea and Tallack to give me a shove when I needed it, we all reached the cliff top as the sun burned through the morning haze. There was not a cloud in the sky as the gulls circled overhead. As soon as we reached the thickets, I began harvesting all that I needed.

"Aunt Mel, those juniper berries are not ripe." He looked at me as though I had lost my wits.

"That's right. Green berries for some medicines, ripe berries for others and flavouring. I'll need to come back just before the frosts set in for the ripe ones. Be a love and cut some of the green shoots and stems for me, would you? I can take the oils from them until my next visit." I carried on picking and taking in the fresh smells of pine and bitter fruits. Brea tried to help me but the burrs and spikes shredded her delicate hands. With enough gathered to last me, I took the branches Tallack harvested and wrapped the bundle with twine. "I'll pick these up when we are on the return journey. Save carting them all the way to the salt marshes and back."

I turned to find the cliff path and saw Brea picking the pretty stems of a tall plant behind me. The distinctive purple blotches colouring the stalks sent me into a spin. "Drop those now!" I yelled at her, dashing over to swipe them from her grasp.

"What did I do wrong?" The flowers fell to the ground. Her hands shook with fright.

"That's hemlock. Don't you be picking that unless you're killing rats. You should wash your hands as soon as you can."

"But it looks just like horse parsley." She turned her palms up and checked her hands. Any sap entering those cuts could be fatal.

"Come on, we'll cut through here and climb down to the beach. The quicker you rinse those wounds the better." I called to Tallack and led the way forwards along the worn track to where the cliffs were not so sheer. Cut into the rocks was the steepest path I'd ever seen. The crumbling layers were mostly covered in dense shrubs. We looked down at the boulders and pebbles below. They seemed tiny from where we stood.

"I'm not sure that you should even try this, Aunt Mel. It's too much for you." Before he could complete his reasoning, I felt a hard pressure behind my heels, a weight bearing down on my footing. The ground gave way beneath me and I tumbled down the rock face. Sliding at speed along the rough ground, the rocks gouged at my flesh and buckled my knees until by chance, I hooked my elbow between the forked branch of a thick shrub. My arm almost dislocated from its socket, but it prevented complete catastrophe. I had fallen more than two boat lengths from the top. Cernonnus must have decided to spare me, for I genuinely thought my time was up.

Clinging to the branch, I could feel the last of the gravels and sands falling from under my legs. I did not dare to look down. Tallack shouted my name in desperation. I tried to call back, but my breath was short and pain flooded my body. With the last of my strength, I locked both arms over the branch and found a foothold near the roots. There I stayed, drifting in and out of consciousness until I heard my nephew whispering calming words into my ears.

Tallack stayed by my side, having climbed down to find me. Brea ran back to the camp to summon help from the crewmen, who arrived sometime later in one of the boats. They climbed up to meet us with ropes, and lowered me safely to the ground. By the time the rescue was over, the tide had retreated once more. They were able to carry me around the headland to our shelters.

Laying me next to the fireside, Jago and Brea fussed about me, washing my wounds and patching me up with cattle gut stitches and plantain paste. I lay still, but for the chewing of bitter willow bark to ease my discomfort.

"I just don't understand what happened." Brea cried, cuffing the tears as they streaked down her face. "One moment you were there next to me at the top of the cliff, the next you were gone."

I tried to calm her with reassuring noises but she would not be soothed.

"You are the only one who is kind to me, Fur Benyn. I would be lost without you." Still the tears poured down her face, until Tallack took her into his arms and rocked her gently in the sand.

"Did you wash the hemlock from your skin, child?" I managed to ask, my chest hurting with every inhalation. She nodded into my nephew's chest, but continued her sobbing and wailing. Anyone would think that she had gone over the cliff, rather than me. I chewed and chewed, but the willow couldn't take away the agony. I gestured to Jago to pass my medicines kit.

"What can I get for you?" He asked, taking the fabric bag and unwinding the ties.

"You know what I need." I gave him a look that conveyed how much pain was coursing through my body. He nodded, but his brow was deeply furrowed with regret. Taking out a tiny pouch, he pinched a small amount of the dried yellow resin and dropped them into a beaker of warm milk. He swilled it about until the poppy resin melted, and held it up to my lips. I drank eagerly, taking down as much of the liquid as he would let me have. Within a few blinks, I could no longer feel a thing. My world spun and danced before my eyes, but the pain was at an end.

Over the course of the day, I was intermittently aware of all that happened around me. I recall being lifted onto a stiff contraption, lined with my furs, and lowered into the boat. The motion of the waves sent me into a dream of my mother's arms. I could swear that I heard her sing, but poppy resin is known to make a fool of the brain. I can see why people get a liking for its effects.

It was dark when they carried me through the compound to my hut. The medicine had worn thin by then and the pain was returning to my limbs. Jago's sweet face never left my side.

"Are any bones broken?" I asked, almost afraid of his response.

"It is a miracle that you are not dead, more so that nothing is broken but your skin." He snapped at the Frynkish girl to fetch this and that, but safe in their care once again, I slept.

***

It is remarkable what a few days of rest can do for the body. With my cuts and bruises healing well, I pulled myself from my bunk to re-join the world about me. My hip and back were still sore, but not so much as to stop me from going about my business. Jago and the girl were busy working on their hut, leaving me alone to dwell on all that had happened. I checked my stores, finding a new jar of salt, my juniper supplies and the rest of the herbs gathered from the trip to the coast. Tallack must have sent someone to trade on my behalf. It was such a kind gesture; I put on my shoes and trod the boards in search of him.

The compound was thick with priests. Everywhere I looked, they were lolling about drunk, or addled from smoking, tattooing each other or looking grim on guard. Two loitered wherever Jago went. He gave the impression that it did not bother him, but I could tell that deep down their presence was a worry. And rightly so, they can hardly be trusted not to turn on him.

I hurried into the Long Hut to find Tallack. He was holding a group of women in thrall with his great adventures. His arms flew about his head as he regaled them stories of his daring warriors, and the people they meet across the sea. One of his audience members was Brea. I approached them and stood just behind the group of elder ladies, listening to his embellishments and amazing tales.

Brea caught sight of me first. "Fur Benyn. How good it is to see you up and about." The ladies parted, and upon seeing me, drifted away from their show. Brea stepped closer and flung her arms about me in a half-hearted hug.

"There now, child." I patted her arm and gently pushed her from me. "Takes more than a little tumble to put me down for long."

"So, it would seem." Tallack stood up from his bench. His embrace near squeezed the life out of me. "I reckon you are hardier than most of my warriors. I should take you with me on my next voyage. What do you say to that?"

"Argh, get on with you, boy." I chided, but his banter always lifts my spirits. My smile was beyond control.

"Brea, what say you get Aunt Mel a cup of ale and something tasty to eat?"

"Certainly. Nothing would give me more pleasure." She scurried off before I could refuse. Tallack and I sat together and spoke quietly so that we could not be overheard.

"Can you recall that day on the cliff? Did you see what happened?" I urged, keen to hear his answer before Brea could return.

"You slipped… didn't you? The edge was crumbling and it gave way beneath you." He pulled me to the top table seats where we could huddle together.

"I thought so too, at first. But I can't help thinking that… maybe it's my imagination…"

"Go on." He said, but his tone had altered from concern to alarm.

"I felt a pressure against my heels, like someone stamping their foot against them tipping me over." I knew as soon as I said it that I had absolutely no proof. His expression was one of tempered fury. Brea had wormed her way into his heart.

"Aunt Mel, there were just us three up there that day. You cannot suspect Brea of foul play; she thinks the world of you. What could she have to gain by causing you harm?" His handsome face withered into a scowl. "You were off your head with poppy resin at the time. Your thoughts were clouded. It was nothing more than a shocking accident. You should be thanking the goddess that you survived." He leaned away from me, as though my accusation tainted his fondness for his old aunt.

Somehow, he made me ashamed of my thoughts. I hated not having his favour. "I saw the salt and my juniper supplies. I assume you arranged all that for me?" He nodded, still seething from my words. I had to make things right between us. "It was good of you to do that for me, Tallack. I am in your debt."

He relented following my display of gratitude. "Can't have our medicine woman go without medicines. You are important to this community, and to me." The grin almost returned, almost.

I rose to my feet and stepped down from the top table.

"Won't you stay for something to eat?" He called after me. I thought about the fox cubs and my recent brush with death. Tallack may believe that Brea is beyond blame, but I am not so sure. The list of people whom I trust is shrinking daily. I thanked him and left the hut before Brea could return with my ale. I didn't want to give her another chance to finish me off.

With so much enmity in the compound, I thought it prudent to pay a visit to Cryda's house. Her pregnancy must be coming along nicely, so long as she eats well and refrains from the willow bark and other dangerous herbs. As soon as I saw her, I made the choice not to tell her about my suspicions. If she is anxious, it might seep through to her child.

She was sitting on the edge of her bunk, with her elbows on her knees and her chin cupped in her hands. Her eyelids drooped, then bolted open when she spotted me.

"Are you not well, Cryda?" I strolled closer on my stick, wincing with the effort.

"Oh no, I am fine, just tired. My swollen belly has me using my piss pot half the night." When she sat up straight, I could see how she had grown. Not a large child as yet, but well underway.

"You might know that a child of Aebba's would be a little warrior." I joked, but she did not grin. "What troubles you, my lady?"

She took her time in framing her answer, and when it came, it was in the form of more questions. "Do you think that Aebba sits with Cernonnus in the Summerlands? Does your slave really hear him speak?"

She put me on the spot. If I admitted the falsehood, I would lose her trust. What then would stop her from revealing my ruse to the entire tribe? At the very least I would be shunned, and the protection Tallack and Blydh give me withdrawn. At worst, they might allow the priests to take Jago for their sacrificial offering no matter my objections. I could not afford to confide the truth.

"I believe that Aebba is looking down upon us all, especially while his bones are above ground. He wants to be sure that his death is avenged, and yet I have no proof for a tribunal." I expected her to seek clarification over my suspicions, but she heard only one thing.

"You think that he watches over us, sees all that occurs, hears everything we say and to whom we speak?"

"Until he has been avenged, Aebba will not have peace among the gods. I do firmly believe that, yes." I thought she might burst into tears. Her eyes glossed over and her breathing shortened, but she held them at bay. Her reaction was not what I expected. I thought that Aebba's presence over us all would have a comforting effect. "Is there something you wish to tell me? I can keep a confidence if that is required."

Her mouth opened and then closed tight. She shook her head, reclined on her bunk and turned her back to me.

CHAPTER EIGHTEEN

Cryda's behaviour played on my mind for the rest of the day, that and the truth behind my fall. The more I wandered about, the easier my hip joint felt, so I took a turn about the compound. Everywhere I looked, menfolk were slaughtering and butchering while the womenfolk salted and dried. Not a single soul was without busy occupation. Tallack's men stacked the smoked fish from the trip, bundling them together in strips ready for the pilgrimage to the solstice circle. The gods had truly blessed us.

As more and more of the tribe saw me up and about, I drew a crowd of worried mothers and injured warriors, keen to secure my help. How quickly the chores back up when you're out of action for a few days. With a tail of coughing infants, limping elders and one or two gashed heads, I returned to my hut and called Jago to assist me. The patients came and went at such a rate, I almost missed the thundering hooves of the messenger, galloping into camp.

I was not the only curious one to abandon my post in order to listen to the news. Others flocked to the Long Hut, peering in between the folds of the door flap. At least my seniority affords me the right to enter Chieftain quarters. I instructed my patients to wait at my roundhouse, while I grabbed my stick and shuffled quickly across the planks. The messenger's pony was white with foaming sweat, and bore the mark of the Alchemists. News from the mining settlement was rarely good.

Pushing through the group gathered in the doorway, I made my way closer to the top table. All of Aebba's family were there, shouting, arguing and spouting their own brand of wisdom. I grabbed young Derwa by the arm and kept my voice low. "What has happened? What's the news?"

She rolled her eyes to the back of her head, sighing and pouting her mouth. "Something about running out of copper and that it's all mother's fault for insulting the Ordo's and breaking her word. Quite honestly, Aunt, it's a good job that she did. Can you imagine me bound to that hairy old Ordo, or worse still, his stinking even older father?" She snorted to herself, proud of her defiance. For such an amiable girl, Eseld is teaching her some very unpleasant ways. Her ignorance hardly helped matters either.

I inched closer to Blydh's side, trying to discern each separate argument as they hurled them at volume across the top table. From what I could make out, Eseld made claims of mismanagement at the mining encampment, placing the blame firmly at the feet of the Alchemists. Blydh countered with the point that Eseld and Paega had dishonoured the tribe by breaking Aebba's promise to bind Derwa to the Ordoviches. This in turn had resulted in their refusal to trade any more copper with the Alchemists in the settlement at Bentewyn.

Surprisingly, Tallack spoke up for his half-sister, reminding us all that their father did not state when the binding would occur. He also pointed out that Derwa was still too young for such a commitment. That was when the cheeky little maid found her courage.

"I am old enough. I just don't want to lay with those backward hairy short people who think that singing is the answer to everything, especially the one who got the Ruvane with child. Mother says I am to be bound to someone handsome and rich. If I have to spread my legs, it will be for amber, jewels and more furs than I can carry." She spun about next to the fire pits, revelling in her own boast. All the widows and every one of her siblings stopped talking and glared at her. She had no idea of the pot she had stirred.

Blydh and Tallack boiled with fury, each of them unsheathing their blades and stepping towards Eseld, the undoubted perpetrator of the slander against their mother. Cryda wept, falling into Aebba's chair and burying her face into the bear fur draped across the frame. Paega stood in front of Eseld, his father's sword held aloft in his hand. I can't imagine what he thought he could do with such an item. It was crafted to show Aebba's wealth and status, not for battle. Like the bronze shield hanging from the wall above his chair, both were for ceremonial use.

"She's just a child and knows not the truth of her words. Rumour and suspicion are not fact!" I yelled, stepping between the boys and raising my arms to their blades. "Aebba's seed grows in Cryda's womb. It's nothing but malicious lies to suggest otherwise." I waited, my pulse thumping in my ears. "This must stop. A tribe should come together in times of grief, not tear asunder over gossip."

Tallack was the first to lower his sword. "Aunt Mel is right. This will not solve our copper problem, and without that, we have no bronze for weapons or trade." Slowly, Paega and Blydh stood down, but remained rooted to their respective spots. Eseld was the only quiet one among them, which is suspicious by her very nature. Brea tugged on Tallack's arm, urging him to sit by her side. I hadn't thought her capable of such manipulations, but he bent to her will and placed his hand on her leg. She poured out two cups of ale, passing one to Blydh where he stood facing off Paega, and the other to her target of affection.

Cryda's tears dried. She looked thoughtful for a moment, and then offered, "Are you sure there isn't any copper on our own land? I mean, has anyone actually looked?"

The twins glanced at each other, and then back at their mother. Everyone present frowned in contemplation.

"Would any of you even know what copper rocks look like if they fell on your heads?" The Ruvane had a point. Our attention had been focused solely on tin. We all assumed that it was the only metal we had in abundance. It irked me that the Ruvane was right. None of us had seen the raw rocks before the Ordo's processed it into pure copper. We could be sitting on a vast hoard of the stuff and none of us would know.

With roiling tempers reduced to a simmer, I opened a calm dialogue. "The way I see things, there are two choices. The first is to make good on Aebba's promise and to re-forge an alliance with the Ordos. With their encampment being so deep in the mountains, it could take a full moon just to get there, let alone establish ties of friendship. They were mighty offended by your rejection, Eseld. I wouldn't put it past them to tell us all to sling our hooks and begone." I paused, letting the suggestion sink through their skulls. It looked to me that Cryda was not even listening, her attention seemed to be waning.

“And the second?” Blydh asked. He had not changed his stance or removed his threatening gaze from his half-brother the whole time I had spoken.

“Well now, doesn’t the Cantii have one or two flourishing copper mines, down at the other end of the coast? I think it might be prudent for Tallack to sail down the channel to trade with your father, Cryda. What say you?” We all looked in her direction, expecting the Ruvane to make a solid decision in the tribe’s best interest. She peeped up at me and looked puzzled. I spelled it out for her. “Cryda, as the current tribal leader, it is by your word that this problem must be solved. Perhaps Tallack should invite the Chieftain of the Cantii to return with him for a visit here. We could explain our difficulties with metal supplies, and you could catch up with your father after all this time. What say you?”

The confusion seemed to linger about her absent look. “Oh, um, yes. That sounds like a sensible plan. Son…” She gestured towards Tallack. “Go and collect your grandfather, if he will grace us with his time.” She returned her face to the bear fur, flicking her wrist at all those about her.

Eseld treated us to one of her discontented scoffs, dragging Derwa from the Long Hut via the rear door. Cernonnus only knows what she will cook up now. That woman eats, sleeps and breathes discord. I suspect that she will garner the support of her father and the priests, and that will not lead to anything good. My suggestion will make it seem as though I am gathering our allies against the priests. I will have to watch everything I eat and drink more than ever. No more feasting in the Long Hut. It’ll be porridge made on my own fire for the foreseeable future.

Common sense told me to return straight to my house to tend to the sick and wounded, but curiosity overcame me. My clicking joints and the thumping noise my stick makes when I lean for support makes it nigh on impossible to creep up on anyone, yet I managed to make my way behind Eseld's hut unseen and unheard. I loitered next to the door linens and bent over to rub my shins. To anyone walking past, it looked as though I was overwrought with weariness.

I heard Eseld speak first. Her voice remained low, so that I was unable to make out what she said. There was no such difficulty in hearing the response, for her father's great booming voice was loud enough to shake the rafters. He was not pleased with the news from the messenger, and even less by the family's decision to send for the tribal Chieftain of the powerful Cantii. He thrust an arm through the door flap and nearly knocked me from my feet in his haste. He shouted back to his daughter, "Leave this to me," and marched off towards the river bank.

Standing on the main boardwalk, I dithered, wondering if I should follow or not. I was in no fit state to do battle with the wicked old man, and I could not send Jago to spy on my behalf for fear of him being captured again. Against my better judgement, I returned to my sickly children and bleeding warriors, and set to stitching, bandaging and dispensing my herbal tonics. By mid-afternoon, I set up my medicines and tinctures on a board outside my house, so that I could keep an eye on camp affairs while I tended my patients.

There were the usual sights, sounds and smells. The roasting meats at the fire pits, the fresh caught fish hauled ashore by the river banks, the tribal wives reprimanding children and dogs while they beat the dirty linens on rocks upstream. I watched the movements of the widows. Those were the most intriguing of all. Brea appeared to have found her confidence in Tallack's company, forsaking handmaiden duties and leaving Cryda to fend for herself. And fend she certainly did, for Cryda seemed to be gathering her furs and linens, metals and trove items into her hut. With each of her trips from her roundhouse, she would stop and glance about her to see who was watching her movements. Whenever Eseld was visible, Cryda slunk back inside until the camp was cleared once more.

Thick black smoke billowed from behind the priests' shelters near to the river, then the drumming began. By sundown, the wailing and chanting started, low at first, and then much louder, drawing elders from the middle camp houses. When all went silent for a few moments, and a bleating cry filled the air, I knew that he had sacrificed a goat to his gods.

I finished dealing with the last of my warriors, and instructed Jago to prepare my meal. With my trusted stick beneath my arm, I ventured towards the gathering crowd to witness the latest staged spectacle of the priests. Unsurprisingly, nearly all the tribe in camp was in attendance, even the Ruvane and her sons.

Brea still clung to Tallack's arm, and from his dazed look, he rather enjoyed her attention. I recalled the scene Jago and I witnessed, confirming my suspicions over his preference for male company. I scratched my head. Perhaps my nephew does not have a partiality at all. Maybe, he likes both boys and girls equally. That revelation I could cope with, but I was not sure that Brea's feelings for Tallack were genuine. Deep in my gut, I was sure that she was using him to further her own ends.

Edging my way closer to the front, elders' wives, children and servants all stepped aside to allow me passage to the front of the circle.

The old man wore the blue jay headdress again, with the carved wooden beak. His wizened chest showed his breastbone through thin skin. He had painted himself with woad and red clay. A string of bones hung around his neck. With the drummers thrashing a beat out on the pigskin and wailing their ridiculous chants, the old man knelt down in the centre of a cleared circle. Eseld sprinkled salt around him, wasting good materials to build a sense of wonder among the elders. Paega lit long grease torches and stuck them into the ground at intervals around the salt circle.

His grandfather was almost ready to begin his performance. He seemed to be waiting for something, or someone. Closing his eyes, he held each of the bones in his necklace, mouthing a prayer to the gods for each of them. In the middle of the row, a small pouch hung from the twine. With great ceremony, he pinched open the purse and pulled out a single bone. It was tiny, like those found in the hand.

Eseld stepped into the salt ring carrying a bronze cup of blood. I hoped that it was from the slaughtered goat and no one I was likely to know or love. The priest stood up and raised the bone high in the air.

"This is the last gift from our much-loved Chief, Aebba the Wild. A brave bear of a warrior, taken from us under shameful circumstances. He will be avenged. Daughter, bring me the blood." She lifted the bowl to chest height and bowed her head.

"Great Aebba, hear us. Here is the bone from your strongest hand." He cupped it in both palms as though it was the most precious item in the land. "Daughter. Take the bones of our forefathers from my neck and dip one into the blood." Eseld did as she was commanded, taking her time and making grand gestures for all to see. "Look how the blood coats the white of the bone. Our ancestors were great, they are at peace with the gods. Their bones have no quarrel with our earthly blood." He paused for dramatic effect; his arms raised to the sky.

"Aebba, hear us." He chanted again. No one responded. "Aebba, hear us." This time the crowd joined in, taken by his showmanship, repeating his words in a unified chant. "Show us your displeasure. I place your mighty thumb bone into the blood. If you are indeed at peace, your bone will be coated in the stuff of life."

Eseld raised the bowl again, allowing her father to dip the end of the thumb bone into the crimson liquid. He swished it around in a circle, and then held it aloft. The crowd gasped. Aebba's bone was pristine. Not a drop of blood stained its shaft.

"This proves he hears us and is much grieved. We will avenge you great warrior. I will cast the runes for you, to point us to the culprits."

The elders and their wives spoke softly together, their suspicions turning fast into rumour and spreading within the gathered throng. Still the old priest captivated all those around. While he and Eseld drew more symbols in the river sands, and fetched a flatter bowl in which to cast the runes, I thought about his neat little trick. A good coating of goose grease would prevent the blood from seeping into the white of the bone. I dare say, that was all it took to stun those watching.

With two more bones from his necklace, Aebba's digit, a feather and some pebbles decorated with symbols like the Triskellion, he rattled them in cupped hands and threw them into the bowl. Falling to his knees he hung his head over the runes and took in a sharp breath. The drums fell silent. The hushed crowd leaned towards him.

The old man covered his face with his palms, transferring the goat blood in great clotting blobs. He wailed with a babble of tongues, a trick he learned from me, when Jago fell ill.

"Father…" Eseld dropped to his side, clasping his head between her hands. "He speaks to the gods. What wisdom do they give us?"

The babbling stopped; his hands moved. "It's worse than I suspected, child. The great Aebba speaks of his killer. He says that they walk among us, feast in the Long Hut, and carry betrayal next to their heart."

"What is to be done, father?"

"There is only one thing that can be done, my daughter. We must root out this evil, and punish them."

Eseld clambered to her feet. "But how?"

The priest took his time to glare at every one of the elders in the front row of the circle. Clutching the bone of Aebba to his chest, he bowed his head, closed his eyes and announced, "Every member of the tribe, must initiate into the faith. If they refuse, then we will know they are guilty."

So, that was his plan, to force all members into his faith under penalty of death or banishment. That would make him the tribal leader over Cryda and the boys.

CHAPTER NINETEEN

From the expressions on my nephews' faces, I expected bloodshed. The priest had laid down impossible terms. Become a member of their sect, under his authority, or face accusations of murder. Equally galling, was the thinly masked insinuation that Cryda was to blame for Aebba's death, and that her unborn child was the reason for the betrayal. That did not go unnoticed. Blydh unsheathed his blade. Tallack signalled his men to disembark from the row boats at the riverbank.

As far as I could tell, the twins were prepared to kill everyone from the Priest Sect to defend their mother. Something had to shift, there had to be a way to diffuse the tension building among the tribe's folk. The elders saw the warriors taking up arms further up the camp and began to back away from the circle. Without Aebba's strong will and respect, the tribe lurched from one crackpot idea to the next. A clear and decisive leader was needed.

Blydh swiped the salt circle with his foot, and stepped closer to the old man. His protectors scrambled to his aid, grabbing their weapons and jostling the spectators from the crowd until they towered over Eseld and the old priest. Blydh didn't back down. Tallack took a large stride to his brother's side, his men rushing to stand at his back forming a united front. The difference between Tallack's men and the priest warriors was about half a day of smoking bad weeds. They were incapable of fighting much fitter and sober men. All who stood there knew that.

The priest glanced about him, weighing up the likelihood of defeat. He must have decided that the numbers were not in his favour, for he affected a pathetic and old air, struggling to get to his feet and groaning as he leaned on his daughter for support.

Blydh was not taken in by the show. "You need to gather your half-baked warriors and leave camp." There was something forceful about Blydh that no one could describe. He had a presence and command that belied his years. One abrupt conversation with him, and you'd think him as old as I and far wiser. In truth, he was one fewer summers than his half-brother Paega.

"We must stay. Our duty is to follow the chosen one, and he is right here in this compound." The old man let his features droop, feigning exhaustion after his time channelling the gods.

Tallack and Blydh looked at each other, and then at me. I shrugged, keen to avoid their argument. I knew precisely who the old man was talking about, and feared that he would use this as an excuse to take Jago for his own. That, I could not allow. I shrank back into the crowd, ducking below elbows and weaving between shoulders. The twins must have known who the old man was talking about, for they were in the Long Hut when Jago had his first seizure. I can only suggest that they were out to make the old man beg. Free from the gathering, I hastened my steps.

"And who is the one you speak of?" It was Tallack's voice. I'd know it anywhere.

"He is the painted boy from your medicine woman's hut. He speaks with the voice of Cernonnus."

I quickened my pace, stomping across the boardwalks back to my slaves and livestock. It didn't help.

"Aunt Mel...?" Tallack, again. I pretended my old ears had not heard him, scurrying as fast as my bones would carry me. "Aunt Meliora!" He bellowed. I stopped, breathed deeply, and turned around. The circle of onlookers had parted, giving Blydh, Tallack and the odious priest clear sight of me. I pulled a face of surprise, as though it was the first time I heard my name called.

Blydh knew I was faking. "What is this about a chosen painted boy?" As always, straight to the point that one. No beating about the bush.

I had to think my answer through with care. I cast my eyes down to the slippery boards, and mimicked the performance of the priest, staggering towards them groaning and leaning heavily on my stick. I could see Tallack covering his grin with the back of his hand. It gave me time to contemplate my response.

"It's true, nephew. The chosen one is under my protection." I played up to their ignorance, knowing that they were using this to exert their authority over the priests. "He relays words of wisdom from the god of gods, to help us in our time of strife." I glared at the old man, challenging him to speak.

Blydh took the reins. "Then you should hand him over to the priests, so that they may leave camp." His tone was forceful and unerring.

"I cannot do that, Nephew. The chosen one speaks in the tongue of his forefathers, and only I can interpret his words. He must stay with me." I stuck my nose in the air and folded my arms across my chest. I would not be brow beaten by Aebba; I certainly was not going to allow it from his sons.

"Perhaps the old medicine woman would like to come with us on our travels?" The smirking fraud suggested.

Eseld snorted without even trying to conceal her amusement.

"I would not, and no amount of persuasion will make me change my mind." I spun about on my stick and tried to strut away.

I could hear Eseld sticking her oar into matters behind my back. "Are you going to let her push us all around like that? Who does she think she is? I am the widow of Aebba the Wild. If I say she has to hand over the boy to my father, she should be forced to do so."

Tallack defended me, blessed gift that he is. "Be quiet, Eseld. You were second wife, at best, and from common stock. Aunt Mel is from a line of great Chieftains, and don't you forget it."

"Watch your tongue, boy, that's my daughter you're slandering."

I left them to fight among themselves. I figured the longer I remained, the more inflamed the situation would become. Dashing into my hut, I rattled off my instructions to the girl and Jago. They were to pack all our things in bundles and load them onto the pony. We could not stay and wait for the priests to carve poor Jago up as an offering as soon as night fell.

Digging out the last buried pot of my hazelnut paste, my meagre treasures, and my tinctures, I wrapped them in my furs. As I was stacking the rest of my belongings with my knives, I could hear the raised voice of the girl, ranting at Jago behind the hut. I poked my head outside to see what the commotion was about.

"I told her that we had to leave, Fur Benyn, but she resists. She has worked so hard on our new hut; it is a shame to leave it behind." Jago told me.

I nodded my understanding. "Tell her that if we don't leave, you will end up as the next main dish over the Long Hut roasting pits, and she will end her days under the priests' bedding. We'll be back soon enough." I gestured to my small herd of goats. "Pick out the best milker to take with us, then see what price you can get for the rest." Before I could return to my packing, I saw Cryda rushing towards me. I had no time for her games and nonsense, so I dashed inside.

She entered my hut uninvited, watching me select my essential herbs and potions from my stores. "You are leaving?" When I failed to answer her obvious question, she continued. "Will you come with me to the solstice circle? I have a few loyal warriors to protect us, and I could use your skill should this child come early."

I stopped and regarded her. Her eyes were puffy with sorrow, her voice desperate and sincere. Her request explained her recent furtive activities. She too was preparing to escape. It was always safer to travel in a group, no matter the destination. At least at the solstice celebrations, I had the opportunity to forge other alliances. "Fine, but I leave this very day."

She looked animated for the first time since Aebba's passing. "If you'll wait until nightfall, we can be along the eastern trail for a half day before they notice our absence." She had a point. The last thing either of us needed was for Blydh and Tallack to force us to stay.

As it happens, it was a good decision. Cryda took Aebba's cart and horses, and made her slaves load them in the forest outside the compound. During the course of the day, we had assembled quite the procession. Some of the elders and their families had caught sight of the goods being transferred and sought out Cryda for permission to join us. I bribed the warriors on guard with the last of my nuts and a little poppy resin. It was all I could spare.

Come sundown, we slipped through the gates and set off at a decent pace. Most of my things cushioned the large beaker containing Aebba's bones. Only one part of his thumb remained in camp, and none of us were prepared to approach the old priest to ask for its return. Jago sat astride my pony, with the girl walking alongside. It was indulgent, and I suffered some uneasy glares from the elders for my decision, but they would soon complain if his injured ankle slowed us all down. For my part, I lay among furs and dried meats, salt pots and treasure trunks, in the back of the waggon with Cryda. I felt almost like a Ruvane myself.

The first part of the night was slow and arduous, taking us over the narrowest stretch of shallow river waters and across the treacherous marsh land. It was not for the faint of heart. More than once our cart got bogged, needing all the brave warriors and slaves who came along to push us from the mud. We made good time through the dense birch and ash trees, probably because the noise we made, scattered all creatures who would threaten us, far and wide.

By sun up, we rested the ponies and made camp. We were distant enough from the compound to give us a head start. Jago collected wood and built us a nice fire, while the girl boiled some porridge for Cryda and me. Her slaves joined the warriors in a hunt to supplement our meagre rations, and give us something to cook at our next stop. It dawned on me that no one at the Chieftain compound knew where we were headed. Older folk such as I knew that this would be the third summer since the last pilgrimage to the largest henge on the land.

Those solstices between, were celebrated closer to home or at the stones at Boscawen Un near Lands' End. This was a summer of special feasting, of tribal discussions and alliances. Whoever became our next Metern, should not miss this opportunity.

"Cryda." I called to her as she returned from emptying her bladder in the shrubs at the wayside. "What is your thinking here?" I spooned out some porridge into a bowl and handed it to her as she sat on a large boulder. "I understand why we left the priests behind, but what of Blydh and Tallack? Shouldn't they have their chance to build their names among the great leaders of the lands?"

She peered at me in confusion. It looked to me that she had not thought this venture through. We should have taken the trouble to bring Tallack into the plan as a failsafe. At least then, they could follow us to the east and still be there to join in the feasts and rituals. I blamed myself. I called to Jago and bid him the task of unpacking my knife wrap. Letting my porridge cool, I took the leather roll and laid it across the ground at Cryda's feet. At one end of the row of blades, was my toughest chisel. It's a handy tool for cutting through bone and sinew.

"Shift your legs woman." I roared. Cryda jumped off the boulder as I took a fist size rock and pound it against the end of the metal chisel, carving out a rough symbol. By the time I was done, my porridge was cold. "There, not too bad I reckon. A bit wonky I grant you." I stood back to admire my handiwork.

Jago was pulling faces and tilting his head. "Forgive me, Fur Benyn, but what is it?"

Cryda grinned. It was an old trick, but a faithful one. She lifted her linens to reveal her ankle. The same circle within another circle was marked on her skin. Still he looked perplexed.

"It is the sign of golden light from the sun, just like Cryda's hair. Aebba sometimes called her that when we were all much younger. The boys will see this on the marker stone, and know that we came this way. They should be able to guess the rest."

The day wore on, and Cryda grew restless, keen to continue our journey. With everything packed and our evening meal skinned and gutted ready for the pot, we set off once more.

"Best look lively, I shouted to Jago, who dawdled behind us on my pony. "From this point onward, we are crossing the Durotriges land, and you don't want to find yourself without warriors to protect you." That put a hot coal in his leggings. We trundled on for the better part of the afternoon, stopping to water the ponies and gather what items we could along the trail. It was slow and tough going over the Blackdown Hills, but it's good to get them out of the way near the start of the journey while everyone was fresh.

One of Cryda's warriors led the way, taking us on a steep curve away from areas where Duro's are known to camp and hunt, like Crewkerne and Coker. I sent one of them to scout ahead and make sure that we had somewhere safe to lay overnight. He galloped off as though the Morrighan was on his tail. Hardly any of us spoke that afternoon. It was as though each of us was inwardly begging the gods to let us pass unnoticed. The henge might be protected land, but we have to get within sight of the cursus grounds before the sacred amnesty takes effect.

It was almost dark when the scout cantered back to us with news from a homesteader that a large group of Duro's were settled near to Fivehead. My back was sore from the bumps along the track and the constant rattle against Cryda's trunk of metals, but it was better than walking. We pushed on in a southerly direction to add distance between us and our best guess as to the Duro's location. I was hoping that we'd get as far as Penselwood, but the wheels on Aebba's cart needed some fixing before we got to Podimore. We had no other choice but to make camp and keep the fire low so as not to draw attention to ourselves.

Jago raked over the embers, keeping the heat on our hare and duck supper as they roasted to tender perfection. Cryda ate enough to feed a small tribe of her own. I took my fill and walked the edges of our camp to stretch my aching limbs.

The scout chose our camp site. From my standing point, I could see the dark silhouette of the tree line as it climbed in all directions around us. For all the scout's wisdom, I couldn't help but think he had chosen our site poorly. We sat at the very bottom of the basin, the smoke from our cooking, wandered upwards to the stars, unhindered by breeze or cloud.

A growing sense of unease took hold of me. Cryda's slaves manned the lookout points, but they were as weary as everyone else; more so since they had walked all night and most of the day, while others rode horses. What use would they be to us if the worst should happen? I relieved myself in the privacy of the shrubs and hastened back to the fireside.

"Cryda, I don't think that we should stay here all night, it's not safe." I said, gesturing for Jago to bundle my knives and begin to pack our things away. He scooted around the fireside and drew back his foot ready to kick the dirt over the embers when Cryda stopped him.

"Don't be silly. This is perfect for us. We are sheltered on all sides from the wind, and there is water and firewood close by. Besides anything else, I am fit for nothing. I must sleep on solid ground, or this baby inside me will kick me all night." She flicked her hand at Jago, sending him scurrying away. He looked to me for his orders. I gave none. Cryda was shattered, as was everyone else, but I just could not settle.

When the moon was high, I took a last wander to the warrior on watch beyond the fires and reed shelters. The closer I got to him, the more I could smell the ale on his breath. His eyes roved the dark lands at the trail head, but I could tell that he saw nothing. He leaned on a trail marker, with one knee buckling beneath him.

He did not hear the owls calling to each other, or the branches snapping in the woods beyond. Neither did he see the glint of the axe as it cleaved his head in two before my very eyes.

CHAPTER TWENTY

The warrior dropped to the ground, his brains spilling out from his skull. I yelled and screamed to warn the others at the fireside, but the raiders knocked me down into the mud. I was lucky that they didn't cave my head in too. More Duro's came, flailing their spears and daggers, bellowing and running at the elders on foot. Their riders encircled those sleeping babes and mothers from the shelters until we were all dragged into a pitiful group of captives. We were too few and ill equipped to fight back. Their raid caught our warriors and lookouts off guard, slicing their throats from behind. We were easy pickings.

They seized our carts and horses, and made us all walk behind them in a long procession to their camp. I tried to plead with their warrior leader on Cryda's behalf, but he sneered at the mention of her name.

"She is with child, take pity man." I roared at him.

He jabbed his thumb towards the back end of the line. "So are some of them down there. Don't hear them bleating about it."

His fierce glare was enough warning for me to hold my tongue. He alone had killed two of Cryda's warriors, his men the rest. We were defenceless old women and children. Defying him would not help our cause. We shambled along behind the waggons and horses, through boggy peat land and rocky outcrops, with barely a couple of torches to light our way. Steering us all south, we sighted their camp at daybreak.

The Durotridge tribal elders came to their firesides as we walked past, some of their young hurled great clods of mud and stones at us. One deranged woman spat at Cryda, the spittle catching in her golden hair. This was but a tiny fraction of their tribal clans. Their main compound is quite a distance further south by the shore and much larger than ours. They may not have our vast lands or tin mines, but they are strong in number and skilled horsemen. Our tribe is too scattered to battle against their frequent invasions.

Was it just bad luck that we were caught in their path, or was our scout paid off for our whereabouts? If he did betray us, it did him no good. We left his body for the crows to pick over.

They pushed us into the centre of the camp. I spotted one larger shelter, made from fine skins and tall birch branches. I guessed that this belonged to the clan leader. It turns out I was right. Cryda was dragged by the hair between the door flaps and into the presence of their Metern. Fearing for her life, I shuffled along the row of captives while the Duro's had their backs to us. It was only when I drew close to entering, that they noticed me and stepped in my way.

"I need to go with her. I am the medicine woman for our tribe. Allow me to enter, and I will furnish you with poppy resin for your troubles." There were at least five big strong men standing outside the shelter. I could see the indecision on their faces. One scratched at his plaited beard, and thrust a stinking forearm under my nose. The gash cut across his muscle, but missed that which carried his blood. I've smelled some rotted wounds in my time, but this one was about the worst. His face flushed with a glow of sweat, his eyes giddy and unfocused.

"You fix this, I let you in." He growled. I nodded, dipping my head beneath his arm and slipping into the tent behind.

At one side of the shelter, a young woman reclined on furs, while a great bearded man prodded Cryda in the chest. I recognised the woman immediately, and she me.

"Aunt Mel! Whatever are you doing on Duro lands?" It was Wenna, Eseld's eldest daughter. She scampered over to me and threw her jewelled and painted arms about my middle and squeezed.

"Careful, child. You'll knock the wind out of me." I patted and smiled and attempted to hug her in return. She seemed too sprightly to have heard the news. I peeled her from my body and looked her square in the eyes. "Do you know about your father?" At the mention of Aebba, she curled her lip. She was so much like her mother; the same tone in her voice, a similar sneer towards that which she found distasteful, and a confident attitude to her stride.

"I stopped calling him my father the day that he and mother sold me to him." She gestured towards the hulking mass of Metern examining Cryda. "Mind you, could have been worse, I suppose. At least they didn't bind me to those hairy Ordo's from the mountains."

I didn't think it prudent to mention that her sister might yet have to endure that fate. Wenna required careful handling if we were to get out of their land with our lives.

Her expression puckered into a frown. "What about him? He's not dead, is he?"

How else could I respond to such a direct question? "He is, Wenna. We carry his bones with us to the great gathering at the solstice circle on your eastern boundary."

She peered at Cryda; taking note of how pathetic she seemed. They exchanged a glance of mutual understanding, one that seemed to confer a degree of sympathy from their shared loss. Wenna did not react as I expected. She was the neglected middle child, sold as chattel to a rival tribe. Her parents were neither concerned nor interested in her welfare from then on. Little Derwa was the spoilt younger sibling, Paega the eldest son and heir. I thought she might rejoice in her father's death, a natural justice from the gods for giving her away. Instead, she took a lung full of air and approached her husband.

"My love. This is the tribal Ruvane for the Dumnonii. She carries my father's bones to the solstice circle. I should like you to let them pass through our lands, for the sake of honour. They have already paid a heavy toll in losing their warriors." She touched his shoulder with such tenderness, I knew that she had more than the Chieftain's ear. What a clever girl. In just a few summers, she has grown from child to wily woman. She has made this land hers, and the men in it her servants and protectors. Wenna has all the guile of her mother with none of the arrogance. She deserves to be the Ruvane of this huge tribe. May the gods keep her on this side of our borders. If they were to invade us while our tribe is without leadership, they could take over all our lands and mines in as few moons as three. I should make an offering to the Morrighan to protect us from such an event.

Wenna's Chieftain turned to face her, his smile spread across his face. His loins crushed against her belly. He grunted, and then lunged at her lips with a grotesque kiss.

She endured him for a moment or two and then pulled away. “Well, my love… do I have your blessing?”

He grunted again before launching himself onto the furs on the ground. A clever girl indeed; he was just a dumb brute. She was the brain behind the entire tribe.

Wenna approached Cryda. “Did he die well?” She fixed on the broken woman before her, as did I. Her response confirmed my theory that she had nothing to do with Aebba’s murder, for she shook her head with some violence and tears streamed down her cheeks. She appeared to be more troubled by his passing than when she first learned of the news. Perhaps it had been a delayed reaction. As satisfied as I was that she did not kill our Metern, it did not exclude the possibility that she carried another’s child.

Wenna stood tall, dry eyed and composed. “I shall come with you and Aunt Mel to the solstice. My warriors and I will take you along safe paths across our borders.” She was a remarkable Ruvane for her young age. It was obvious that they were all loyal to her, and that included the slob on the furs.

I needed to catch her in this amenable mood and press my luck. My dear niece, your warriors took all our belongings… my knives and herbs…” I gave her my most imploring look, wringing my hands in front of my chest.

She waved her understanding. “It’s fine, Aunt Mel. I’ll sort everything out.” She clicked her fingers at a slave girl standing by the doorway. “Rest, while I go and arrange everything.”

I followed her outside the tent, intending to keep my promise to the man with the wounded arm. By mid-morning, I had a great deal more injured and sick folk lined up at the cart than I would tend in a quarter moon back at our compound. Jago and the girl made a fire, boiled herbs, gathered more and generally ran around after me, while I stitched wounds, squeezed out pus, burned out the rot and sliced off black growths.

By high sun, Wenna was all set to leave, and my stocks had run down to nothing. I climbed into Aebba's cart with Cryda and buried myself in my old furs to rest. I got hardly any sleep, before the new members of our procession were lifting babes and children into the back of the cart for my healing skills.

And thus it was so for the rest of the day. I helped those I could, and sent others to fetch plants and materials from the wayside, as we crossed the Duro's land to the plains and homesteads at the furthest reaches of their borders. Here, the clans had divided the cropping areas with stone markers and hedges. Their farming had an impressive order, with each family marking their own land with carvings and symbols. This must be the way of those across the seas. It bore the same traits as that which Jago spoke about from his native home.

We made camp for the night at sunset, less than a morning's walk from the stones. If we were to enter the sacred spaces come sun up, we all needed to wash and gather offerings to the gods. The lakes on the River Wylye gave us all that we needed, a plentiful supply of white birds and ducks to roast for our supper, or to offer in sacrifice at the cursus. Wenna took charge of all our affairs, allowing me time to bathe for the morning ritual.

The days may have grown warmer during the last moon, but the waters were chill, silted with slime and mud and choked with weed. I wandered around the bank looking for a cleaner spot to dunk myself, passing reed beds and clumps of willow. Cursing myself for not having brought a blade with me with which I could harvest the bark, I waded in up to my waist, gasping with the cold. The muck and filth would have been preferable to sharp flints and rocky fragments under my sore feet. Cursing and slipping, I decided to stay put and immerse myself beneath the surface, uttering my praise to Cernonnus and the Lady of Lakes and Seas while I washed.

I pinched my nose tight, closed my eyes and mouth and bobbed down, letting the murky water seep into every nook and crevice of my body. Shuffling in my crouched position, I felt a sharp pain between my toes. At first, I thought it might have been a pike, intent on biting me for invading his lake, but as I moved my foot, I could feel the straight edges of something sharp. Before my lungs could burst, I grubbed about in the sediment and pulled up a long grey sword. In the dim light, I could still see its magnificence. This was no common man's blade. This was created for a Chieftain of greatness. It outshone Aebba's fine ceremonial sword and bronze shield that hung from the rafters of the Long Hut. I scratched the surface with a thumbnail, expecting to find the old brown of the bronze gleaming new. It did not. The mark I'd made through the tarnish looked to be silver, but it was harder. There was no give when I tried to bend it to my will.

Struck with indecision, I stood in the lake admiring the fine metal work on the handle. It was clearly thrown into the lake as an offering to the gods, but had they guided me to the spot in order to take it for myself? It seemed a shame to leave it there, growing dull with age. In the darkness, I completed my chants and ritual cleanse, and made my way to the bank with the sword. Dressed in a clean tunic, I wrapped the metal in my dirty clothes and carried them back to camp, awaiting a moment when I could pass the blade to Jago for safe keeping among my medicines and tinctures.

That night, I slept better than I have ever done. Maybe the gods favour me after all. Jago showed me a small ledge beneath the wheels of Aebba's cart where he had hidden the exotic blade. I told him to pack it with my belongings when no one else was around to see. He's a trustworthy lad. I'm still not sure about the girl though.

Cryda and I took bread and meat with Wenna come dawn, each of us keen to continue our journey. With everything stowed away, we set off in a north-easterly direction as soon as the horses were watered and fed. By midday, our procession drew level with the stone circle. Many tribal leaders were already encamped, their warriors guarding flocks and cattle, and their shelters built to last out this important summer.

Before we could stake our small section of the sacred ground, we had to walk on to the cursus to make our offerings. Jago and the girl carried my basket containing two plump ducks. Wenna had her slaves carry enough for both her and Cryda.

I looked all about me as we paced along the track towards the vast procession ground. "Wenna, where is your husband? Did he not ride ahead of us?"

She glanced about furtively, and then at her feet. "He had some tribal business to take care of first. He'll join us when he can. I will stand in his stead, if it pleases the elders for me to represent him."

I thought it odd that he should miss one of the most important meetings in three summers, but I said nothing. While her kindness extended to me, Cryda and my slaves, I was not about to sour the relationship with more questions. We passed the burial mounds of the tribal Chieftains and moved towards the long ditch beyond. Here lay the longest processional ground anyone has ever seen. It's been there for longer than I can remember, certainly built before my time, and that of my grandfather. He lies in the mound over yonder too. I pressed my thumb to my forehead and sent my best thoughts to him in the Summerlands.

Inching along to wait our turn to cross the bridge over the ditch, I kept my eyes peeled for anyone leaving the cursus who I might know. My family spread far and wide thanks to Aebba's forefathers and their tendency to bind daughters to clan and tribal leaders. Eventually, it was our turn to cross. Jago and the girl hurried along after us, as we each walked to the east for the first offering.

With the sun high overhead, we reached the massive tree trunk half buried in the ground at the farthest end of the enclosed strip of land. The base was dripping with fresh blood.

Wenna went first, taking a kicking hare by the neck scruff from her basket and slicing open its throat in offering to Cerridwen. "Mother, crone, wise keeper of all life. Take this hare in payment for the abundance you give our tribe, this day and every day hence." The blood spattered over the tree trunk and dribbled down her arm. She laid the twitching creature in the pile of other dead and dying animals, knowing that they would form the basis for a massive feast come nightfall. Cryda and I stepped up and repeated the ritual, facing the east where the sun wakes from its nightly slumber; our giver of life.

Bloodied, but energised, we strolled the full length of the cursus to the most westerly point. Cryda seemed a little brighter. She and Wenna compared jewels and furs, metal torques and bracelets. I was itching to tell them about the exotic metal of the sword I found, but I was afraid that they would force me to return it to the lake.

At the other end of the processional ground, an entire oak tree, branches and trunk, leaves and shoots, was buried upside down in the soil. All who looked upon the roots would be reminded that when the living pass from this world, they must climb down the trunk into the Underworld. Only the valiant who die in battle are afforded a place in the Summerlands, where my grandfather rests.

Cryda seemed most eager to complete this part of the ceremony, welcoming us into the sacred space. She lifted the lid from Wenna's basket, and chose a white bird with long legs and a sharp beak. It pecked at her as she reached in to grab it by the legs, but she would not be deterred. Facing full west, within sight of the tree to the Underworld, she drove a dagger into its guts.

"I give this bird in offering to the Morrighan. May she keep my boys safe in battle, and choose our next Metern with care." She swung it by the limp legs, its innards falling onto the ground as she flung it into a roaring fire a short distance from the tree. Again, Wenna and I repeated the process, each of us asking something different from the Goddess of Battles and Judgement.

We had just one more act to complete before leaving the cursus for the circle, a gift of our own blood to the god of gods, Cernonnus. By now, the entire tract of land was buzzing with visitors, lines formed by each of the giving trees. We made our way towards the centre, waiting for the chance to spill blood. I wiped my small blade on the hem of my tunic and offered it to Cryda. The crowds moved aside, allowing her to step up to a wooden altar carrying a large ceramic bowl. As she walked up to prick her hand with the knife, we heard that familiar scoffing sound.

There stood Eseld, on the other side of the altar.

CHAPTER TWENTY-ONE

"How is it that you are here?" Cryda shrieked.

Eseld fumed from the other side of the offering altar, tapping her foot and clenching her fists. "Did you think no one would notice your little disappearing act, with *my* husband's bones?"

I was stunned. We had taken so many precautions before leaving. "How did you get here so quickly?" I stammered, aware that we were blocking the processional activities and people were crowding behind us in a line.

"Paega and I rode here as soon as you were missed. Derwa, the priests and your boys, will follow along shortly."

Neither of us had any words for her, we were thrown into a daze of confusion. Her scowl sharpened. She leaned forward producing a blade from a scabbard at her waist. Cryda and I jumped back, frightened that she would take her revenge out on us there and then, in front of the entire gathering.

"Well, are you going to just stand there? Make your offering to Cernonnus and step aside." She spun the knife until the handle faced me and thrust it into my hand. Panting with relief, I took the blade and stabbed the point into the fleshy side of my left hand, letting the blood ooze into the bowl and mix with that from other tribes. I spoke my blessing to the god of gods, and passed the knife to Cryda. Her offering was swifter than mine. She muttered beneath her breath, trickled no more than a couple of drops into the bowl and hurried away, leaving Eseld to collect her blade from the altar stone.

We were washed, blessed and bound by the terms of peace within the sacred space. I should have felt untroubled and safe within the area, but with Eseld fuming and vengeful, I could not rest. The knife at her waist stayed at the forefront of my mind for the rest of the day. We followed her to the area that she and Paega had claimed for our tribesmen. It was not the best position by any means, nor was it large enough to accommodate all that were set to arrive. Determined to make the best of a bad situation, we set up camp and tried to barter for enough provisions to keep us going until the evening. I needed to restock my supplies of herbs and willow bark, since I had used up most of my stores on Wenna's warriors and tribe's folk.

With the priests due to arrive at any time, I insisted Jago came with me to the lane of merchants and sellers. I buried what tin nuggets I had beneath the bedding in our shelter, and took just a small amount with me to trade. The closer we walked towards the stone circle, the quieter Jago became. His eyes darted from one great rock to the next, his mouth hung open in awe.

"Don't they have circles where you're from then?" I asked of him.

"They do, I have heard tales, but I was taken from my homeland before I was old enough to leave our fields for the pilgrimage. I never got to see them. From what my father told me; they were nowhere near as large as these." He screened the sun from his view with a raised hand. I chuckled, leaving him to his amazement. Sometimes I forget how magnificent the stones are up close. His admiration and my memory are just more things that dull with age.

The seller's huts were varied and equally impressive. Goods from far across the seas, and from closer to home were displayed for our consideration; amber jewellery, worked silver, golden hair fasteners, pots and beakers, furs and oils, and much more besides.

One stall at the farthest end of the row interested me the most. It traded seeds from all over the land. Some I recognised, the tiny black spheres of the poppy, the golden yellow of the big mustard seeds and of course, the grains of wheat and barley, but there were some that intrigued me more. I bartered for some flaxseed, a little hemp and a tiny bag of poppy.

At the end of his table was a pot filled with a clear green oil. I had tasted this in the Long Hut before. Tallack was always bringing home jugs of pressed oil, but the olives themselves were given to the Metern and his wives as a prize beyond value. Eseld once tried to feed me one of the fruits. The trader let me try one. It dried my teeth as I bit into the black flesh, but the tangy flavour stayed with me for some time afterwards. I cannot decide whether I liked the taste or not. Either way, I have eaten a tiny piece of fruit from such distant lands and found the experience enjoyable. Now I understand Tallack's desire to be at sea and travel to foreign lands in search of new and exciting foods, beads, jewels, songs and stories. Cleaning off the last of the olive flesh, I pocketed the pit from its centre.

Jago was still entranced by the massive stones casting me into shadow. At least, that was what I thought he was staring at, until I turned around and saw the horses galloping into the sacred space carrying tattooed and shaved priests. Jago's look was of fear, not awe, for each of the priest warriors were painted in woad and chalk, just as I had found him that day by the river.

As luck would have it, the pitch Eseld had marked for our use was not sufficient to house the Priest Sect. They made their camp further from the stones, closer to the cursus, not that distance would stop them from taking poor Jago. I could offer him small comfort, being feeble against their might.

"I won't let them take you lad. Stick close by and you'll be fine." He gave me a force smile. I understood his doubt. "Here, try one of these olives. Bet you've never tasted anything like it before in your life." I pushed the black fruit close to his mouth, expecting him to take it from me. Instead, he stepped backwards, and turned away from my small gift.

"Forgive me, Fur Benyn. I never liked the taste of them. My father brought an olive sapling back from a long pilgrimage. It grew well in my mother's garden."

It was the first time I had ever seen him with glossy eyes, close to tears. I paid the trader with my tin, and gathered up my precious seeds. On our return to our allotted section of camp, we found the girl running errands for Cryda. The fires burned low and there was no wood left to stoke the embers into life. There was only one thing left to do. I borrowed an axe from young Wenna's tribesmen, and wandered off into the woodland beyond the processional grounds with Jago.

At least he could still chop wood. I twisted a few lengths of green branches together and bound the sticks in a bundle while Jago carried the larger logs. I was loathed to send him back on his own to fetch more, but with Cryda and Eseld at each other's throats, I had to do as much work as the girl. I could see Wenna smirking from some distance at the sight of the two widows snarling and spitting like wild cats. At the time, it hadn't crossed my mind as to where the third of Aebba's wives could be. The last I saw of Brea; she was preening by Tallack's side before he set sail down the Channel towards the Cantii lands under his grandfather's reign. Had she sailed with him and his crew?

With the fires lit and some salted boar in the pot, I tied a flour ball of crushed nettle, sorrel, dandelion and salt in a linen pouch, and dangled it into the stew. With the last of my milled barley flour, I rubbed in a little butter and salt and mixed it to a flat dough with some beer. While that cooked on the hot stones, I set about calming the widows down.

Their argument was so loud and fast, I couldn't hear what each of them were saying. Eseld was red in the face and grunting with rage. She was lethal enough at the Chieftain compound on the River Exe, who knows what she is capable of while all eyes are fixed on rituals and ceremonies. We may all promise to preserve the peace within the sacred space, but who among Aebba's widows keeps their word?

Leaving instructions for the girl to mind the stew and grind more flour, I hooked my arm beneath Cryda's and marched her away from our camp. Sewn into a pocket in my tunic was my most treasured possessions. I carried them everywhere with me. At this most unsettled time for our tribe, it was important to forge new alliances and allies, even if that meant donating my collected wealth to the cause. I paused, thinking through my approach before reaching for a gold chain to offer in trade. My hand rested inside the pocket, moving the links between my fingers. "If your father can't provide us with copper to trade, we need to source it elsewhere. What do you suggest?"

She looked at me as though I was speaking in tongues.

"Cryda, you are the Ruvane, until Aebba's bones are laid to rest. You must steer the fate of the Dumnonii. Without copper, we can't make bronze. Without bronze, we have no way to repair weapons, no worked metals to sell, only our tin to trade."

Her forehead pinched together. "Can't we just trade more tin? There must be heaps left to mine. Send word to dig faster."

I sighed and scratched my forehead. Sometimes I forget that she gets scatter brained when she is with child. "They are processing all they can down there, and anyway bringing up more tin would do no good in the long run. Flood the trading stations with lots of the stuff and its value will go down. Tin is our power. No one else has any at all, not here, not across the water, not anywhere as far as I can tell. It must be traded with care."

She listened, and then looked pained, as though the responsibility was just too much to bear. Flicking her hair over her shoulder, she said. "Then let Blydh take charge of negotiations. I have a husband to bury."

Perhaps she was right. Blydh was level headed and as stubborn as a hairy boar. No one was likely to coax him into an unwise trade agreement. "When shall we expect to see him, do you suppose?"

She shrugged, pulled her arm away from me and wandered off in a dream. This solstice was going to be most taxing. Returning to camp, I found the girl breaking bread for Eseld, and Wenna approaching her mother from her tribal enclosure. This was their first encounter since Wenna's binding ceremony. I held my breath.

"Mother." Wenna offered, her fingers knotted together in front of her belly. She stood tall, peering down at Eseld.

The cold reception seemed to take the wind from Eseld's sails. "You came then, child." She moved closer, looking for signs of forgiveness, comfort even.

Wenna's eyes narrowed, halting her mother's progress. "I stopped being a child the moment you sold me."

Eseld swallowed, her hands flitted about her. "But look at how well you have done for yourself. So many fine clothes and jewels. Are you not glad of your alliance?"

Wenna did not respond. Her glower of pure hatred was answer enough. I thought she might enquire about her father's ceremony, whether there was a part for her to play in the rituals, but she turned on her heels and left our fireside. Jago reinforced the posts of our shelter and lay fresh bedstraw in thick layers beneath my furs. With a woven reed panel over my head, I settled down for the evening next to the fire. The youngsters heard about a fighting pit on the outskirts of the sacred space. Folk said there were wagers running on a fight between a lynx and a wolf. Maybe in my younger days, I would have been tempted by such sights, but age has made me see the cruelty from a different slant. They are not natural enemies. They should not be pitted against each other, especially for sport.

I ate the nettle and boar stew, drank my ale, and turned in for the night with my knife roll tucked into the bed rushes. Jago returned to the fireside with the girl before the moon reached its full height. They banked up the fire and slept behind my shelter. If we are to be here for long, we will need to build something longer lasting. We have been lucky with the weather so far, but I can't see that lasting for long.

When morning came, I ate my porridge, and returned to the woodland to gather supplies. Much of what I needed had already been scavenged by other tribes, but I was able to harvest some plantain and birch bark. It's a good job I had Jago strip some willow when we stopped at the lakes to bathe.

I stopped on my way back at the Metern burial mounds to dig out a little chalk powder. There were many elders gathered at the entrance to the newest mound. Cryda was in the centre of all. I moved closer, curious to hear what they were discussing.

"But he belongs with his forefather's Cryda. You can't make this decision without discussing it with us. He was our leader. His burial should mark his importance in tribal matters." It was one of the more vocal of the elders. His reasonable statement was met with murmurs of agreement from many others.

"I don't care. I want him to rest at the top of a tor in the middle of the moors. He can watch over our lands for all time, and make sure than no other tribe can take possession. It's what he would have wanted."

"Then why bring him all the way here to the summer solstice? We could have buried him on the way."

"Because I want the god's blessings from the ritual processions on the longest day. Then we can build him a cist fit for a true Chieftain." She looked wistfully into the distance. I could see that the elders were not happy with her decision, but she was the Ruvane. It gave her a temporary status above them. The murmurs this time were more reserved and in disagreement, but none were brave enough to gain say her, until a familiar voice boomed over the noise of the lot.

"I don't think that is a very good idea, mother." It was Blydh. He stood tall and tanned behind Cryda, with his hand resting on the hilt of his sword. He looked for all the world like a young Aebba.

She turned to him, stepping backwards to accommodate her swelling belly. “Son, I am glad you have come. Where is your brother? Did you leave him in charge of our compound?”

“You sent him to fetch our grandfather. He can’t be in two places at once. For all his fancy boasts, he is not yet a god.”

“Then who watches over our crops and the camp?” She tilted her head at him, perplexed.

“I left Lorden in charge with a few of my men. The slaves have their orders and he’ll keep them in line. It’ll be fine. I made sure little Derwa got here safely. She’s with her mother.” Blydh set his jaw and narrowed his eyes at the interrogation, but Cryda missed the cues.

“What about raiders?”

“What about them? They’re all here with us.”

Cryda blinked several times, mildly shaking her head. Her gaze was drawn to the entrance of the burial mound. People from all different tribes wandered in with offerings to their ancestral Meterns and those special family members who were afforded space to rest next to the greatest Chieftains of all time. It brought the discussion of Aebba’s bones back to the fore.

“We should inter father here, where Cernonnus can grant him passage to the Summerlands.” Blydh was not asking permission, or making a suggestion to be debated. This was his decision, and he expected the elders and his mother to comply.

“But to rest so far from home would upset him. I want him to be near to us, to watch over Dumnonii lands.” Cryda screwed her face up, on the brink of an emotional outburst.

Blydh held his chin, striking a dominant pose as he thought. He could hold an audience as well as his brother, but with greater gravitas and fortitude. “For a warrior such as Aebba, there should be two rituals. His long bones will stand in a stone cist at the top of Higher Tor, with the skeletons of his horse and favoured hound. We will inter his skull here in this barrow, with his forefathers, after the death march and funerary rites, along with his ceremonial bronze shield and sword."

"And his bear fur. He will need that in the Summerlands." Cryda whined.

"This is most irregular. How will he find the Summerlands without his head?" The vocal elder had raised a valid point. It was unusual to even have a burial, in place of cremation, even more so to scatter his bones in different locations.

"My father was a skilled navigator. He will use the stars to guide him."

Their conversation continued for some time, going over old ground and questioning the reasoning behind their decision. I scuttled off in the opposite direction. Something peculiar had caught my eye. Eseld was hurrying towards the tree line, wearing a thick hooded cloak on a balmy day, carrying a bundle wrapped with linen. Her furtive manner and quick pace had me stumbling and cursing with my stick to catch up with her among the undergrowth. Hiding behind a broad trunk of an ash tree, I watched as Eseld knelt on the ground and placed the bundle by her side. Grabbing a firm branch from those fallen, she scored a hollow in the soil until it was about two hands deep. She placed the bundle in the hole, and pushed the loose soil over the top.

CHAPTER TWENTY-TWO

I watched Eseld, stamp the loose earth down over the bundle and cover the fresh soil with dead leaves and twigs. With one final sweep of her foot, she glanced back at her handiwork, pulled her hood up over her head before running back towards camp. My stomach felt heavy inside. I had a shrewd idea of what lay at the bottom of the shallow pit, but I had to know for sure.

When I was certain that she had gone, I unearthed the bundle and peered down at the linen strips binding the form together. It smelled of death, and mint. A few blue petals poked out from between the layers. Closer inspection told me it was penny royal. That confirmed my suspicion. An aborted baby lies in the ground at my feet. From its size, I would say that it was less than six moons old. If it was Eseld's she was remarkably spry and unharmed by the affair. No, I suspect that she was helping another get rid of the mistake, but who? It could not be Cryda, since she was busy introducing Blydh to the Chieftains of other tribes near to the stones. Her belly grew rounder with every sunrise. It certainly couldn't be Wenna, as I was sure that she would rather carve out the child with a hot knife than ask her mother for assistance. I puzzled over this discovery, as I picked and gathered all that I needed for my medicine kit.

Over the course of the next two days, word got around camp that a skilled healer could be found in our enclosure. I set up my stall in the mornings, and had everything from scalded children, dislocated shoulders, cursed mothers, archery mishaps and festering sores. From many, I received welcome gifts of food and ale, from others, the offer to build a nice shelter from the elements. By the second evening, Cryda and I had a warm hut with fresh bedding grasses and a roaring fire for my bartered venison. The gods were good indeed.

Eseld fumed all the more, since there was not enough room for her inside our new hut. She stomped around shrieking about little Derwa catching a chill and needing better shelter, but I was not about to be turfed out of my new bed by Eseld. I know her scams and ploys. Given the chance, she would push both me and Cryda out into the cold damp air.

"Why don't you ask the priests to help you build a hut? I'm sure they would lend a hand to one of their own." I was expecting her usual scoff of derision, but it did not follow.

She looked pitiful. "They're all busy speaking with the gods."

I took that to mean that they were all half-baked on hemp to be any use to her. Still, it was not enough to shake me, and good news for poor Jago.

"What about Paega, he's a strapping lad, surely he could build his mother and sister a reasonable shelter for while we are here?"

Eseld shook her head. "I haven't seen him. He went to the fighting pits and didn't return."

I wanted to shout from the thatched top of my hut, *you reap what you sow*, but I held my tongue. Clearly, the priestly blood in him is more dominant than our side of the family. Give the boy a whiff of weed smoke, and he'll be dancing with the pixies and sprites until he climbs down the Underworld tree to meet Cernonnus. Gods help us if he ends up our next Metern.

Jago and the girl created a lean-to with the reed hurdle at the rear of my hut and bedded themselves down.

By the sixth day in the sacred space enclosure, Blydh had forged strong ties of friendship with a couple of overseas tribal leaders. He told me that language had proven a barrier until he gave them some of my ale, and then it did not matter what was spoken. They giggled and laughed until sun up. I sent young Jago to interpret their words, and a bargain over our tin was struck. Sadly, they were not able to provide any copper, so our options are limited to Cryda's father and making amends with the Ordo's from the mountains.

On the seventh day, I rose early and dragged myself across the chalky plains to the forest for more herbs. My healing stall kept me busy from dawn until dusk most days. This morning, Cryda had risen before me and was neither in the hut, nor the enclosure beyond. I thought nothing of her absence, until I carried my bag of fresh plants and bark strips back through the woods to the edge of the camp. Huts had sprung up all around the standing stones, each tribe keeping mostly with their own kinfolk. I knew that the enclosure closest to the cursus housed those elders of the Ordo Tribe, which is why I was not shocked to see Cryda creeping out from one of their shelters.

Hanging back behind the tree line, I watched as the taller of the Ordo's who had visited us, ran after her out of the doorway. Wearing only a cloth to cover his pintel, he reached out to grasp her hand, pulling her to a standstill. Cryda gave him a ferocious glare and snatched her hand away, before stomping off in the direction of our hut. I waited until he had given up on trying to entice her back inside with him, and sneaked past unseen.

When I got to our house, Cryda's eyes were raw with upset. We exchanged glances; mine offering her solace, hers warning me to back off. The girl had fried pork with steaming hot barley beer bread. With all my new patients, we could eat like the gods all the time. The salty sizzle put life in my old cheeks and set me up for the day.

It was late in the afternoon when we got word that Tallack was in camp. I didn't hear his tidings until nightfall. He and Blydh had discussed their options prior to delivering the news to Cryda and me in the hut. Eseld lingered in the doorway as they squeezed in and greeted their mother. She hugged them each tightly, and sat on her furs with Tallack at her side.

"I come with bad tidings. Grandfather is very sick and not fit to travel. Your mother is trying to hold the tribesmen together but she is old and frail and they do not listen to her. I tried to discuss terms of trade with your brothers, but they would not listen. The entire area is burning and fighting. All I could do, was to give offerings to the goddess, and ask for his recovery." Tallack slipped his hand under his mother's palm and clasped it tightly. The boys peered at their mother, expecting a response. She simply stared into the fire without a flicker of acknowledgement for her father's imminent death.

"Mother… did you hear what Tallack said? Our grandfather is dying. We have no trade for copper." Blydh knelt by her legs and gave her a little nudge. It seemed to revive her a little.

"I heard you. We have no copper."

Blydh had her attention. "You had most to do with the Ordo's, do you think you could approach them about renewing our alliance with them? If you apologise, it might not be too late to arrange for the binding of Derwa to one of the Ordo leader's sons."

Cryda recoiled, pushing Blydh back away from her, and scooting across her bed rushes.

"It has to be you…and before you start barking at us again, Eseld, you know this has to happen if our tribe is to continue to trade." Blydh jumped to his feet, anticipating backlash from Eseld over her daughter's betrothal.

Everyone looked shocked, me most of all, when Eseld stepped closer and said, "I understand. If it will help, Cryda, I am prepared to go with you to the Ordo tribe and apologise for my insult." She looked at each of us and frowned at our silence. "I'll go and prepare Derwa for the meeting."

When she had left, Cryda levered herself up from her furs and laid a hand on Tallack's shoulder. "If Eseld is prepared to apologise to the Ordo's, there is no need for me to go too. You are far better at negotiations than I, and those mountain people would take the word of a man over that of a woman any day." She cradled her bump as she moved towards the door. "Good, that's settled then."

In the end, both Tallack and Blydh accompanied young Derwa and her mother to the Ordo enclosure. From what I hear, Derwa kicked and fought Blydh all the way, scratching and biting and pleading for mercy. It makes me wonder what had happened that could have changed Eseld's attitude over the binding. Tallack told me much later, that Derwa's binding gifts were of particular interest to the Ordos. Not many of their

Chief's sons received a chest of tin ingots and several amber bracelets in the exchange.

Word spread quickly among the elders of our tribe. The women braided flowers into their hair, wore their finest tunics and jewels, while the men slaughtered animals for the feasting to join the tribes together.

Wenna met us at the edge of our enclosure and gave Derwa a silver brooch to wear on her gown. Carrying a posy of wild flowers, Derwa took Tallack's arm as he led her along the track toward the wooden henge by the river. I walked next to Wenna behind Eseld, Cryda and Blydh

"Where is my brother?" Wenna asked me. All I could do was shrug. It was really his place to give Derwa to the Ordos, not her half-brother Tallack. Wenna smiled sweetly every time her anxious sister turned around with a look of panic plastered across her face, and then in a hissing whisper she berated Eseld.

"How could you do this to her. She is younger than I was when you sold me."

"Will you be quiet? She has caused this family enough problems, things you know nothing about. It's her duty to bind the tribes." Eseld spat back. We could all hear their exchange despite their attempts to keep it hushed.

"Duty? It's the worst kind of punishment. Those hairy mountain men stink. You want your youngest child to spend her days popping out more hairy little miners from the valleys?"

Derwa began a quiet but incessant sobbing. Tallack tried to comfort her, but the wailing grew in volume the closer we got to the henge. As luck would have it, we were not the first family to have a binding ceremony planned. The couple receiving the ritual blessing before us, looked a great deal happier than our small group.

The Ordo family were waiting on the river bank, washing their hands and faces in the water. I gave Derwa a hug and stepped aside. It was not my place to interfere. Eseld did nothing to curb her daughter's worst fears, leaving everything to poor Wenna.

The sisters linked hands and wandered a short distance from the crowd for a private word. Listening carefully, I could just make out what the elder of the two was saying.

"My dear little sister. You must alter your thinking." She placed both her hands on Derwa's shoulders and stared directly into her eyes. "See this as an adventure. You are no longer under the control of mother, or that disgusting old goat of a priest either. If you can bring this Ordo into your heart, and worm your way into his, you can steer him to do your bidding. You will be the next tribal Ruvane of the Ordoviches. That is a position of power, if you will just use it to your advantage." Wenna wiped away the tear streaks from her sister's cheeks, and gave her a knowing smile. Derwa fully understood her meaning. "Buck up, girl. This is your moment." Wenna approached me for the flowers I held and gave them to her sister. With a gentle kiss to her cheek, she directed her towards the emptying wooden circle of life.

I slipped the pipers a nugget of tin, and they began playing a slow and soulful tune as Tallack led her to the portal struts and left her standing opposite the Ordo boy on the far side of the circle. As the pipers played faster, Derwa and the boy began their dance, he skipped south around the outer ring of posts, and she north. When they reached the opposite sides, Eseld gave the boy gold and amber beads, while the Ordo's gave Derwa gifts of a similar nature. Each of them pocketed the jewels and metals, before the dance began a second time. Weaving in and out of an inner circle of posts, Blydh and Tallack stepped inside to give their sister more wealth. On it went until the couple reached each other in the centre most circle, their pockets bulging with gifts to begin their days together.

In the very centre of the henge waited a holy man of the old faith. A simple robe covered his body, the mask of the green man over his face. He stepped forward and gestured for the couple to raise their hands together. He produced a silver blade from his robes and sliced across each of their palms. Derwa flinched, drawing in a sharp breath. The Ordo boy smiled at her and steadied her with a few muttered words. I could not hear them. Blood mingling, the two palms were bound together with a length of green dyed linen and tied at the wrists.

"Say the words, Derwa." The holy man prompted.

In no more than a whisper, Derwa began her oath. "By the grace of Cerridwen, mother of us all and keeper of wisdom, I pledge myself to the Ordoviches Tribe, my new family and husband. I will honour them, break bread with them and give them many sons and daughters. If I should ever fail him, may the gods strike me down."

Derwa looked at her smiling Ordo boy, he was obviously thrilled by the deal.

"And now for your oath."

The Ordo tightened his grip on her hand and stammered. "By the wrath of Cernonnus, God of all that is wild and vengeful, keeper of death, I will protect my Derwa and honour her family with plentiful sons and daughters. I swear that she will never want for food or clothing, shelter or affection. If I should ever fail her, may the gods strike me down."

Eseld handed a large copper armlet to her daughter. With a little assistance from her new husband, she slipped it over his free hand and secured it against the widest part of his muscles.

A woman from the Ordos passed him a smaller band of silver, and he repeated the struggle with Derwa. She seemed most pleased with her expensive metal gift, rubbing it against the beaver pelt covering her shoulders to buff the shine. It may have seeded the smile on her face, but as the pipers played a jaunty jig to cement their new binding and hasten them from the circle, I noticed that she walked at arm's length from her new man. Perhaps Wenna's little talk had not helped after all.

The stroll back across the plains to the feasting tables set out in our enclosure was speedier than our outward journey. We were all keen to wash our throats with several cups of ale and taste the selection of pies and meats either family had provided. Eseld sat on a stool at the farthest end of the long table. She looked ashen grey and not in the slightest bit happy. Only the Ordo's and Cryda looked mildly pleased with themselves.

We were a sombre crew. Derwa wept openly when the Ordo Chieftain raised his ale and blessed them, welcoming her into his family. I thought it was a nice sentiment, but then I don't have to leave my kin and travel to the mountains with people I met yesterday. I don't have to bed down with a grinning Ordo boy who might turn vicious and beat her for the sake of retribution. Poor girl, I understand her tears.

With the feast underway, I sneaked back to my hut to check on Jago and the Frynkish girl. They were already in their lean to, and giggling beneath the furs. I cleared my throat and make them jump out of their skins.

"Fur Benyn, we did not expect you back from the binding ceremony so soon." Jago straightened his tunic and glowed with embarrassment.

"Hmm." I grunted, pretending to be annoyed. I wasn't at all, but best to keep them on their toes. The girl stood up next to him and looked shame faced.

"We were wondering, great lady, if it is possible, may we be bound in the big wooden circle while we are here? It would make us both very happy. Of course, we would still serve you that goes without saying…" He wrung his hands together in supplication. How could I be strict when all they wanted was for their love to be formally recognised?

I couldn't help myself. Digging into my pockets, I pulled out my tin pouch and gave him a few nuggets. "This should be enough to get the girl a new tunic and to pay the holy man. Just don't tell anyone how soft I am, got it? Best get along and do it tonight. The union is hallowed this side of the solstice."

Bless their little faces. His grin nearly knocked me off my feet. They rushed away to make their preparations as giddy as children. I glanced about our enclosure. There was no one left to guard our belongings. With all the healing I had done in the last few days, our huts brimmed with attractive wealth. Anyone could slip in and strip us bare of everything. I hurried over to Wenna's tribe and looked for the warriors and slaves who had accompanied us from their camp. There was not a single one. I would have assumed that they were gambling at the fighting pits, were it not for the absence of their horses and all their belongings. Other than Wenna's two personal slaves, her tribe had gone.

CHAPTER TWENTY-THREE

This could not be right. Where were the Duro Tribe? None of the other Chieftains or elders would dream of leaving the circle until the solstice was over. There were still so many rituals and ceremonies to finish. I did another sweep of Wenna's enclosure, looking for signs of livestock, provisions, weapons, anything that could explain where the Duro's could be. Her slaves were remarkably tight lipped on the subject when I asked them for information on their whereabouts. None of it added up.

I tucked my knife roll into the back of my belt, and risked leaving the rest of our things unattended. Tired and filled with a sense of dread that I could not shake, I made my way back to the feast and sat as close to Wenna as I could. The flowing ale had loosened some of their tongues and there was enough noise for me to conduct my conversation without others overhearing.

"Where is your husband this evening, Wenna? Does he not realise that the solstice is almost upon us?" It was a direct question; I expected a direct answer. Instead, she shuffled over on her bench and reached for some wild raspberries in a dish and offered them to me.

"Why worry about the menfolk, Aunt Mel, try one of these. They are worthy of the Summerlands they are so sweet." She virtually pushed the berry between my lips to shut me up, but I would not be deterred.

"Your camp is deserted, child. Where are all your warriors?" I raised my hand up to halt her attempt to force more food into my mouth. She looked about the table, a few of the family were beginning to notice our strained debate. "Well? How is it that you are all alone here, on the eve of the most important festival in three summers?" Tallack and Blydh heard my insistence, each of them turning to listen to her answer.

"We…um… were low on supplies. I sent them out on a hunt and told them not to come back until they had caught enough provisions to last us until our return." She gave us a forced smile. It was quick thinking indeed. Tallack and Blydh seem contented by her response. They continued drinking and laughing with the Ordo's over tales from the sea. I was less convinced.

"They took all their belongings with them on a hunt? That seems most unlikely to me."

"Why should it? They are warriors, other than their weapons, they have no belongings. Relax, Aunt Mel. This is a celebration." She poured more ale into my cup, but I couldn't drink anymore. The uneasy feeling wouldn't leave me. I stayed for a little longer, said my farewells to a tearful Derwa, and returned to my hut.

Jago and the girl returned late into the night. I could hear them giggling and stumbling about in their lean-to behind my little round house. As long as they keep their affections a secret, it should cause no trouble among tribal members. It's not generally permitted for slaves to wed one another. That assumes that they are free to be bound, but who am I to stand in the way of love. Both have had such dreadful lives since they were snatched from their families and homelands. It's a blessing that they have each other for comfort. I don't know what I would do without either of them. I owe them my life. Keeping their secret is a small price to pay in return.

Their noise did not stop, and I could not sleep for fretting. I pulled my largest fur over my shoulders and heaved myself up from my bedding. Cryda was not in her bunk. I don't need too many guesses as to where she was spending the night. The sky was black with every star beaming down on me. The gods must be polishing their metals for tomorrow's celebrations. One fire glowed from Wenna's enclosure; her warriors were still missing. I don't believe her story for one moment. All the healthy and fit tribal leaders were asleep within this sacred space. Why would her husband abandon the site the night before the solstice?

Come dawn, I let the lovers lie in while I stoked the fires and cooked the mushrooms and salt pork, with fresh barley bread and thickly spread butter. Cryda returned, her hair sticking up in all directions, her tunic worn back to front. I suspect that she had hoped to slip into her bunk before I awoke, but my fretting put paid to that idea.

With all illusion stripped bare, she brazened it out. "Morning, Meliora. That smells good. I could eat a whole hog."

I ripped a chunk of bread off the flat loaf and stacked the fried boar strips on top, passing it over to the Ruvane. "Better get yourself smartened up before your boys wake up." I nodded to her tunic. She took the hint and the food, and went into the hut to sort herself out.

The more I looked over at Wenna's camp, the more convinced I was that she was behind something sinister. When I had eaten, I walked over to Tallack's shelter. He and Brea were still in their furs.

I kicked his foot. “Nephew! Wake up.”

He didn’t move. I tried another kick. “Hey! Get up, I want to talk to you.”

He groaned, yawned and turned over. “Not now, Aunt Mel, my head is killing me.”

I sat on the edge of his bunk. “Did you speak with Wenna at the feast? I honestly don’t believe her. Those warriors have fully packed up and gone.”

“So? They are hers to command.”

“Exactly, and there is no love lost between Wenna and our tribe. What if she has sent them to sack our Chieftain compound?”

He flapped a limp arm, shooing me from his presence. “Lorden and Blydh’s men will stick a sword through them. Stop worrying about it, Aunt. Now let me get some sleep.”

I was making no progress with Tallack at all. Picking myself up, I rushed to the next hut to try Blydh and got an even less welcome response. He threw his bronze torque at my head. Thankfully, he did not aim well. With all avenues exhausted, I walked over to Wenna’s fireside, offering her a token of peace in the form of warm salt pork and barley bread.

“Hmm, I could smell you coming, Aunt.” She accepted my gift and took a huge bite of the greasy meat. “Do you remember when I was little and you would come and sing me to sleep?”

“When you thought the wolf pack would jump the barricades and find their way into your hut? Yes, I remember.” I sat on a stool by her fireside and threw another log into the embers. “So many things frightened you back then, child. Now look at you.”

She smirked. “You were the only one kind enough to soothe me. My mother spent all her time with Paega, or Derwa. I was just a constant thorn in her side.”

"She loves you though, I'm sure." As soon as the words left my mouth, I heard how insincere they sounded. We both ended up chuckling. "But your father did love you. I do know that."

Wenna took in a long breath through her nose, thinking about him. "Perhaps. Didn't stop him from bartering me to the Duro's for a pathetically weak peace agreement."

"You're a Ruvane yourself now. You understand the politics of neighbouring tribes. What would you have done in his position? The Duros were raiding our homesteaders and killing hundreds every moon. I'm not sure that he had any other choice." I peered at her, weighing up her state of mind.

"Of course, he had a choice. There are always other ways, different outcomes. He chose the easiest and cheapest path for him. I paid the price." She finished off the food and stood up. "Thank you for the pork, Aunt Mel, but I must get on with my chores. Lots to do today."

I had no idea how sour her feelings were for her parents. I left with a leaden heart and a churning stomach. My visit did nothing to quell my fears.

When I got back to the roundhouse, Cryda was polishing Aebba's skull on her lap. It looked a monstrous thing, all yellowed and stained from the journey. Some of his teeth had fallen out in the jar. Cryda asked me to dig about among the long bones and find them. I made some excuse about needing to gather herbs and rushed away. A quick glance back, and she had collared the Frynkish girl to fetch them in my stead.

People were already gathering for the great walk from the river, around the barrows to Stonehenge and the burial mounds. Cryda was to carry his skull, while the boys were to take his ceremonial bronze shield and sword. Cernonnus only knows what Eseld and the priests will have Paega carry to out-do them all. I lingered in the woods until the sun was high. I could hear the drums marking the start of the rituals, and so hurried to my hut to collect my offering.

As I neared our enclosure, Jago met me with a long bow and finely crafted arrows. "Is this what you came back for, Fur Benyn?"

Patting his shoulder, I took them from him. I have never seen him so happy; it warms my heart to look upon them both. "It is. You're a good lad, Jago. Mind you don't get seen." I chided, pointing to the girl. He grinned. Turning my back to them, I looked across at Wenna's camp. The fire was out, the huts all empty. There was not a single slave to be seen. Where was she?

My stiff joints creaked and groaned against my haste, as I tottered towards the river and our family group awaiting the procession. There was Cryda at the front, with Aebba's skull laying in a large wooden bowl and surrounded by a wreath of ivy and yellow hawkbit flowers. Behind her stood Eseld, her gift to the gods she kept hidden beneath the wide sleeves of her cloak. Brea next, clutching a bronze dagger that I have seen Tallack wear in his belt. The boys came next, with shield, sword and spears. Little Derwa stood at the end with her new husband holding her by the elbow, as though she would run off at any moment. Where was Wenna?

I approached Derwa. "Have you seen your sister?"

She shook her head, adopting a glower to rival her mother's. "Not since last night at the feast."

"Boys, have any of you seen Wenna?" Each of them looked along the line of our family members. None of them had realised that she was missing. Perhaps she was right, Wenna had been invisible to them all. They neither noticed her presence or absence.

In desperation, I returned to the front of the line. "Eseld, where is your eldest daughter? Surely she would not miss her father's ceremony like this?"

Eseld shrugged, and then moved at the sound of the pounding drums. The procession had begun. I joined the end of the line, before the next tribal family, whose leader had fallen in battle, in the hope that she would be waiting for us at the end of the march. With my heart thumping in my chest, I tried to look calm and serene as the occasion demanded, but my mind raced through all possible reasons for her absence, before alighting on one. She had joined her tribe on their way to take over our land.

Trapped between grieving families, I completed the slow walk through the crowds in a giant arc to the hallowed ground of Stonehenge. Every tribe we passed, honoured the fallen in their own way. Some whooped and hollered, others wept quietly, some wailed loud enough to rattle the stones loose. Our elders stood with warriors and those from the Priest Sect, closest to the henge. The ground was smoother at this point, the grass worn away to bare chalk by the constant footsteps of the pilgrims over the course of two full moons.

I could see Eseld's father loitering at the northern point of the circle, close to the ditch crossing. He wore his crow head and blue feathers which trailed down his painted back. Behind him gathered members of his sect, itching to divert attention to themselves. It must really stick in his craw to see so many keeping faith with the old ways. His new religion may be popular with the youngsters, but it's all show and bluff over substance. A couple of the other families carried the bodies of their recently deceased on boards raised up by warriors. I could hear the priests shouting, *burn them*, as they walked past. Their interference would not be tolerated in this arena. After the second body was yelled and jeered at, a great number of warriors moved to face them down. Outnumbered ten to one, they soon shut their mouths.

Cryda was almost at the circle boundary. Only she could approach the outer ring of stones, while the rest of each family filed around the circle within the limits of the ditch. Those carrying the dead stood face to face with a holy man in each doorway. At the sound of the drums, the bones passed through the portals into the realm of the dead. Almost all of the doorways passed a fallen tribesman, but few were as high in status as Aebba.

From the outer portal, Aebba and one other Metern, were passed to the larger inner portals, where priests stood cloaked in the red robes of the Summerlands. The drums fell silent, as Aebba's skull was held aloft.

A booming voice from the hooded figure said, "I sense a conflict with this soul." No one gathered in the sacred space spoke. The plains were eerily silent, but for the whistle of the wind. "How did this Chieftain meet his end?" He turned to look at Cryda for the answer. All eyes fell on her, awaiting the response.

"My husband was poisoned." Cryda muttered in a hesitant voice.

"And was he avenged?"

"He was not."

The crowd gasped, the priests stirred, murmuring their angst and jostling against the warriors.

Eseld stepped forward from our group. "It's not true, Holy One. Aebba choked on his food."

Cryda shot Eseld a scathing look. The ceremony was falling apart before our very eyes. Both women opened their mouths to protest, but before any sound could be made, the priest yelled above them.

"Enough! Aebba the Wild cannot pass into the Summerlands until his death is avenged. He will remain between worlds until he is at peace with the manner of his passing." The holy man turned around and placed the skull on a stone plinth in the very centre of the circle. The bones of the other Chieftain passed through the giant doorways and were laid alongside Aebba to await the shortest night, and his spiritual journey to the Summerlands. All being well, the other Metern will be permitted straight into the realm of gods.

Cryda began sobbing. Aebba would have to wait until the next solstice marking the shortest day to gain entry into the Summerlands that is supposing his death is avenged by then. His soul would be left to wander alone until that day. When all the bones, and in a couple of instances, fresh bodies, were passed within the confines of the stones, it was the family members' turn to approach with grave goods in payment to Cernonnus. I leaned to the side to watch Eseld lay her offering. It was a golden band, studded with amber and polished to a sparkle. It was big enough to have sat on my head. Cryda narrowed her eyes at her rival. Where had the head piece come from? The boys each laid Aebba's ceremonial weapons, followed by Derwa who laid down his favourite black bear fur. I waited for Wenna to step out from the crowd, but she was nowhere to be seen.

Flushed with panic, I stacked my archery gift alongside the considerable hoard. His grave gifts were vast compared to that of the others. At least that should offset the scandal hanging over his death. Maybe Cernonnus will permit him entry this night in light of the great wealth we bestowed on him.

The drums and pipers played, while the holy men and priests performed their ritual sacrifices of ducks and goats for the lesser men, and a fine bull for each of the

Chieftains. The blood drained into the chalky ditch and trickled for some distance until it sank into the pale soil, and beyond into the Underworld.

I scanned the rows of people in search of Wenna, until my sight stopped at a grinning Derwa standing next to her new husband. Lumbering as quickly as possible, I moved to her side and nudged her elbow. Her expression was not that of a grieving child nor a reluctant wife.

“Where is your sister? Did she say anything unusual to you at all when you last saw her?” I whispered in a low growl.

Derwa’s grin was fixed and growing in size. “All I know is that she told me that I can come home, as soon as she is Ruvane of our lands.”

CHAPTER TWENTY-FOUR

There was no time to lose. I had to make the boys see sense and insist that they return to our land. I stood between the twins and placed a hand up on each of their shoulders. My face must have shown them how worried I was, for they listened with a respect I hardly thought possible. After explaining all my suspicions and the conversations Wenna and I had over the last few days, they too thought it odd that she should miss all of Aebba's rituals.

"Look about you, lads. Can you see a single Duro here? Even the Cantii are represented, despite your grandfather being so ill." They did as I instructed, peering about them trying to spot tell-tale tattoos on their warriors faces and the arm bands of horse leather.

"Why didn't you say something earlier, Aunt Mel? They could be days ahead of us."

I gave Tallack a purse-lipped snort for his stupidity. "Where did you moor your ships?"

"Due south in a little bay I know. It's more than a day's ride from here, but quicker than killing our horses trying to outrun the Duro's on their way to the compound.

"Can your ships carry Blydh's men too?" I had already began leading them away from the circle, I didn't care who tutted and sneered at my disruption.

"They can, but they won't be large enough for the slaves, women or provisions. Even then it'll be a tight squeeze." Tallack said, scampering after me and Blydh as we marched back across the plains to our enclosure.

"Then we leave your mother here with Eseld and the slaves to walk back in their own time." I said, panting with the exertion.

"We? You can't come with us. There will be fighting, and terrible bloodshed, especially when I get my hands on our dear sister."

"Then who will sew your wounds and amputate mangled limbs?" I stopped walking and put my hands on my hips, glaring at the pair of them.

Blydh gave in to my stare. "That's a good point. You're all skin and bone anyway, you can ride with me."

I wasn't sure whether to be annoyed or pleased, and had no time to argue. With hurried instructions given to Jago and the girl, I packed all that I could carry and slung my medicine bag over my shoulder. In no time at all, I was lifted onto the back of Blydh's horse and we set off amid a great swathe of angry warriors heading south.

Keeping the River Avon within our sights, we rode hard while the going was good and dry. When the horses began to tire, we rested and watered them for as long as we dare, while I ate strips of salted boar with the men and stretched my legs. If it had been any other time, I would have lingered to collect much needed plants and bark, but before I could straighten the kink from my spine we set off once again, thundering through the landscape towards the cove and Tallack's boats.

His men were surprised to see their clan leader, when we arrived long after nightfall. The horses were in a state and desperately needed time to recover. We left some tin nuggets and a couple of Blydh's men to tend them and lead them back to the Chieftain compound in a few days. With the boats stripped of spare rigging and supplies, there was just enough room to accommodate both Tallack's and Blydh's men as we set off west from the cove in the dead of night.

The moon was high above us, lighting our way, and the seas were calm and hypnotic. It looked as though we had the blessing of the gods, as Tallack steered the leading boat around the headlands towards the mouth of the Exe. Blydh's men and I slept as best we could in cramped conditions, while Tallack's men rowed the massive oars against the prevailing current in shifts. When the sun crept above the horizon, Blydh's men took control of the oars, and paddled us around the massive peninsula that marked the end of the Duro's land. With the sails catching the breeze and the men pounding the oars, we made good time along the Channel to the mouth of the Exe.

The sun was high through clouded skies when we navigated the estuary of our homelands. I spared a thought for Jago and the girl, Cryda and Eseld as they sat at Stonehenge awaiting the divine light to carry Aebba's spirit away. With the growing menace of what we might encounter when we reached the compound, I wondered if I might meet Aebba in between worlds later this day. What had Wenna unleashed on our weakened tribe?

I looked up at Tallack as he piloted the vessel as far up the river as he dared to, without marooning us on a sand bank. With just a short distance from our camp, we fastened the boats to a jetty and crept along the marshy banks and red clay earth tracks. I hung back a little, watching the twins unsheathe their swords and make gestures to their men to split up and approach the gates from either side.

Something was terribly wrong. Black smoke snaked up into the air from several areas at once, there were no community sounds, no dogs barking or children playing. Moving into the clearing beyond the woodlands behind the men, it was clear that we were too late. The gates swung open, one falling off its hinges, the other juddered in the wind.

The earth was churned up with countless hoof prints and pools of blood. Inside the compound, the stilted grain silo burned and crackled, the thatches of each hut smouldered with floating embers, the goats and sheep slaughtered in their pens. Such carnage, such waste, and I knew that this was the least of the losses. Creeping ever closer, Tallack and Blydh kept an eye out for ambush, but I knew the Duro's had slashed and burned, before leaving with all that they wanted.

Those warriors who fought under Lorden's command, now lay dead over the ramparts, or fallen from the lookout tower, pinned to the fences with dozens of arrows. There were no slaves anywhere. Either they had run for their lives or were captured as part of the loot. Blydh ran into the Long Hut and surveyed the scene. More of his men lay butchered over the benches and tables. They didn't stand a chance against the entire Duro Tribe warriors.

The fire pit in the centre of the room had long since burned out, but the smell of charcoal and burnt flesh remained. Aebba's high bench and table were smashed to pieces, revealing the hiding place of the tribal wealth stores. Wenna knew everything about us, when we would be away from camp, when our men were most vulnerable and disorganised, and more importantly, where we stored the Metern tributes to pay for new crops and trade. They had cleaned out every bead, tin nugget and amber jewel to our name.

I spun about unable to offer up any words of wisdom to help, when I heard a faint groan from under the splintered planks of wood. Tallack heard it too, tracing the source back to a mortally wounded Lorden. Blydh lent a hand in clearing the debris away from their fallen friend.

"Where did they go?" Tallack asked him, but he was fading fast.

I took out my water bladder and raised the edge to his mouth. He was beyond sipping anything. "Are they heading for the mines?" I spoke gently and watched his blood shot eyes cloud over. He managed a tiny nod, before his last breath left his body. I held his head for a few moments more, but he was gone. We each raised our faces to the sky and uttered our incantations to Cernonnus. Lorden may had slipped from the righteous path, but he was a good boy once. Whatever turned his temper sour, could not have been his fault entirely. He was one of us, and deserved a respectful end.

"What should we do now?" Tallack said, his sense leaving him at this crucial time.

"All we can do is to try and outrun them. The land between here and the mines is treacherous, and slow going, especially if you don't know the paths well. We must grab whatever food is left here, and get back to the boats. There is no time to lose." They did not stop to argue, or question my resolve. Without control of our own tin mines we were all finished. If Wenna became tribal Ruvane to all Duro and our land, she would be unstoppable, and us her slaves, or worse. I have little doubt that what affection she once had for me is long gone.

I was exhausted, but I knew that I could not let the boys down. They were still young and green when it came to decision making, and I was the only elder around. I hurried as fast as I could to the boats, but every muscle and joint throbbed with a pain that would not relent. At least in the bow of Tallack's largest boat, I could wrap my cloak about me and try to sleep.

As soon as we were underway, the men took their shift at rowing, resting in between turns to keep the forward motion constant. Even still it was a long way, against an increasingly strong current. Tallack steered away from the rocky outcrops and left a trusted man in charge while he rested next to me for a time. I shared my water and the last of the salted boar strips and sat close to preserve the warmth.

"Even if we can get down there before them, they will still outnumber us by a massive amount. How are we to ever defeat them?" He whispered, so that his men would not hear the anxiety in his tone.

"I've been thinking about that. There should be a fair number of slaves in the mine; good fit people with axes and tools. If we can keep this speed going, we will have time to barricade the path."

"What if they're not headed for the mines at Bentewyn? What if she is taking them to Droskin? That's on the north coast, we'll never get around there in time."

I hadn't thought about that. We had no means of defence if she decided to split the warriors into two groups. The only way I could see us beating them, was to catch them in a narrow part of the trail and shower them with lethal arrows from above. With a few well-placed palisades and fences, we could pick them off a few at a time. If their target was Droskin, we didn't stand a chance. The site was a mass of tiny tunnels in the cliff face. There was no centralised part to attack. Wenna had already decimated our largest settlement, she would make short work of smaller ones.

There was still one thing in our favour. The alchemy clan leaders are shrewd and forward thinking. They have strict discipline over their slaves, who are many in number. If we could just get there to warn them, they would have time to put further defences in place. I can't imagine that they would not have some method of deterring those traders who pass Lands' End on their way to the Ordos or further tribes north.

I ruminated until my head hurt, and then slept with my cloak pulled up over my eyes to keep out the strong rays of the afternoon sun. If we get through this, we need to set up some kind of early warning system, to send a signal to the mines about potential dangers of invasion and such.

This was the one time when I wished that the priest warriors were with us. Their numbers and carefree attitude towards death makes them useful allies. Everything banked on the horsemen taking time to rest after the raid on our camp. As much as we needed a similar break, we simply could not afford one. On we sailed, with Tallack adjusting the rigging to capture every wisp of wind. The warriors were almost at fainting point with exhaustion during their rowing shifts, but on we sped.

When at last, we pulled onto the beach at Bentewyn, daylight was scarce. Blydh was the freshest of the twins, helping me off Tallack's boat and onto dry land.

"Find a couple of trustworthy scouts with fast horses. Send them with all the speed of the Morrighan to the Mount at the end of the lands, and to the mines on the north coast in warning. Get the boats hidden in the rushes upstream and hurry!" I didn't think my legs would take anymore, but I pushed through the pain and the wheezing as the warriors streamed past me and ran towards the valley. Every footstep I took was taken in the knowledge that we might be too late. If Wenna and her men had reached the river before us from the northern direction, then all the Alchemists could be slaughtered and left to rot on the gravel mounds.

By the time I reached their main settlement, Blydh and Tallack were already making a great noise and rousing the elders to take action. I breathed a massive sigh, and closed my eyes. They were unharmed. We still had time to save them. Struggling up the incline to their clan leader's hut, I leaned in the doorway and puffed until I could speak.

As luck would have it, he remembered me. I had treated an injury of his that had blurred from my memory with age. He welcomed me into his home with such respect, I was taken aback. I am so used to the dismissive tone of Eseld and her kin, that I had forgotten what it felt like to have my opinions valued. He listened to my dire warning, and told me what defences were already in place. With a few suggestions from me, he called his clan together, along with all the slaves from their mine tunnels up and down stream of the river, and issued specific orders.

We had no idea how much time we had before the Duro's arrival, assuming that they were not heading north for the Droskin site on the coast. The clan leader, Kenver, sent his eldest daughter to ride to the top of the ridge with the instruction to whistle a certain call when the Duro's were spotted. His sons were sent to cut the ends of new oaken shaft props into spikes and join them together in deadly barricades. These were to be spaced at regular intervals between the trees, funnelling their riders into a trap at the bottom of the valley.

Slaves filled baskets with discarded rocks from the mine and scattered them along the trail to slow or hobble their horses. Others sat and made weapons from their supplies. All in all, the settlement was well stocked for such occasions. With a short wait ahead of us while the alchemy clan prepared, Blydh and Tallack held strategy talks with their men. I took a few moments to myself, gathering plants by torchlight and sharpening my blades.

A horde of bloodthirsty horseback warriors is a terrible force to battle. They have the advantage of swift and agile movement. Our warriors were all on foot, or hidden up trees and at the top of the valley ridge. They could trample a dozen of our warriors before the first arrows were set in flight.

Kenver offered me stew from his own hearth, but I couldn't eat. My gut twisted in terrified knots and my knee jogged constantly with apprehension. Kenver did not seem at all flustered by our news. He was calm and orderly. His children were similar, each of them carrying out the orders from their father and leader, with efficiency and precision. They were a far cry from the shambles of the Priest Sect. If the Alchemists ever decide that their mining empire was not enough to satisfy a lust for power, I have no doubt that they could oust our family in an evening without breaking into a sweat. No wonder why Eseld was keen to marry her daughter to Kenver's eldest boy.

With a torch dowsed in grease and set ablaze, I walked the length of the valley floor to check on their progress. The cunning old men of the settlement had strung their fishing nets from the branches of tall trees. If any of Wenna's riders decided to break away from the trail, their horses would be tangled, or the warriors strangled. I could still hear the noise of axes against wood in the distance, the barricades were not finished.

The moon was high above me, without a cloud in the sky to dampen its glow. The gentle rustle of the shrubs on the river bank gave the valley an unsettling air. I wondered where Wenna and her tribe were spending the night. How close were they to reaching the settlement and its hidden loot? The last of the baskets of rocks were strewn on the wayside, and the mine entrances shuttered and wedged closed. We were almost ready. Where were the twins? This would be their first battle without Aebba to lead them. Blydh had the most experience with driving off raiding Duro's, but how would he fair without his trusted horse? Tallack was a talker and a trader. Apart from breaking up fights between his sailors, he had few skirmishes to boast.

I emptied my bladder behind some bushes, and started back for Kenver's house to rest. With the torch held high, I stepped lightly between the rocks weary for sleep. As I put one foot inside the hut, I heard the shrill whistle of warning. Wenna was attacking in the dark.

CHAPTER TWENTY-FIVE

I was frozen to the spot. This was so unexpected. Attacking in the dark put everyone at a disadvantage. Perhaps Wenna realised that we would prepare for her arrival. Maybe her warriors caught the scouts on their way to warn the rest of the clan at the other mines. Whatever her reasoning, she succeeded in surprising us. The barricades were incomplete, the slaves were not finished crafting arrows and the warriors were all exhausted and away from their strategic positions.

"Fur Benyn," Kenver said, placing his hand on my back. "There is one tunnel left open for the wives and young children of the elders. Please go with them. You'll be safe there until this is all over, and then I…" He realised that he too might die this night. "And then I, or another, will come and fetch you." His face was all quiet kindness amid my utter turmoil. It was certainly a tempting offer, but how could I leave the boys to make decisions on their own? What if they needed my herbs and healing mid battle? If they were to fall this night, Paega would automatically become the new Metern, and then we would all suffer. Under those circumstances, the tribe would fare better under Wenna and her husband's rule.

"I thank you, Kenver, but I must stay. I have my task to complete as have you. If you will permit me to work from your cooking hut over yonder, I can set up my tinctures and blades there?"

"Of course, but should you get cornered…"

"Then I'll stick em with this." I picked up my largest knife and waved it about under his nose.

He grinned at me. "Then they had better watch out. Luck be with you, fair lady, and may the Morrighan choose to save us all this night."

"And with you."

I gathered my things as he grasped his sword and ran out to his allotted position. My legs were like those of a new born calf, I was so frightened. I laid out my things, and cleared the meat preparation table for my potential patients.

It was the howling and yelling that I heard first. Screeches and screams to terrify those in camp. Little did they know that the settlement was deserted but for me and a couple of slaves to do my bidding. All those fit and able to fight, sat high in the branches, waiting for the trap to snap shut. Next came the galloping hooves of more Duro's than I ever knew existed. The louder the sound became, the more I could feel the rumble travel up my legs to rattle my heart. It was no use, I had to see whether all our plans would work.

Moving through the door linens, I closed my eyes for a few moments so that they could adjust to the moonlit scene before me. From my position at the bottom of the valley, I saw the vast number of horsemen hurtling down the riverbank into camp. Their swords were held high, their spears poised in readiness to fling at anything ahead that moved. As they raced towards me, I watched a few of those warriors at the back peel off into the woods, but moments later return to the main crowd. The barricades were working.

My entire body quivered in fear as they drew back their throwing arms and aimed in my direction. The deep trumpet of a ram's horn echoed throughout the valleys, signalling the start of raining arrows. They fell in a massive storm of piercing barbs, felling warriors and horses by the dozen. Others rode on, pierced in shoulders and ribs with bronze tipped darts. A few held shields aloft, deflecting the worst of the onslaught. The forerunners of their tribe, kicked their heels into the horse's flanks, speeding their progress towards camp.

Tallack shouted, "Now!" And two of his men tightened a rope across large tree trunks at head height. There was no time for the warriors to stop, the first lost his head, the rope slicing clean through flesh and sinew, the blood gushing high into the air. The two either side of him, kept their heads, but snapped their spines. The horses ran on without them, leaving the riders limp on the ground. More showers of bronze tipped barbs flew into those at the back, killing, maiming and scattering the group into many different directions.

Thinned to a manageable number, the horses spooked and reared up at the fishing nets. Others tried and failed to jump the spiked barricades, impaling the riders as they were bucked from their steeds. Those that attempted to shelter among the trees met with flying daggers and spears. The valley was littered with dead or dying Duro's, limping horses and broken arrows. Blood seeped into the river, swirling about in frothy pink pools at the water's edge.

There were now two small groups of Duros left. Those at the farthest end of the valley, turned their horses and fled. Wenna was closest to me, trying to regroup in readiness for attack. Blydh's men jumped down from the trees and unsheathed their swords, moving in a coordinated line from behind. Tallack's men did the same from downstream, blocking off all routes to escape. Wenna kicked her horse and broke through the group until she could see me, standing next to Kenver and Tallack.

"Don't let them finish us, Aunt Mel. You wouldn't let them betray their sister like this, would you?"

Her plea was a feeble one. I could sort of see what she was trying to achieve. With one south-western tribe controlling all the metal distribution and wealth, she could ensure that the priests were driven from the region, that daughters got a fairer say in the binding rituals and alliances, that woman had a chance to thrive without the fear of male retribution. It was a noble quest, but one that involved slaughtering her own brothers first.

"There's only one shameful betrayal here, girl, and it's not with the Dumnonii. You killed our warriors, you torched our compound and grain stores, took all the tributes from the hidden troves. I can't spare your life, child. Only the clan leader and your brothers have that power." I looked over at Tallack and squinted in the darkness to spy Blydh at her back.

Tallack shouted up to her. "Where did you stash the metals and jewels, Wenna? Tell us that, and we may yet spare you."

She swallowed. Her fear transmitted to the animal beneath her, who skittered on the rocks and gravel, whinnying its anguish and pulling on the rein. "We didn't stash it anywhere. I sent it back to our Chieftain compound with some of my men."

Tallack shook his head at her gall, and then twisted to look at his brother. "What say you, Blydh. Are we to strip her of all her metal and let her go?"

"So she can gather more men and come and kill us in our sleep? No. We have to send others a warning. Family or not, no one tries to attack us without paying the penalty. I say we send her head back to her tribe." The men at his side each raised their swords grinning, cheering and agreeing. Those behind him pulled the strings back on their bows and aimed at her chest.

"Will you not let me trade for the lives of my men? I have gold."

Tallack's brows raised with interest. However much gold she had, it would not make up for the vast wealth she had plundered from beneath Aebba's bench. I noted her anguished expression and heard the note of fear in her voice. Perhaps she could be dealt with and punished in another way.

Blydh rubbed his chin, and then shrugged with his palms facing the sky. "Then we'll take your gold, and that of your men, when you are dead and your guts are spilling into this river for the fish to eat." He signalled his men and an arrow found its way into the hearts and necks of each marauder, including Wenna. She looked shocked, and then horrified, as her hand clutched the bloodied hole in her chest. She slid from her horse onto the mud and rocks, alongside her fated warriors.

I have seen so much death in my time, I thought myself hardened to its chilling effects. Nothing prepares you for watching a loved one die. I rushed over to her convulsing form. She choked on the blood erupting from her lungs and through her mouth. Great gurgling bubbles surfaced from her throat. Cradling her narrow body in my arms, I shushed and rocked her as her life slowly faded from her eyes. With her last breath, she reached up and touched my face, trying to smile through red stained teeth. She was gone.

Kenver carried a torch over to where I sat. He offered me his hand to pull me to my feet. I didn't want to let her go. All I could think about was the night terrors that kept her from sleeping as a child, the songs I would sing to soothe her back to sleep. She still looked like a child to me. For all her bravery and grand schemes, she was just a little girl trying to make herself heard among a self-centred family. Well they all heard her this time. They'll never hear her again.

Eventually, I laid her head down to the ground and closed the lids of her eyes. She'll burn come the daylight, along with all her tribal warriors. Did the Morrighan take her to the Underworld, or will Cernonnus grant her the right to sit with the greatest warriors of all time in the Summerlands? Only time will tell.

I didn't want to see the men stripping the wealth from their bodies. I couldn't face the prospect of Blydh carrying out his threat to behead his sister and send it back to the Duro's Chieftain compound. That was one atrocity too much. I took Kenver's hand, and let him guide me back to his hut, where I wept for the spirit of my young niece.

Come the dawn, I found that Blydh's men had taken the bodies away up stream to a clearing ready for cremation. Kenver extended his hospitality in return for help in building more defensive structures in and around our mines, both here and on the northern coast. With nowhere to call home it was an easy decision to make, plus the climate is more forgiving this far south. Tallack took some of his men and his ships back along the coastline to the Exe. He was to stay until his mother, Eseld and the elders returned from Stonehenge and transport them to Bentewyn. It rains a fair amount, but the comparative warmth would ease us through winter.

***

I was quite looking forward to seeing Jago and the girl, when the sails of Tallack's boats were spotted heading for the beach. It had been quite a while since Wenna's cremation, and I was keen to get back to a normal routine before the frosts began. During that time, I had grown fond of Kenver's children, and his wife was most welcoming and friendly, but it's not the same as having your own people around you. Jago and the girl's absence made me realise how much I loved them. To me, they were family.

With many others from the settlement, I walked down to the beach to greet them. The sails billowed in deep red and green stripes. Tallack stood at the bow, shielding his eyes from the low autumn sunshine. Eseld stood behind him, with a fixed smirk. Derwa was with her, and incredibly, her new husband from the Ordo Tribe. How had she persuaded him to come to our settlement, instead of returning to his own tribe?

A second boat carried Cryda and her slaves, her furs and a few of Tallack's men. I could not see Jago or the girl. It had been my only request of my nephew, to bring them to me at all costs. For one horrible moment, I thought of all the dreadful things that they could have been exposed to without my protection. The Priest Sect had remained with Eseld and Paega in the sacred space, while I left Jago at their mercy for all this time.

Hurrying onto the wet sand, I met Tallack as he jumped over the side and splashed through the shallows to greet me. His men began unloading the boats, and carrying the ladies to shore. Still, I could see no sign of Jago and the girl.

"Where are my slaves?" I grabbed Tallack by the ruched fold of his tunic and shook him.

"Before you go screaming at me, Aunt Mel, talk to the Lady Eseld over there. She would not travel with them and there was no room in the other boats."

I let him go and stomped over to Eseld with a glower that could freeze the ocean. "Well?"

"Oh, for the sake of Cernonnus, don't snap at me." She hitched up her linens and pulled a face at the water lapping against her feet. "Your precious painted boy is perfectly safe. My father is bringing him with the sect over land."

"How dare you let your father take him like that? You had no right."

"Take him? Should we have left him at the stones for anyone to claim then? I made sure the creature was fed. I made sure he was rounded up and taken back to the Exe. You should be thanking me." She stuck her nose in the air and stormed off. I was left bewildered and more frantic than ever. Spinning around, I watched Cryda struggle up the incline. She looked ready to burst.

Eseld yelled back at me. "They left a couple of days before we set sail. They should be here any day soon." I suspect that was her idea of kindness, to let her debauched father take charge of the prize he coveted so much. There was nothing I could do but return to the settlement and lend my healing skills to anyone in need. At least it took my mind off Jago and the girl's whereabouts for some of the time.

Cryda was close to birth. Pressing the side of her belly, I could make out the little one's feet wriggling about. I laid my ear down to her bump and listened. Its heart beat fast and strong.

"What do you think, Meliora? Will it be soon? Can you tell what it is?" She needed reassurance so badly.

"Aye, it won't be long now. Better stick close to camp for a while."

She sat on my bunk in Kenver's house. They had vacated their home for our use over the winter. I felt bad for pushing them out, but he assured me that new huts were already under construction nearby. His small settlement would more than triple with us all descending upon the mining community. Blydh was still patrolling the eastern borders with his men, while Tallack made noises about sailing to the island, west of Lands' End. He said he'd heard about a possibility of a copper trade. At the very least, he might be able to barter tin for grain to see us through. I could understand why he would not want to overwinter with Paega, Eseld and the priests in this cramped settlement. Rivalry and clashes were inevitable, especially since our Ruvane continues to be vague, and still holds the jug containing Aebba's long bones in the corner of our house.

I asked Cryda why she had not completed the burial on Higher Tor as planned, but she told me that she wanted the boys to be a part of interring the bones and building a massive quoit to stand over his stone-lined grave. It seemed a lame excuse to me. In truth, I suspect that she had grown used to making decisions for the tribe and did not want that privilege to end. Can't say I blame her. It was what Wenna wanted for herself too.

The following day, the priests arrived at a canter, calling and shouting as they drove their horses down the valley. It looked to me that they had taken quite the detour, since they arrived with a long string of unbroken wild horses behind them. Their noise and commotion were disturbing, setting the children and babes in arms crying. Eseld's father was at the front of the other sect members, along with the sullen Paega. The old man's tunic was crossed by a pair of dark arms, bound together at the wrist. Jago was tied to the priest on the back of his horse.

He pulled the reins up, halting the pony in spitting distance to my feet. When it was safe to move closer, I rushed over to the priest to give him a piece of my mind. Poor Jago's face was squashed against the old man's back. He couldn't move. Only when Eseld's father cut the ties from his wrists, did my Jago slide sideways from the horse and onto the gravelled ground. I tried to slow his fall, but I was not strong enough to fully catch him before he landed. He hit the river bank with a thud, but didn't utter a word. I thought he might be pleased to see me, but he lay on his side still and limp.

"Jago… are you in pain? Tell me what they did to you." I crouched over him, touching his shoulder to get a response. He simply closed his eyes. I glanced over his arms, his neck and legs. I could see no sign of injury other than the marks from the rope about his wrists.

"What did you do to him?" I screamed at the priest.

The old man displayed both palms to my face. "Nothing. The restraints were to stop him from running. He's your property, you made that very clear. I thought you'd be happy to see him, you seemed so fond of the boy."

I squinted at him, looking for evidence of falsehood. He appeared genuine, but you can never tell. Crouching again, I lay the back of my hand on Jago's forehead. There were no signs of fever, he was not sick. I could not understand why he was behaving in this way.

"Jago. You must speak to me. Tell me what has happened?" Still nothing. I shook him by the shoulder. "Jago!"

His eyes flickered open and he whispered something so faint, I could not hear him. I leaned closer to his mouth and asked him to repeat his words.

"They sacrificed my wife."

CHAPTER TWENTY-SIX

I couldn't believe what I was hearing. Looking around the priest warriors and their horses, I tried to spot the girl in the crowd. She was nowhere to be seen. The priest looked shifty; his eyes darted in all directions to avoid my stare.

"Is this true? You killed my Frynkish slave?" I stepped closer to him, balling up my fists and panting with fury.

"We got news that the Duro's had burned the compound and were heading west for the mines. We had to give praise to Morrighan to gain her favour in defeating the raiders. What else were we to do?" His shoulders crept up to his ears. He tried a placatory smile. My emotions were boiling over. All I wanted to do was to stick one of my sharpest blades through his eye and into that twisted brain. He saw my state and quickly sought to calm me. "I can pay you her worth if it helps, but I was true to my word over the chosen one. We harmed not a hair on his head."

Losing my balance in the giddiness, I sat heavily on a boulder and held my head in my hands. My innards pained me; my mind crushed with weariness. I could stitch gashes, amputate legs or pour ointment into wounds, but I could not mend a broken heart. How would he ever forgive me for leaving them with these butchers?

The old man took my silence for bartering. "Look, I can pay you more than she was worth if it means that much to you."

At this point, Eseld decided to intervene. "It was just a slave, Meliora. You still have the other one." She pointed at Jago, who lay motionless still. I was too tired to fight. No amount of explaining would get through their thick skulls how much she meant to me. For Jago, she was beyond all value, she was priceless. I hoisted myself to my feet and approached the Chosen One.

"Come along, Jago. Let's go home." He did not move. I bent lower.

His sight was fixed on the river. "Kill me, Fur Benyn. Put this wretch out of its misery. She was my reason for living."

I grabbed his wrist where the ropes had chaffed him sore. He neither flinched nor yelped in pain. Gently, by careful steps, I pulled him to his feet. "You cannot die, boy. You are *my* reason for living." I hooked my arm around his waist and guided him to my hut. His ribs were prominent and he was weaker than a new-born foal. Whatever food I laid before him; he would not touch. Fine roasted boar, blackberries, duck eggs, anything to tempt him to eat, but he refused. I knew what he was trying to do, but I would not let him starve himself to death.

I laid fresh bed rushes and a fur for his bed next to the fire and encouraged him to lie down. He did, and stared at the smoky roof until I had fallen asleep. I woke in the middle of the night in search of my piss pot, and saw he was gone. Running out into the darkness I called and called his name, until Tallack and Brea were woken by my noise.

He could see my state of anxiety. “Does he mean this much to you, Aunt? I can get you as many slaves as you like, why is this one important to you.”

I couldn’t answer him in a way that he would understand. He and the girl had saved my life, cared for me and protected me when I was most vulnerable. In return, I had abandoned them at a time when they needed me most. I had let them both down. “I can’t explain, Nephew. Will you help me to find him or not?”

He and Brea put on warm clothes and lit torches and went in search upstream from the settlement. I went downhill, towards the beach. As soon as I left the gravel walkways next to the mouth of the river, I could see the light footprints in the sand. Quickening my gait, I stumbled across the flowing water and down to the water’s edge, holding my torch high and peering into the gloom. As my eyes adjusted, I saw his silhouette just before he bobbed down below the waves.

“Jago! No!” I waded in, throwing the torch to one side, and fighting against the incoming tide. My clothes dragged me backwards making the going even harder, until I walked on tiptoe with my head tilted away from the surge. When I reached the spot where I thought he had disappeared, I held my breath and sank below the water. Clouds of tiny bubbles, plus the darkness made it impossible to see more than an arms distance away. I surfaced, screaming his name over and over, hoping that he would have a change of heart and want to live. Swimming now, in the freezing tidal currents, I could neither see nor hear him splashing. Another breath and I bobbed under the waves, keeping my body fully upright and allowing myself to sink towards the bottom.

Just when I thought I might be too late, and had lost him forever, my foot hit something as I kicked out. Uncertain what I might find, I crunched into a ball and reached my hands down to touch the object. It was the wiry curls of his hair. Without thinking, I grappled beneath his chin and yanked, sending his body upwards. With my arm hooked under his, I swam until my lungs burned to the surface, and gasped in the fresh air.

He was not moving; a dead weight, pulling me under. "Jago, snap out of it and fight, damn you!" I don't know how I kept us afloat for so long, my muscles were on fire and my joints stabbed pain right through my hips. Thank Cernonnus that I had woken Kenver and his family with all my shouting and scurrying about. With their help, we managed to haul Jago to shore and lie him on his side to push out the water from his lungs. He coughed and spluttered for a long time, but he was alive.

Kenver and his son carried him to my hut that I shared with Cryda, and laid him on my bunk. I couldn't let him out of my sight until the urge to die had passed. I sat on guard, day and night for half a moon cycle, trying to get him to eat and drink. Tallack and Brea visited me, bringing food and news from the camp. Even the old priest came to see if I needed him to perform a healing ritual to cleanse the bad spirits marring his recovery.

It was Cryda who was most patient, a Ruvane of a great tribe, sharing a round house with a heartbroken slave from foreign lands and a crotchety old lady. She seemed to understand why he meant so much to me. Every time I managed to get a spoonful of stew down his throat, she would smile and stroke her belly.

One morning, after a three-quarter moon, a slave came running to our hut to take me to the mine shaft at the top of the valley. Kenver had sent for me to heal an injured relative who had been trapped by a rockfall. I looked at Cryda and then at Jago.

"Go, it's fine. I'll watch out for him." Cryda said, waddling from her bed to the porridge pot simmering in the fire. I grabbed my knife roll and my medicine bag and began the trek up the hillside. Winter was fast approaching. I could feel the icy sleet as it hit my face and neck. The walk reminded me how little exercise I had taken since caring for Jago; every muscle felt tight and stiff.

I wasn't sure what to expect when we arrived at the entrance to the mine. The roof of the tunnel was supported by wide beams of oak, and the walls were coated in a thick layer of wattle and daub. It gave the impression of permanence, although from the state of the cave in further along, that was only an illusion. Rocks the size of sheep littered the tunnel just beyond my patient, layered with a finer mixture of gravel and pebbles. The injured man was covered in fine black dust. I could see by torchlight that the bone of his forearm stuck through his skin in jagged spikes. I'd seen breaks this severe before. They never healed well and often resulted in amputation later on, when the bad humours built up and sent them half mad.

"Please, Fur Benyn, you have to fix me. I have to work or my children will starve." The young man must have been in agony. Apart from the sweat dripping off his brow, he made no sound when I put my foot against his shoulder as he sat there and yanked his arm with all my might until the bones snapped back into place. I washed the dirt from his flesh and stitched him with fibres from the back strap of a hare. With the worst done, he was able to shuffle along the narrow passageway until he was out and into the light of day. Kenver helped me to find some strong branches to fashion a splint, and I used strips of fabric from my kit to tie them to his arm.

"Try and keep it held high or it'll swell and throb." I turned to Kenver. "Well, if only one person got hurt in this cave in, then you didn't do too badly."

His brow cinched together and his lips disappeared against his teeth.

"What?" I asked, puzzled by his response.

"He was the only one that got out. The others working that seam were crushed beneath the rocks."

I gasped. He hadn't given any clue as to how bad the accident was. "How many lives?"

"More than twenty, some children too. Mining is a family concern, generally speaking. The little ones dig alongside their parents. They can get into the smaller tunnels where the grown men can't."

Words were not enough to express how I felt. This was far beyond anything I ever imagined. We have been blind to the dangers that members of this clan face every day, yet happy to profit from their work. Instantly, I was humbled and ashamed. When I mentioned this to Kenver, he raised his brows and inhaled slowly.

"It's the way it's always been. Someone has to dig the stuff out of the hills now that the metal nuggets in the streams have all gone. We are the only suppliers of tin for bronze from here to the Summerlands, as far as we know. Stop mining, and there'll be no more trade."

I understood what drove us all to exploit the mines, but I had no idea that small children faced the same terrors as their elders. "How often do rock falls happen?"

"More than they should." He turned away from me. I'd hit on a bruise. He might seem like a genial and intelligent host, but he controlled all the mining in the region. He had the power to make shafts wider, allowing men to dig and not children. He had slaves to fell timber to sure up the tunnels. He could ease back on expansion and add extra props and beams. He could, but that would slow down tin production and trade.

My guilt drove me to the shacks and huts at the farthest end of the valley. These were the shelters for the poor families and slaves. Their cramped living quarters and dreadful working conditions left them with buckled spines and brittle bones. They spent all the day underground, breathing in black dust and drinking dirty water. Their food was what thin rations could be spared from the settlement lower down the valley, which by the looks of them, was not enough. I wandered about the shacks, examining bony children with coughs that could rupture a lung. This area was the richest in the land, and yet their people were worse off than their animals.

These were the people who had lost loved ones in the rock fall. I peeped into a couple of the huts to see those who worked shafts further down the valley, quietly sobbing and comforting each other. There was nothing I could do to help. As Kenver and I made our way back down towards home, a man staggered out in front of me, with wild eyes and drool leaking from the side of his mouth. He spun about as if he was lost, and then fell to the floor. His arms moved in jerky spasms while the muscles in his face twitched.

Never before had I seen anything like this. I looked at Kenver for an explanation.

"It's just smelter's twitch. He must have breathed in too much of the fumes." He said, stooping to help the man to his feet, before pushing him towards his hut.

"You've seen this before?"

"I have. Sometimes when the tin rocks are mixed with white crystals, it sends the Alchemists twitching like that as they are burned. Most of us try to stick with rocks without those crystals. It makes for a purer tin and stops you losing your mind."

"Is there anything we can give him to ease his suffering?" This was all new to me, and deeply troubling.

"Not really. He might get better, or he might get worse. We'll know by morning." Kenver helped the man down onto his bunk and returned to where I waited for him on the riverbank. For once I felt like my healing skills were sadly lacking. I ought to know how best to help these people with their bowed backs and pale skin, their smelting sickness and Cernonnus knows what else.

Thoroughly dispirited, I wandered back down the valley with my host, stopping every so often to harvest what nature afforded me. I had little to say to the clan leader, except an apology for the behaviour of the priests on the flood plain of the river. They had erected their tents in a circle and dug a fire pit in the middle. Around the outer edges, warrior men and women of their clan breathed in the fumes from smothering the flames with green hemp. The more they took into their lungs, the louder and more irritating they became.

"Is their state similar to that of smelting sickness?" I asked curious as to whether the priests would start crushing and burning the rocks to achieve their talks with the gods.

"Not at all, no. The white crystals have no smell, and the dizziness is disturbing and unpleasant. Hemp is for the feeble minded, although I suppose the end result is the same. They both eat away at your common sense." He chuckled, the first time since earlier that day when I first learned of the cave in. It was not as though we had forgotten those lost, but we were powerless to change the outcome. Kenver left me as we passed the priests to inform the clan elders of the rock fall.

I carried on towards my house. The closer I drew, the clearer the screams were. At first, I was shaken, thinking that we were being raided and Cryda was in great peril, but then I realised the source of her pain. She was in labour. How long had she been in this state with me away up the valley?

I increased my speed, dodging the boulders and wading through adjoining streams until the moaning and shouting grew louder, then stopped. Panicking, I hurried as fast as my aching legs would carrying me. Every possible problem flitted through my mind. Had she died from blood loss, or passed out from the pain, or was the baby dead or… so many terrible things can go wrong during childbirth, and Cryda was all alone.

Except, she was not alone. After the long pause of silence, I heard a faint tremulous cry. It was followed by a man's voice, a deep melodic laugh of delight. Skidding to a halt in the gravel at our door, I burst through the linen hangings and there they were, Jago stood by the bunk clutching a baby to his chest, the wrinkled pink skin in stark contrast to the smooth darkness of his. The beaming smile of joy would not be quelled. Cryda lay on her soaked furs, pushing out the blood sack with a look of thunder over her sweat streaked face. The babe stopped crying in his arms and tried to open its eyes.

"Look, Fur Benyn. A little girl."

There was little left for me to do. Jago had even double tied the cord and snipped it with the knife I had given to his wife. It was all he had left of her.

"Looks like you are halfway to taking over my job, lad." I grinned. The relief I felt overwhelmed me. Jago was finally on the mend, and Cryda was through the worst of the birth. The little one had a thatch of the blackest hair you'd ever seen. If I were the judgemental sort, I'd say she looked the image of the Ordo visitor Cryda spent so much of her time with. The babe had her mother's eyes though, bluer than the sky at midsummer.

Word got around camp that a new family member had arrived. Tallack and Brea were the first to bring gifts of baskets and furs for a crib. Derwa and her new husband arrived with Eseld. The young wife could be heard protesting right up to the moment her mother thrust her through the door linens. The Ordo gave Cryda a golden hair clasp, and a few kind words of praise on the healthy size of the babe. Eseld handed over a small bracelet, made from woven horsehair studded with tin beads. It was a fine piece. Cryda accepted the gift with thanks. Her perplexed frown was almost as deep as my own.

Young Derwa stood by the door, transfixed at the sight of Jago clutching the child. She trembled from head to toe, her eyes slick with welling tears.

"Well, child?" Eseld screeched at her. "Give her your gift."

Before Derwa could hand over whatever she held in her fist, she turned tails and ran from the hut.

CHAPTER TWENTY-SEVEN

"That bloody girl will be the death of me. What trouble she creates for us all." Eseld scratched her head and flounced around the hut. "Well? Go after her man. She's your problem now."

The Ordo did as he was told and scurried from the room.

"I knew Derwa should have given you a good milking goat. Such a godsend when you've had enough of them pulling on your teats."

For the life of me, I could not understand why Eseld was being so amicable. Had she and Cryda reached an accord while they were at the circle gathering? Perhaps she had convinced herself that Cryda's days as Ruvane were numbered, and that her son's elevation to Chieftain would raise her own status. I was not about to rock the boat by commenting on this observation. Harmony in such a cramped settlement is difficult to achieve at the best of times, as the boys could attest. Tallack and Paega avoided one another in camp. Paega stuck with his grandfather's clan, and Tallack stayed near to the boats on shore, awaiting the next trading voyage.

Kenver suggested a celebration to welcome the new blessing into the tribe. It was a kind gesture, but one that sat heavily with him. How could we celebrate new life, when twenty or more of his clan had taken the trip to the Underworld? Those at the top of the valley were in deep mourning, while those near the estuary were free to feast and dance. My solution was to make it a small affair, a single long table with family and a few elders.

He and I walked along the river bank watching the priests tattooing their youngsters and forcing them to inhale hemp smoke. Paega was among them, the white of his eyes were shot through with red vessels. His inane grin told me that he'd taken more than hemp. The further we walked up the valley, the more I could hear the roar of hooves, galloping in our direction. For a moment, my heart leapt, recalling the same sound when Wenna's tribe descended on this little community. Kenver and I stopped and waited for the first sighting of the arrivals, and breathed easily when Blydh and his men came into view.

"What a relief." I cried out. "At last we have someone with common sense to knock our family into shape."

Kenver scrutinised me with a puzzled look. "How is having all three brothers here, as winter sets in, a desirable outcome for my clan?"

I was dumbfounded. "What do you mean?" I asked, trying to keep my tone level, as riled as I was.

"From what I have seen, all three have such opposing views on how the tribal affairs should be run. Conflict will follow them wherever they go, and our dwindling numbers cannot sustain injury or worse from brawling and taking sides. Every tribe in the land knows that we are without a Metern, and we are vulnerable. The Duro's will be out for revenge, and that is just the start of our problems. We need a strong leader, and sooner rather than later."

His words took the wind out of my sails. As prepared as I was to defend my family's honour, I knew that what he said was true. The longer we waited to declare the next Chieftain, the greater the threat from rival tribes. I took a breath to calm myself, considering my response. "There are plans to subject the boys to an endurance test laid down by my ancestors in the spring."

"Fur Benyn, I fear that will be too late."

We were just a day away from the winter solstice and grain was already running low. The trawling nets caught fewer fish as the shoals ventured further south and local woodlands were stripped of easy prey. As resources grew scarce, in-fighting was a real possibility. Kenver was right. The tribe needed a decisive and respected leader as a matter of urgency.

"Do you have any suggestions?"

"You say you had an endurance test set to weed out the weakest?"

I nodded. "A race to swim across the bay to fetch a falcon's egg from the cliffs come spring."

Kenver smiled with a little snuffle. "So, you are only testing their physical strength, not their courage?"

It threw me for a while. I had thought that my ancestors were testing both. "You have something better in mind?"

Kenver gestured to a fallen tree trunk where we both moved to sit. "We have similar trials for our clan, although I did not *have* to endure the Nos Gans an Marow, since I was already marked for leadership, but there was an expectation for me to prove myself. It tests the bravest of warriors."

I was intrigued. In all my years I had never heard of the challenge. How would a *night with the dead* be arranged? My expression was enough for him to continue his explanation.

"There are cursed mine shafts, abandoned by my forefathers along the cliffs next to the sea. My people believe that the servants of the Morrighan await those who dare to enter. The tunnels were well propped and shuttered, and yet they claimed the lives of any who dug there. Fearing that those wicked spirits might escape into our settlement, the entrances were covered and sealed."

"And the trial involves spending a full night inside those shafts?" I asked, my mouth agape at the thought.

"It does, but first they must swim the treacherous ocean currents and climb the cliff face. Find the tunnels and break down the seals. There are many entrances, but once inside the tunnels branch and cross. It takes all your wits not to get lost or turned about. When they find the mouth of the Underworld, they must snatch the tin studs from the ear of a perished miner and return it to the beach at dawn."

That was a hefty challenge indeed. I had spent but a short time underground, tending to the man with the broken arm, but I still felt the chill of death hanging over me. As old and frail as I am, I don't think I would have the strength to fight against servants of the Underworld. My heart was pounding at the notion of sending the boys into such danger. There would be no protection other than their own wits and stamina.

My respect for Kenver and his people swelled until I felt unworthy of his friendship. How had this clan weathered such harsh conditions for so long? "But how would you know if they had fully completed the challenge and not cheated?"

"That's easy, because we will be standing on the cliffs watching them."

How could I present this alternative as a necessary course of action? With the perils of dancing with the dead, I could not see me garnering the support of Eseld or Cryda. I mentioned this concern to Kenver. His response was to allow him to present it directly to the boys. Coming from an impartial clan leader may be better than from an aunt, whose bias towards the twins was obvious to all. I blushed. For all my attempts at subtlety, I had failed to hide my preferences. Having those damn priests steer our tribe was beyond my patience.

Wandering back towards my hut, we watched Tallack greet his brother with the usual boisterous spirit I had come to love about them. How many days had they left to share in such camaraderie? How will the losers of the trial react towards their brothers when the new Metern is pronounced?

On our way past the priests' tents, I made a short detour to ask Paega to join us outside my hut. He did not object, since I ask very little of him and pay even less attention to his antics. The twins sensed that something was afoot when they saw Kenver and I calling for Eseld and Brea. Cryda was nursing the babe on the edge of my bunk. I pinned the door linens back so that she too could listen to what Kenver had to say.

With an authoritative tone, Kenver began his speech, pointing out the urgency and emphasising that great warriors of the past, told tales of their might and cunning, in deceiving the keepers at the gate of death. Their legends live on in the clans of the west, and songs of their courage will last for an eternity. I watched the faces of each of my nephews as they listened to the ordeals ahead of them. Blydh narrowed his eyes and took a slow breath, his arms crossed over his stout chest. Tallack squinted, concentrating on the details, absorbing every ounce of advice with care. Paega looked as though the blood had drained from his entire body. Even when he inhales too much hemp, he was never so pale as while he listened to Kenver explaining the Nos Gans an Marow.

When Kenver had finished explaining the procedure, Eseld peered through the doorway at Cryda. Both looked worried by the prospect of their children provoking the servants of the Underworld. I admit, I had my reservations too, but if there was a chance that Paega would drop out of the quest, it would be worth putting the boys in danger.

Eseld spoke first. "I think we should wait for the spring trials as we originally planned. Don't you agree, Cryda?"

Everyone looked at the Ruvane, nursing her infant to her breast. Her concerned frown, flattened out as she looked at Blydh and then Tallack. "The Chieftain selection cannot wait. Kenver is right. Without a Metern, more will come to take our lands and the mines from us, and that victor must be wise, strong and courageous." She glanced at Paega who averted his eyes. "I am convinced that my boys are more than capable of the challenge. Are you afraid for your son, Eseld?"

It was almost habitual; the scoff was loud and derisive. "Of course, I am not worried about Paega. My son has all the qualities of his father and none of the shameful tendencies of his half-brothers."

"Hah!" Was Cryda's reply.

Tallack squared up to Eseld, jutting out his chin and baring his teeth at her. Blydh could see her for the stirrer that she was. Every sleight directed at her son was met with diversion tactics. He put his arm around Tallack's chest and pulled him away.

"Leave it brother. She is not worth your ire. One of us will succeed in this trial, and we will feed that hemp addled low-life to the dark spirits of the Underworld, and then we'll be rid of him for the rest of our days." He manhandled Tallack until they were face to face, Blydh's cool reason deflating the animosity. "Come, let us prepare for the challenge. Tomorrow will see a new Metern for the Dumnonii." The twins strode away without a backward look.

"They mean to do this thing tonight?" Eseld said, the wobble in her voice clear to all. She peered at each of us, in hope that there would be an excuse to delay. No one spoke. She scuttled off, pushing Paega by the shoulder towards the priests' tents. Kenver excused himself, citing the need to organise the cliff top shelter for the watch.

I was left with Cryda, standing with her babe in arms, and Brea looking a little lost.

"We ought to make a bundle of food and take our furs with us. It'll be a cold and long night before they complete the quest." I said, mainly to Brea, but it was Cryda who answered.

"The baby will get cold up on the cliffs all night, and it is a long way to walk after giving birth. I'm not as young as I was, Meliora."

Jago stuck his head up high from his seat on the rushes. "I can carry the child for you, if you wish, or I can build you a fire and warm your ale for you, great lady."

I looked at him with raised brows and scrunched up my nose. Had he taken a shine to the baby, or Cryda? I couldn't figure out his reasons at all, but was glad that he had motivation to do something other than wish he was dead. Baffled, I left them to decide what they would do, while I wrapped half a flat bread and some cheese in a length of fabric and restocked my medicines bag.

In the end, Jago convinced Cryda to walk up the steep slope of Bentewyn hill and amble across the fields to the cliff edge. In the distance, we could see some of Kenver's slaves securing the hazel posts of a number of hurdles together with twine. They built a series of smaller pens, like the ones we used to separate the rams from the sheep only these had additional hurdles strapped across them to form a roof. It was bleak and windswept at the highest point. Jago built several fires and made many trips to fetch logs to last us throughout the night. By late-afternoon, the sun began its descent to the horizon.

Eseld joined us on the cliff edge as we stood at the outer most point of the headland looking down towards the beach. The breakers lashed the shore, spraying Kenver and the boys with globs of white foam. Even with my old eyes, I could see that he was giving them the benefit of his advice and wisdom. Whether they chose to act on it was doubtful. Each of them is so headstrong in their own ways.

The boys lined up facing the sea. Kenver raised his arm, waited for them to signal their readiness and then shouted for them to go. His arm fell as the boys hopped and jumped the lower waves and dived into the ocean. I shivered at the thought of what lay ahead of them. Just the approach to the jagged cliffs was perilous, let alone the swirling currents which could just as easily drag them beneath the surface as smash them against the rocks.

Tallack was by far the strongest swimmer, as we all expected, but Blydh was hot on his heels. Paega thrashed about trying to keep up. From our high vantage point, we could all see their progress around the corner of the headland. Looking down on them, also made it easier to see Paega's attempts to slow Blydh down.

Every time he drew close to his legs, Paega grabbed hold of Blydh's ankle and dragged him down.

Cryda turned to Eseld. "Your son has no honour."

Eseld shot her a shrivelling glare. "Honour is worthless in the face of death. This tribe needs a ruthless and feared Chief."

Brea almost burst with laughter. I must admit, I found it hard to keep my face straight. Eseld chose to ignore the outburst. We walked along the cliff edge slowly, keeping pace with the boys as they struggled against the pounding waves. Tallack took a wide route away from the cliffs, adding distance to his swim. Blydh and Paega stayed close to shore, but the buffeting swell threw them backwards more often than their forward motion. As Tallack drew level with a tiny cove nestled in the crook of the next headland, he turned his direction towards land. Paega and Blydh were still in danger of being smashed against the rocks. They bobbed and kicked out against the surging waves, but were powerless to alter their course.

As Tallack powered towards the small beach, letting the drifting currents take him ashore, Blydh realised his brother's wisdom. He pushed off an enormous boulder and swam out and away from the cliffs. Without the battering of the waves, Blydh swam in a wide circle to land at the same point as Tallack. The twins were safely ashore. Cryda heaved a great sigh, and went to check on Jago and the babe resting in one of the shelters.

Tallack was still fresh and full of energy, he scrambled up the beach and began climbing the rocks to the area Kenver had suggested. Blydh took a few moments to catch his breath. He bent double and rested his hands against his knees, panting. Paega was still in the water, clinging to a boulder. At the high-water mark, Tallack found three torches, all primed with grease, which Kenver had left for them. I watched him examine all three, before making his choice. From a pouch hung around his neck, he produced a couple of flints. Shielding the greased moss from the frigid breeze, he struck the rocks together until a tiny spark set the grease aflame.

As Blydh caught up, Tallack lit a second torch with his own and passed it to his brother. Even in the midst of competition, these boys cannot help but protect each other. I brimmed with pride. If only Cryda had seen them as I had. Brea yelled down the cliff edge, her hands shielding the sound from the wind.

"Don't help him you fool!" She growled in anger, although the boys had not heard.

Eseld and I looked at her with fresh eyes. Where had the mousy Brea got to, leaving us with this brash and social climbing harpy? We all leaned over the edge of the cliff. Eseld chewed at her hangnails as Paega appeared to be stuck in his present situation. There was nothing anyone could do to help him, even if it was permitted.

Tallack stuck the handle of his torch between his teeth and started to climb. They were right above Paega in the sea, who we could all hear whining feebly as he was buffeted by the waves.

"You can do it, my darling boy. Climb the boulder, Paega, climb!" Eseld yelled, but his only moves were those defined by the swell. Just as we had all but given up on him, a freak wave carried him high into the air, depositing him on dry land a stone's throw from the twins. Eseld sneered. "My boy is favoured by the gods. He carries the thumb bone of his father for protection."

Cryda screwed up her fists and glowed with anger. I signalled to her to let the comment go, but she couldn't. "That's supposing that Aebba was his father. He doesn't seem to carry any of Aebba's traits, and you are very fond of that cousin of yours." The jibe was not well thought out.

"Oh, we're going there, are we? When you have just given birth to another little Ordo bastard." Eseld was so close to Cryda's face they shared the same breath. I couldn't let it descend into a scrap. I stepped between them and pushed them apart.

Brea provided a timely diversion. "Tallack has found the first entrance."

We rushed to the cliff edge and squinted into the darkness. From the light of their torches, you could just make out the silhouette of the twins, pulling the undergrowth away from a shuttered mine tunnel. Blydh handed his torch to Tallack and slipped his fingers behind the wooden planks. With all his might he yanked until it rattled loose. With a foot against the rocks, he tugged one last time and the door gave way.

Tallack held out the torch for Blydh to take. Paega dashed past, snatching the lit pole and dodging into the tunnel.

CHAPTER TWENTY-EIGHT

We looked squarely at Eseld. She had raised a despicable creature for a son. Even she had the grace to look a little sheepish. She walked back to the shelters and helped herself to some of our food. The rest of us watched Blydh climb back towards the beach for the third torch, before he and Tallack entered the tunnel and out of our sight.

There was very little that that could be said to excuse Paega's behaviour. We sat around the fires, eating bread and cheese and wrapping our furs around us to keep out the wind. Jago busied himself, adding more wood to the fire and fussing about Cryda and the child. It was a relief when Kenver and his eldest son joined us for the night watch. He kept us bright and cheerful with tales of his forefathers and how they were great travellers and traded with people from distant lands and foreign shores. He untied a tiny leather pouch from his belt and poured the contents into the palm of his hand.

"These belonged to my grandmother. She had a whole necklace of them brought back from a place where it's so warm, the most exotic fruits grow throughout all the seasons." In his hand lay a dozen or more polished blue beads. I picked one from his palm and took it closer to the fire to see. It had a swirl of white running through in a perfect layer.

"What are they made from? I have never seen blue clay this fine before." I asked, returning the bead to its owner.

"It's not clay. They are made from glass. The finest and purest sand is fired to an incredible heat. It turns to a red-hot gloop and when it cools, this is what you get. She had others that were red, some were green and other colours too." He seemed pleased by our reaction to his treasures, his smile broadened above his greying beard. "I should like you all to have one." He began passing each lady a blue bead. Eseld grabbed hers as did Brea.

"You should give them to your wife and daughters, Kenver. You have already given us your home. You'll have nothing left." I said, frowning at the greed of Aebba's widows.

"I want you to have them. When you go from this place, and rebuild your Chieftain compound, you will look at those beads and remember us down at the end of this great land." He pushed the largest of the jewels into my hand and folded my fingers around in acceptance. It was a beguiling thing. How many days travel had it taken for this to find its way all across the seas and land to get to this corner of the world? It made me hunger for my youth. How fortunate Tallack is to be young and the master of swift boats. His stories keep our tribe yearning for more trade partners even further afield. What I wouldn't give to go with him, but an old woman is of little use on such a voyage when space aboard ship is so critical.

The moon was broad and rose slowly above the clear sky. As it reached the highest point, Cryda was yawning and keen to bunk down with the babe. Jago had spent the evening adding a layer of grasses to our shelter, blocking out the wind from whistling through the gaps in the hurdles. All in all, it made quite a difference. By the middle of the night, I half expected to see Paega come running out of the tunnels with the Morrighan on his tail, but all was quiet.

Kenver removed his furs and walked to the cliff edge to check for any sign of them. Satisfied that none of the boys had sneaked out onto the beach, he returned to my side and banked up the fire.

"Have you ever been down the cursed shafts?" I asked quietly so as not to wake the others.

Kenver nodded, his eyes widening with memories of the experience. "It takes a lot of courage to face the servants of the Underworld. I felt it was my duty to enter and spend the night, even though I was already set to be clan leader. I had to prove my mettle."

"What was it like down there?"

"Colder than you could ever imagine, and with wet clothes it chills you to the bone. That's if you can keep your teeth from shattering against one another. The tunnels start fairly wide until you meet the first fork in the path. Whichever one you choose; they narrow soon after and reduce in height so that you have to crouch to pass through." He looked at me to assess my interest. I was captivated by his descriptions, my stomach twisting in knots at the thought of what the boys would be suffering right beneath our feet in the hillside.

He chewed on a strip of cold boar and swallowed. "Of course, as disturbing as the confined spaces and the cold gets, it is nowhere near as bad as the emotional toll. It can send a man crazy after a while. Tallack is the slimmest of the boys, so he stands a chance of clawing through the gravel and dirt at the furthest reaches of the shafts. And that will still involve wriggling on his belly through openings better suited to young children. Blydh will need nerves of stone to cope with the tight spaces against his great bulk. Although, he might be able to navigate the passages towards the largest of the rock falls. That, as far as I can remember, is a fairly big cavern, but it is the most likely place to get snatched by the Morrighan's servants."

I took in all that Kenver had to say and closed my eyes, imagining what they must be suffering as we sat above eating fine food and drinking warm ale. Their torches would not stay lit for long. When they burned out, all sources of warmth and light would be gone, plunging them into a black despair. I wondered if the twins were still working together or whether their keen sense of competition had driven them apart. What if that treacherous lout Paega had squirrelled a weapon in his tunic and had sneaked up behind one of them?

"How do you think Paega will fare in the tunnels?"

"Hmm, from what I have seen of him, and the priests' fondness for hallucinogens, Paega might well do the best of them all. The imagination plays tricks with you in the darkness. You start to think that the soul eaters are creeping up your body, and with nowhere to run or hide, you get yourself in an awful frenzy. Paega would be well used to strange visions and feelings. He'll more than likely shrug it off as a side effect of bad mushrooms."

That was not what I was hoping to hear. Paega was a shameless cheat at the best of times. The thought of him having an advantage over the twins was galling. I said nothing, but inside my head scenes of terrible demons and Underworld creatures, wreaked havoc on my temper. The wait for dawn to come on the shortest day of the cycle was horrendous. For the boys, it must be torture. When the fires burned low, I retreated to the bedding in our shelter, and tried to get some sleep.

Kenver was content to take shifts with his son in watching out for any early emergence from the mine shafts.

It was a restless night for me. I turned so often under my furs that Cryda awoke and yelled at me to lay still. After that I did, but I could not close my eyes again. I watched the orange flicker from the fire light up the hurdle slats above my head. They danced and licked the wood like serpents' tongues. The small child inside me quickened my heart, thinking that the evil spirits had escaped the tunnels and were determined to coax my life out of my body, like the poor miners at the top of the valley. Those poor lads had to fight the demons and still dig through the rock slide to the long-forgotten remains of Kenver's ancestors and slaves. Only then, did they stand a chance of liberating a tin ear stud, to prove their quest was not for nought.

I gave up my attempt to sleep just before dawn. Walking to the edge of the cliff, I scanned the rock face and the beach, but could see no signs of them emerging. How would they know when it was time to swim back to shore if they were lost in the labyrinth of tunnels? Kenver's son returned from the copse in the distance and added fuel to the fires. Kenver awoke as the logs toppled over one another.

He yawned and stretched his arms out, nodding to the pink skies warming on the horizon. "Best wake the others." He said to me, before walking a short distance to water a clump of shrubs. Jago cooked us porridge and then held the babe, while Cryda got herself organised ready to suckle. I paced along the cliff edge, watching the day grow brighter with the ebb and flow of the tide.

"There's no sign of them." I ranted, hoping Kenver would provide me with a much-needed reason. He had no answers for me, just a kindly but pitiable smile while he ate his food. “Shouldn’t they be on their way back by now?” Everyone ignored me. My anxiety was not helping their digestion one bit.

“What if the Morrighan herself caught them, Da?” Kenver’s son whispered, although we all heard him as clear as day.

Kenver shushed the boy and continued to pack away the foods, tools and furs. “I’ll make my way down to the beach and sound the settlement bells. The rest of your clan should be waiting for them to announce the victor as our new tribal leader.” He urged the ladies to return to with him, picking up their belongings and beckoning them to follow.

Now I was torn. I wanted so much to see them emerge from the tunnels and begin the climb, and then the swim back to the main beach, but I also wanted to be there when they arrived to congratulate whoever won. Perhaps I could out walk their swimming speed, if I really hurried. Jago could carry most of our things back to the hut. The rising sun was full in my eyes now, and high enough to shine directly on the steep slope beneath my feet.

The first thing I heard was falling shale and gravel. It skittered down into the sea in time with cautious footsteps. Peering over the edge, I saw the tattooed scalp of Paega as he tumbled down the shallower sections of the cliff towards the water. My heart sank. How was he first from the tunnels? Where were the twins? I waited, my hand over my mouth, hardly daring to breathe. Within just a few moments, Blydh’s head appeared and surveyed the rocks under him. There was still hope. At least one of the twins escaped the maw of the Underworld. He raced after Paega, taking a bolder approach to the descent, skidding and falling until he was almost at his half-brother’s heels.

Where was Tallack, that dear boy with a merry song in his heart and a kind word or two for his old aunt? Paega eased into the sea, carefully pawing his way around the boulder that had caused his ascent so many issues. Blydh hopped onto the top of the giant rock and jumped feet first into the ocean, less than a man's length from Paega's nose. I could hear them yelling and cursing at one another, Paega struck out first with a fist, and then with his feet, kicking and pounding at Blydh in spite.

Sickness crawled up my throat. The two lads were already starting back for the main beach and Tallack still had not appeared. I thought about sending Jago to the settlement for help, but who would be prepared to enter the cursed shafts of the dead to find him? My mind raced, thinking about how his final moments could have ended in such terror, when his narrow frame peeked out of the cliff face. He was alive, thank Cernonnus. Thank all the gods, the boys made it, and in the most important race of their young lives.

Tallack watched the other two thrashing against the currents, way ahead of him. He stood out on a jutting part of the rocks and put his arms above his head. With the most graceful dive, Tallack plummeted in a sweeping arc, clear of the boulders and into the sea. Walking alongside them, I wondered who would tire first until I reached the headland marking the start of the trail back to camp. I lost sight of them while I scrambled down the path, darted between the huts and shacks and joined the large group of spectators on the beach.

Those from the Alchemist Clan, Blydh's Head Hunters and Tallack's crew shifted, allowing me to the front of the crowd. I stood next to Derwa and her Ordo husband, and the widows of Aebba, each of them shouting and yelling to encourage the boys to swim faster. Cryda did her best to root for each of the twins in turn, but it seemed to me that she favoured Tallack of the two. I could be wrong. Brea screamed for Tallack to win, her voice was hoarse and raspy. It was obviously not used to such exertion. What had happened to this timid and gentle young lady over the last few moons?

Standing on tiptoe and leaning on Jago for support, I could just make out their heads above the crashing waves. The priest warriors were jostling behind us, some called out for Paega, others carried on smoking hemp and blowing it across our faces. The smell made me heave, but I did not have the courage to chide them. Eseld and her father stood at the furthest end of the group next to Kenver. Eseld bit the sides of her fingernails, spitting out whatever her teeth could detach.

Tallack's superior swimming style put him ahead for the first time since their escape from the tunnels. Paega and Blydh were close behind, their arms almost tangling together.

"What's going on? I can't see properly." I shrieked, as Blydh's head vanished under the water.

It was Jago who answered me, being taller and no doubt still growing. "It looks like the great Head Hunter is in difficulty, Fur Benyn. He sank beneath the waves twice, taking a long time to reach the surface."

Tallack glanced behind him, as Paega kicked out at Blydh's face, knocking him unconscious. With both arms limp and his body upright, Blydh sank to the depths. In a panic, Tallack stopped, turned about and pounded the water until he reached the spot where his brother was last sighted. Filling his lungs to the fullest, he upended and dived through the freezing waves.

With a nauseating grin plastered across his face, Paega eased his pace and swam to shore and victory. Eseld and the priests went wild with joy, hoisting him onto stout shoulders and parading him along the beach, singing and hollering.

Cryda, Kenver, Brea and I were not so joyous. Each of us shuffled closer to the rising tide, our eyes trained on the patch of ocean where we hoped the boys would surface. Time almost stood still. Cryda's brow furrowed with concern. I held my breath. They had survived a terrible ordeal, surely the Lady of Lakes and Seas would not be so cruel as to take them from us now? Was this my punishment for taking the ornately decorated blade from the lake near to Stonehenge? I promised to any god who would listen, that if they saved the boys, I would give away the sword to the new Chieftain.

It was as though the Lady heard my prayers. Tallack broke through the surface with his brother hooked into the crook of his arm. Kicking out in powerful strokes, Tallack sped through the tidal surge to the shore. Blydh came to his senses as they reached the shallows, standing for himself and coughing out great quantities of salt water from his lungs. Cryda rushed to hug them. Brea burrowed under the Ruvane's arm and levered Tallack away from her grasp.

As I approached them, I noticed a large gash to Blydh's shoulder. The wound narrowly missed the big vessel in his neck. "What happened?"

Panting and spluttering, Blydh pointed to Paega as he sat on the shoulders of larger warriors. "Better ask him."

Kenver stepped up. "Are you saying that he knifed you on your way back here?"

"Knifed, punched and finally kicked me in the face." He spat the blood from his broken nose onto the wet sand.

I rushed to pinch the sides of his cut together until it could be stitched.

Cryda looked to Kenver. “That can’t be a fair trial. What are the rules about deliberately slashing another opponent?”

Kenver looked to his feet. “I’m afraid there are no rules in this regard.”

Paega slid down from the warriors and squared up to Blydh. “See, no rules against defending yourself.”

“Except I was not attacking you. Had I known you would cheat; I would have twisted your fat head off your shoulders last night.” Blydh stood fully upright, his massive fists clenched in readiness. “This weedy little shit stayed in the tunnel entrance all night. He made no attempt to find the lost souls.”

Kenver’s expression dropped into a scowl. “Is this true? Show me your proof. Where are the tin ear studs of my ancestors?”

Tallack and Blydh each produced a small tin stud from pockets sewn into their leggings.

Paega smiled with smug assurance and fished for his proof, holding it in an outstretched palm. “You must stop telling so many tall tales, brother. It upsets your gods.”

Cryda started to cry. Brea looked incensed, stomping away and muttering foul language under her breath. I sensed that there was more to this test than Kenver was letting on. He took the studs from the twins, smiled and then turned back to Paega.

“Hand it over young man.” Kenver commanded.

Paega squirmed, shuffling backwards towards the priests. “What for? You see my proof from there. Make the announcement. I am to be the next Chieftain, which since I am the eldest is how it should have always been.”

Kenver took a massive breath and let out a loud sigh. He thrust his open hand closer. Paega relented, popping the stud into the man’s hand. With a brief examination,

Kenver cleared his throat and announced, “This boy is a fraud, and a liar. He did not complete the trial; therefore, the runners up are equal victors.”

CHAPTER TWENTY-NINE

Eseld and her father were livid. They jostled Kenver, pushing him into the crowd of priests in an attempt to bully him into submission.

"Take that back. My son is good and brave and honourable." She squealed; spittle flew in all directions with her fury.

Kenver would not be intimidated. "The terms of the quest were simple. They were to swim to the rock face, gain entry into the tunnels, find the tin studs belonging to my kin and return at daybreak. Your son is neither honourable, nor truthful."

"You have the proof right there in your hand. The old priest exclaimed.

"I have two studs from my ancestors, and one recently made tin stud. See the difference." He held out both hands and moved the studs until the flat sides were upper facing. Those from the twins bore a symbol unlike anything I have ever seen. They were delicately scored with a pattern of lines marking a tiny maze. The craftsmanship was truly remarkable. Paega's stud was plain. "Which one of you gave this boy a new stud before the trial began?"

Everyone watched the faces of the old priest and Eseld. They held their stare and gave no indication of their collusion.

After a few moments, Kenver snatched his hands shut and pocketed the metal. "It matters little. Paega is disqualified." His eyes searched me out in the crowd. "Fur Benyn, I am right in thinking that the final decisions for our tribe are made by the current Ruvane, are they not?"

I nodded.

"Ruvane Cryda, please give us your decision as to which of the twins will become Metern for the Dumnonii?"

"Wait just one moment, if you please." The old priest shouted. All the family members crowded around him and Kenver. "A new Chieftain cannot be announced until Aebba is at rest and buried. Aebba cannot be at rest until his death is avenged, but no one knows who killed him."

"Yes, we do." Derwa piped up. Everyone shrank back at her boldness. She had not uttered a word in days. Her sullen disposition was a marked difference from her usual bubbly character. She stepped forward to point. "Mother killed him. I saw her with the poison berries." Derwa's look was pure vengeance. I could hardly believe what I was hearing. Of course, I suspected Eseld, she did pick the berries from the wood, but for her own daughter to have openly condemned her was inconceivable. "You think so too, don't you, Aunt Mel?"

The crowd's attention veered to me. I had no absolute proof of her guilt, just many pieces of a much larger suspicion. "I... um… did see her with a pouch of black berries in the woods outside our compound, and she was behaving most erratically, especially when her cousin came to stay. I heard them forging plans about the priests making their moves by a certain moon as Eseld was going to *make the way clear for them*."

Eseld simmered with rage. "I said no such thing. Those were harmless berries and none of your business, you nosy old crone. How dare you accuse me of harming my own husband? If anyone killed him it was Cryda and her hairy little Ordo lover."

"Hey!" Cryda yelped. The twins were snarling and rounding on Eseld. Things would end badly with many more family deaths at this rate.

"Let us examine the evidence." I raised my arms, walking between them all and hoping that they had more honour than to strike an old lady. "Apart from what I saw and heard, Eseld had access to all of Aebba's food. She also insisted that I had a dish of squirrel stew, containing the same poison which killed the Chief. Jago had to nurse me back to health, but I have no doubt that I was near to death for a number of days.

"Then there was the time when Tallack took us to the estuary to gather juniper and other herbs. I left the food which Eseld cooked outside Cryda's hut as she was feeling sick. The following day, two young fox cubs had eaten her meal and died from the poison. Cryda would not taint her own food. It has to be Eseld. She was also present when Gwyn, the roasting pit slave, mentioned that she had seen something useful the night of Aebba's death. That poor girl had her throat slashed for her troubles. Nothing else fits. Eseld wanted Aebba out of the way to let Paega take leadership." All the while I spoke, Tallack and Blydh's men were moving closer to the centre of our gathering. They outnumbered the priest warriors two to one.

Cryda suddenly found her voice. "Then as my final act as Ruvane, I declare that Eseld will be sacrificed to the Lady of Lakes and Seas in punishment for her crimes against our tribe."

The explosion of discord was deafening. The priests snarled and drew their weapons, the Head Hunters did the same. Tallack's crew awaited a signal from him to join in the melee. Blydh and Tallack put their heads together and muttered something inaudible. Before things could get too far out of hand, Blydh pushed through the crowd and climbed onto a large rock overlooking everyone.

"There will be no fighting between our clans." He bellowed. The entire tribe stopped and looked up at him. "That is not the Dumnoni way. Put down your axes and swords." He gestured with a lowering hand for them to comply, and surprisingly, most did. A few addled priests took a little longer, but they too did as they were commanded. "The sons of Aebba have completed the trial. A decision is made. For the first time in history, there will be two Chieftains to lead this great tribe. Tallack and I will rule together. In place of one great warrior, you now have two."

Every Head Hunter and crewman roared with delight. I looked at the old priest as he clasped his daughter's shoulder. His face sagged in defeat. Eseld too, knew that they were beaten. They had manipulated every outcome and it had led to their downfall.

Blydh had not finished his proclamation. "We declare Eseld, second wife of Aebba the Wild, guilty of murder. She will drown at high tide and take her spirit to the Underworld, where she belongs."

Two of Tallack's men grabbed Eseld and marched her down the beach to the rocky outcrop at the low water mark. Two others, hurried after them with stakes and rope to bind her against the slope. The Head Hunters formed a line in front of the priest warriors, preventing them from a possible rescue. Derwa was front and centre, watching her mother scream and squirm against the bindings at her wrists and ankles. I thought she might see her mother's distress and retract her accusation. If she had, I would also be at risk of retaliation from the priests. My evidence were simple observations, nothing more. My fate was in Derwa's hands.

With dry, narrowed eyes, she watched the waves gently lapping up the shore until it covered Eseld's ankles. A faint smile lifted the corners of her mouth when the water rose to her hips and Eseld's cries became more pleading and insistent. When the surge of sea spray soaked her face, making her cough and choke, Derwa did not move. Her Ordo husband edged closer to comfort her, draping his arm about her shoulders. She shrugged him off.

What was stoking the hatred to this level of spite? Had Eseld caused Derwa a pain too great for forgiveness? My mind raced back to that moment in the woods at the circle gathering when I witnessed Eseld burying a tiny bundle; the child too small to live. The abortion must have been for young Derwa. When I think about how we all thought her too young for the binding ceremony. She must have been seeing another behind our backs for a considerable time. Perhaps Eseld felt that the Alchemists would not accept the union if Derwa already had a child by another. It is a puzzle indeed. Who could Derwa have been seeing, and why was she amenable to the binding with the Ordo's after such a long protest?

Whatever the reasons, Derwa revelled in her mother's anguish. The splutters increased until Eseld's cries were mere garbled sounds. The whites of her eyes were flecked with blood from the strain of straining against the ropes. The ocean entered her throat, and did not recede. All her thrashing and frenzy finally ceased. The Lady of Lakes and Seas took her to a watery grave.

No one on the shore moved or spoke, each person reflecting on the justice served to their Chieftain. Aebba was at peace, and could now fly to the Summerlands, and sit next to Cernonnus and the warriors from the past. Blydh was still standing on the massive rock, looking down on his people. He waited until each member of the tribe turned to face him before speaking.

"This settlement is too small to provide winter quarters for each of the clans. Paega, you will go with the priests to the moors and live out your days among your own people. Tallack and I will take some time to select new leaders for the Head Hunters and his crewmen. When that is done, the hunters will ride out to protect our borders. Go now and mourn. We have all lost those that are dear to us."

The muttering and murmurs were a mixture of smug jubilance and sorrow, but eventually the vast mob began to disperse. Blydh jumped down from his rock and spoke softly to his brother. Jago came to me and asked if there was anything he could do to ease my suffering. My guilt flushed across my face. He thought I would be saddened by Eseld's death, when in truth, I felt nothing but relief. Aebba was a favourite of mine from his birth onwards. He and his father before him, treated me with nothing but kindness and respect. Now that he was avenged, we were able to let him go.

I watched Tallack signal Brea to follow him towards camp. She skipped past me, fumbling with something in her hand. The item dropped at my feet. Stooping low, I picked up a beautiful bone comb, carved into the shape of a dolphin. My hand trembled as I held it out for Jago to see.

"Fur Benyn, it is the comb I gave to the cooking slave. She whose throat was slit behind our hut."

I nodded, confirming that I recognised it too. All the pieces slotted into place with sickening ease. Brea had killed the servant girl to stop her from telling me what she saw the night of Aebba's murder. It was Brea who had access to all our houses and the cooking pits behind the Long Hut. It was Brea who despised Aebba with all her might, and she who took the berries from Eseld's dwelling to lace my stew. She had deliberately stamped against my foot on the cliff edge causing me to fall.

I called after her, displaying the comb in my palm. She came scampering back to take it from me.

"It was you all along." I panted, the full weight of my accusation hitting me like a rock. "This belonged to the Long Hut cook."

Brea scooped up the article from my hand. "Who's going to believe you now, Meliora? You have just brought about the death of the priest's daughter. Are you willing to risk what they will do to you if you tell them that you've changed your mind?" She raised one brow at me and smirked. "Aebba had to die, he was a monster, and if you know what's good for you, you'll keep your trap shut." She flounced off towards the new Meterns and slid her arm about Tallack's waist.

What had I done? Far from settling the affairs of our tribe, I had raised a murderer into a position of power. Jago and I were the only ones alive to call her out on her treachery. How long would it be before she declared us as monsters too? I opened my mouth to acknowledge my fear to Jago, but he already knew.

"I don't think we are safe here anymore, Fur Benyn."

***

If you enjoyed this novel, and have a moment spare to express your opinion, **a review on any of the distribution sites would be greatly appreciated**.

For more information on the rest of the series, please go to: www.carantocpublishing.com

The next book in the series is entitled **Pagan Curse**

About the Author

Sam Taw is the pen name for fiction author Sam Nash. Sam is committed to delivering novels in two distinct genres, historical thrillers and a unique blend of science fiction and international espionage stories.

She lives in a small market town in the south of Leicestershire, in the UK but dreams of one day owning a woodland on the Cornish coast.

For information regarding the work of Sam Taw, please visit:
http://www.carantocpublishing.com

For information regarding the work of Sam Nash, please visit:
https://www.samnash.org

Printed in Great Britain
by Amazon

62877323R00172